May
Enjoy Tara's
journey of
"Sweet Glory"!

Lisa Y. Potocar

Sweet Glory

a novel

LISA Y. POTOCAR

TATE PUBLISHING
AND ENTERPRISES, LLC

Published by Tate Publishing & Enterprises, LLC
127 E. Trade Center Terrace | Mustang, Oklahoma 73064 USA
1.888.361.9473 | www.tatepublishing.com

Tate Publishing is committed to excellence in the publishing industry. The company reflects the philosophy established by the founders, based on Psalm 68:11,
"The Lord gave the word and great was the company of those who published it."

Book design copyright © 2011 by Tate Publishing, LLC. All rights reserved.
Cover design by April Marciszewski
Interior design by Nathan Harmony
Photography by Charles Lambert

Published in the United States of America

ISBN: 978-1-61346-714-5
1. Fiction / Romance / Historical
2. Fiction / Romance / Suspense
11.11.10

Dedication

To my husband, Jed, always first in the barn to saddle up my steed and spur me on to my writing muse. And because he genuinely sees people as "people," with equal rights and opportunities, he would have stood behind any woman who wanted to brave their way into soldiering, nursing, and spying during the American Civil War.

Author's Personal Note

Dear Reader,

I *hate* history!

Now that I have your attention…I'll tell you that I actually *love* history, but I didn't always. So what made me want to go digging up facts to weave around fiction—especially for a debut novel—when I could have easily plugged my primary protagonist and her plot into a more familiar setting? And why target young adults for my story's readership?

I was in my early thirties when my mother coaxed me into touring some of Newport, Rhode Island's historical homes. At the time, my career in health care was often stressful due to a rapidly changing atmosphere and incessant backlogs; any getaway was a welcome diversion. While at the Hunter House, the melodic voice of the tour guide, dressed in colonial costume, lulled me back to a moonless night during the Revolutionary War. In this Georgian-style mansion, overlooking the harbor, I pictured Admiral de Ternay, commander of the French fleet, seated on a rose floral sofa in a parlor paneled with pine board grained to imitate rosewood. Under the glow of candles, resting in pewter holders crafted by local artisans, he is discussing with his staff strategy for defeating the British navy in support of America's colonial forces. As I imagined the admiral unrolling a map to show the offensive position of British ships along the coast, I was rudely seized from my trance by the tour guide's demand to proceed to the dining room.

Bam! It struck me then that my apathy for history was rooted in the dull, lifeless presentations of it all through my schooling (no offense intended to my educators; I respect that they had a ton to impart in a short time). Viewed in this vivid, more personal way, some of the same, long-forgotten facts and figures, which had been crammed into my head in the classroom, suddenly sprang to life. I developed a new appreciation—indeed lust—for history! And I was determined to learn more. The very day I returned home, I became an ardent reader of historical fiction with lots of adventure. Amongst my favorites: the *Kent Family Chronicles* and *North and South Trilogy* by John Jakes, master weaver of history around complex plots and subplots. Through his colorful descriptions, I absorbed much about the times and the people. The bigger pattern sewed by our country from its beginning to the present became neatly ordered and clear to me. I suddenly found myself gravitating toward nonfiction, diving for greater pearls of wisdom where historical fiction teased. Wow! I became eager to nurture our young adults down the same footpath. If I had been armed with the potent knowledge of how the past shapes our future, I most definitely would have taken an active interest in my country and its politics long before I hit my thirties.

Researching for historical fiction is just as much fun as reading it; fascinating things turn up everywhere. What seed actually sprouted my story? While reading about Civil-War curiosities, including places haunted by ghosts, I discovered that around three hundred known women, both Yankee and Rebel, disguised themselves as soldiers to fight for their country, and thousands more reinvented themselves in other ways, such as nurses and spies. There is enough documentation for this era to sink an armada of ships, but scant about these pioneers. Besides the more famous cast (Nurses

Dorothea Dix and Clara Barton, Doctor Mary Walker, and Union Spy Elizabeth Van Lew), one female kept reaching out to me from the graveyard of records: Sarah Edmonds, alias Frank Thompson. She trimmed her tresses, enlisted in the infantry, and set off on a journey to play soldier, nurse, and spy. Aha! My primary protagonist was born: the bold, adventurous, sixteen-year-old tomboy Jana Brady who seeks to create a new meaning of what a woman can do during the tumultuous years of the Civil War.

I shall stop here with trying to convince you of the merits in knowing history, especially as belongs to your country. But I challenge you to visit your nearest historical site and see what ghosts come out to play with you. I'll bet you say you had fun!

Warm regards,

Lisa Y. Potocar

Brady Homestead
Elmira, New York
March 1861

Jana Brady gazed across the barn. Under the glow of a single lantern, sinister shapes floated across the latched shutters. A chill of dread shivered through her. She prayed for the safety of the runaway slaves she'd help her pa hide later but hoped for a chance to confront a slave catcher. She dreamed of adventure in everything she did and loved how Ma and Pa had trusted her for several years to watch Pa's back during missions like tonight's. Pitching another forkful of hay over the loft for Ma to level out in the wagon bed below, she remembered the many ways Pa had trained her to divert a bounty hunter, short of shooting him. She'd give almost anything to ram into one with her stallion and unsaddle him while Pa fled with his charges. That'd teach the thief never again to try robbing a people of their God-given right to freedom. Thrilled with the notion, she called down to Ma, "Are we done yet?"

"One more load and we're all set," Ma said. She looked as silly as the scarecrow they put in their cornfields every summer, with wisps of hay sticking out of her long, sandy-colored curls and knitted shawl.

Jana sent down the last forkful and stopped to watch Pa saddling her stallion. She puzzled over his hesitation earlier when she'd told him how excited she was to accompany him. Why'd he suddenly waver when he and Ma had always taught her abolition was worth the danger? He'd been treating her differently lately but wouldn't say why. She decided to steer clear of asking him when the sound of a horse galloping toward the barn made her jump. Who'd even think of visiting now? All abolitionist-minded folk around Chemung County knew the Bradys would be getting underway in minutes.

Dropping the reins he was winding around the saddle horn of Jana's black beauty, Pa bustled from Commodore's stall to thrust open the great barn doors. In whooshed the wintry air, the moon's silvery beams, and their visitor.

John Jones reined in his mare, her tawny winter coat all lathered up and her nostrils flared and puffing steam as she skidded across a layer of dry hay. She came within a whisker of colliding with the mules hitched to the wagon before breaking her slide.

When Ma saw it was Elmira's Underground-Railroad agent who'd come to call, she stopped shuffling about and stood at attention, straight and still like the silo behind the barn. She must've sensed trouble with the escaping slaves because John kept track of them all along their escape route.

"Thank the good Lord you're still here, Thomas," John said, fishing a paper from his saddlebag and passing it down to Pa. "A courier pretty near rode his horse to death bringing this to me from the agent at Alba."

The dispatch crinkled in Pa's large, leathery hands as he unfolded it and read its coded words aloud:

Freight load of potatoes arriving on Northern Central with the wind blowing from the South.

Jana's enthusiasm resurged—a real adventure at last! A slave catcher had failed to nab his targets at the small town in Pennsylvania. Surely, he'd try here, the next stop on the Underground Railroad. She pictured herself staring down the barrel of her hunting rifle at a man who was foolish enough to step north over the Mason and Dixon's Line when seven southern states had seceded from the Union to form their own government. The Confederate States of America had its own laws apart from the federal government now, so Jana deemed it the way most Northerners did: any laws agreed upon between the North and South about aiding escaping slaves no longer applied. And this confirmed for her the slave catcher was greedy and stupid. She wanted to be there when he made the wrong move.

"I'll understand, Thomas, if you won't put you or your family at risk," John said.

"No Brady ever backed down from a fight. Will you be tagging along, John?" Pa asked.

Fear froze John's dark eyes and cheeks. "No, sir! I won't be shackled and dragged back to Virginia as no substitute for a slave the slave catcher can't catch so he reaps his reward. I'll be getting home while the getting's good."

Pa said, "I understand," and turned a stern eye up at Jana. "You'll stay behind too, young lady."

Opening her mouth to protest, Jana choked on her words.

Pa helped Ma down from the wagon and clambered up into its seat. "Riding around in men's britches, toting a rifle for a run-in with a slave catcher's no place for womenfolk," he grumbled as he unhitched the wagon brake, whipped the mules' hides, and tore out of the barn.

John tipped the brim of his black slouch hat at Ma, then Jana, and wheeled his horse around. He left the barn before they could thank him for his warning with a chair fireside and a slice of Ma's award-winning apple pie.

To Jana's bewildered look, Ma said, "I'm sure Pa has another to watch his back in your stead."

Jana snapped out of her stupor and stabbed her pitchfork into a mound of hay, scattering some of its straw in a tizzy and jarring her funny bone. "What burr's gotten into Pa's craw lately?" she asked, rubbing her stinging elbow. "He eyes me as though he's got something to say. Then he stomps off with a huff and a puff." She felt her anger reddening up her cheeks. "There's no time for Pa to find someone else to watch his back. He's gone off half-loaded and you know it, Ma."

"You've done nothing to beget Pa's ire. It's aimed only at himself."

"Then why'd he cut me out of what could be the greatest adventure of my life?"

Ma sighed in exasperation. From behind an evaporating cloud of her breath, she inquired, "Isn't helping slaves to freedom adventurous enough for you?"

It was gratifying, not adventurous enough, Jana thought. *Slipping into the South and sneaking slaves north under disguise, as it was well known in the Underground Railroad that former slave Harriet Tubman did… now that'd be bigger than a barn full of fun and daring.*

As though Ma read Jana's mind, she said, "Honestly, dearly departed Grandpa Brady filled your head with too many patriotic stories of him and his father wielding a musket in their wars."

"You still haven't explained why Pa cut me out."

Ma's annoyance tapered some. "It's too complicated to discuss now. I must nurse Molly." She removed a flickering lantern from its wall hook. "Come up when you're done here, and we'll discuss what *both* Pa and I have on our minds lately." With a sway of her plump hips and a swish of her cotton dress, she left the barn.

Turning the wall lantern's knob, Jana doused its flame as fast as Pa had her prospect of excitement tonight. She choked on an oily fume that crept into her throat. Quelling her coughing fit, she snatched up her musket and descended the creaky ladder. Its splintered rungs pierced her palm all the way down as though they were needling her for not taking off after Pa.

Commodore pawed the floorboards with his hoof, anxious to get going.

Jana set down her rifle and went to her horse. She reached under his belly and slid her hands over the smooth leather of his saddle belt. When she started to unbuckle it, Commodore grunted and bucked, resisting his tack's removal as though he too was angry about being cut out of something grand and glorious. Jana tugged on his bridle strap to steady him and ran her palm down the prickly bristles of his muscled cheek to calm him as well as she could with Pa's words still clapping around her brain like thunder.

Pa's behavior made no sense at all to Jana. It wasn't about her age or that she was a girl or that there could be danger. Pa would've been more concerned about her helping him with risky ventures back when she was twelve rather than now at almost sixteen years old. And he and Ma had let her keep on hunting even after Pa's near-hunting tragedy last year. A black bear had reared up on him with its razor-sharp claws about to swipe the back of his head when Jana killed it with a shot straight through the heart. Word got around that Jana could outshoot any bigheaded male. A few months later at the County Fair, the crowd goaded Pa into letting her step up in petticoat rustling beneath her Sunday best. She borrowed a rifle and, from one hundred feet away, shot down every can placed on a tree stump to the chagrin of every male who challenged her and missed by a mile.

In public, Ma protested such unladylike behavior. At home, she, like the other women always trying to prove how they equaled men, praised Jana. Pa didn't need convincing of that. He believed women deserved the right to vote and own property and tackle anything men did if they had a mind to it.

And Jana did. She slid her riding gloves from her waist belt and pulled them over her hands. She rammed her musket into the saddle holster, hoisted up her riding pants, and swung into the saddle.

Commodore snorted; his grain-scented breath billowed out his eagerness, bolstering Jana's confidence.

Unwinding the reins from around the saddle horn, Jana clicked her tongue, to which Commodore sprang from his stall into a swift canter right out of the barn. She wasn't about to let Pa get shot with no one to back him up or let him get away with cutting her out of what could be the greatest stir on home soil since the Revolutionary War's Battle of Newtown.

Within minutes, Jana and Commodore reached the western fringe of the city just as the whistle blew from the Northern Central's locomotive. She swore it always rang with a more urgent shrill only when it steamed into the station with human freight needing stowing. Too late to make the depot and hide in Pa's shadow, she led Commodore to a wooded canopy roadside. They'd wait there for Pa to pass by and then trail him on his way to a neighbor's farm. The strong scent of pine reminded Jana of Christmas. She prayed for this night to deliver an adventure wrapped up in a bow.

Jana visualized, right about now, as was his usual routine, Pa would be backing the wagon up to the open doorway of a freight car where a stevedore stacked empty crates and boxes just for show. Meanwhile, the escaped slaves would be sneaking through the opposite door unseen and crawling beneath the train to Pa's wagon. As he loaded the crates and boxes atop the wagon bed's hay, the runaways would slip beneath the hay and conceal themselves.

Buttoning Pa's old gray wool coat up to her neck to combat the chill, which sliced through to her bones, Jana ventured to guess how many runaways would come this time. Last time there were seven … the most ever, although sometimes groups rolled in one after another. Once, thirty runaways needed shelter. Elmirans took turns hiding them in corn cribs, haymows, church steeples, potato cellars, attics, secret rooms, or tunnels until time to re-board them on the next *Freedom Baggage Car* to St. Catharines, Ontario. As in Canada, Jana believed the United States should allow black people the right to vote, hold office, sit on juries, and choose where to live. Actually, she wished that for everyone, no matter what their differences. Even more, she'd love for everyone to treat each other equally and with respect.

It was no wonder she held these values, having grown up in the melting pot of people around Chemung County. For as long as Jana could recall, her Irish family had been living harmoniously with their German neighbors, and they had been worshipping in their Methodist church while tolerating the many diverse faiths of their friends. And former slaves, like John Jones, were welcomed into the community too.

She was pondering how proud she was of the folk in her home-town when Commodore's ears pricked back to the sound of rattling wheels over a rutted road. Ruffling his coarse, stringy forelock, she cued him to keep quiet as she'd taught him while hunting; his rip-pling muscles immediately relaxed beneath her.

Pa rolled by, awash in the full moon's glow.

Before starting her horse forward, Jana checked that no one tailed Pa. The soft needles of the pine branches caressed her face as Commodore picked a muted trail through the woods. With more than half of the road to the hideaway traveled and no action in sight, disappointment crept through her.

"Whoa!" Pa called out and reined in the mules hard.

Jana pulled up Commodore, her pulse prancing with nervous excitement. At the road's fork, blocking Pa's left turn up through the hills, a man sat tall in his saddle. She slid her rifle from its saddle hol-ster and spurred on Commodore as close as she dared to the stranger.

With the moon's glare upon him, Pa lowered his broad-brimmed slouch hat over his face to avoid recognition.

The horseman struck a match and held it over his pipe's bowl while puffing on its stem. His flame swelled high enough to show a gaunt face covered with a grizzled beard, a face Jana didn't recognize.

Fanning the foul smells of sulfur and tobacco to Jana's nostrils, the wind warned her there was something rank in this man's business too.

Pa barked at the lone rider, "Who are you and what do you want?"

Between puffs, the man responded in a surly voice, "By authority of the Federal Fugitive Slave Law, I've come to reclaim what you've stolen from the South."

He was no lawman, Jana knew. He would've said so right off, and his jacket flashed no star-shaped badge pinned to it.

Pa reached for the rifle on his lap.

"Keep your hands where I can see 'em," the slave catcher said.

"I've nothing of interest to you. Move aside, and I'll be on my way peacefully," Pa said.

"I saw five darkies jump into your wagon," Grizzly Face said. "Hand 'em over, and I'll be on my way peacefully."

"As I said, I've nothing of interest to you. Move aside or be run down," Pa repeated.

Grizzly Face drew his pistol and aimed it at Pa. "After I kill you, I'll tell the sheriff I was defending myself against a lawbreaker."

"The way we Northerners see it, any laws made between the North and South were nullified when the South left the Union to form its own government. That makes *you* the lawbreaker. And it puts you in hostile territory. If I were you, I'd ride far from here before you regret it," Pa said.

Grizzly Face clicked back his pistol hammer. "I don't like to lose, and I'm mighty fast on this here trigger."

Pa flicked the reins, setting the mules in motion.

Had Pa gone mad to make such a bold move with no weapon showing and no backup? Jana wondered. She kept a cool head and turned to Mother Nature for help—both things Pa had taught her. What luck!

Grizzly Face was set up right below a gangly pine bough, already nearly snapped in two, probably by a burdensome snowfall. Tucking her rifle in her armpit, she sighted the barrel at the splintered strand that held the branch together and pulled the trigger.

Crack! The lower half tore away and swiped Grizzly Face from his saddle. His pistol fired, spooking his horse and sending it hightailing away through the valley.

Pa's head wrenched downward toward his feet.

Jana blinked twice to make sure she really saw John Jones trotting out of the woods opposite. Why had he changed his mind about helping tonight when he was terrified of being this close to a slave catcher? She shrugged it off. Pa would be relieved she had happened along; only they together had rehearsed all sorts of scenarios to escape a slave catcher, should they ever run into one.

Pulling up alongside Pa's wagon, John shielded his eyes against the night's glare with a gloved hand and scanned the woods for their conspirator.

The slave catcher moaned, and Pa and John seized their reins and fled before he came to.

Jana sat up proud in her saddle. She'd gotten the job done the way she and Pa had always figured it: nobody got badly hurt, and Pa got away with the runaways. Turning toward home, she let loose a victory cry that could rival a wolf's howl.

Brady Homestead
Elmira, New York
March 1861

About an hour later, Jana entered the farmhouse, humming her own spirited version of "Home Sweet Home." She laid an armful of oak logs upon the orange-brown bricks of the floor-level hearth and fed the fire.

In the midst of nursing Molly, Ma looked up at Jana. Her eyes clouded over with suspicion. "Why your sudden cheerfulness?" she asked.

Jana turned away from Ma's penetrating stare and stacked her remaining logs in the shelf cut into the fireplace's bricks. "I'll tell you when Pa gets home," she said, putting a crackle of mischief in her voice. She hoped to steal her twelve-year-old twin sisters' attention away from crocheting the green and yellow squares that they'd eventually weave together to make a large afghan. They'd finish a bunch more of different sizes, colors, and patterns to sell at the County Fair come fall. Though not a stitch interested in crocheting, Jana marveled at how her sisters' hands made their single needles fly to the point of invisibility as they worked the yarn.

Rachel and Rebecca looked up but continued weaving their needles around the yarn. "Oh, please tell us now," they cried in unison.

Neither had a thimbleful of tomboy in them; they loved that Jana did. She'd entertained them plenty over the years with her stories of adventure and mischief. Their favorite story was when Doc Carter had plucked ten-year-old Jana from some roadside bushes after she'd dented his carriage with a walnut-sized rock from her sling-shot. When Doc brought her home, Jana explained that she'd grown bored with fixed targets. Ma and Pa couldn't help finding humor in it, and Jana had escaped punishment.

Miming sewing her lips together, Jana cued they'd have to wait until Pa got home. Removing her hat, she let her thick, auburn tresses tumble down over her shoulders.

The twins puckered out their bottom lips and fell silent.

After hanging up her coat and hat on the pewter wall hooks in the front hall, Jana reentered the sitting room just as Ma finished but-toning up her housecoat and mopping Molly's milk-smudged face with a cotton towel. She took the squirming baby from Ma, nestled her in her arm, and settled into a rocking chair before the crackling fire and its pleasant oak smell. The firelight set the room aglow and warmed Jana as she gazed lovingly upon her three-month-old sister. Cuddling with Molly, she rocked her the way she'd done with all of her sisters when they were babies.

Five-year-old Eliza slid off the sofa, leaving a tiny comb stuck in her doll's hair. Clad in knitted slippers, she padded across the wide-planked floor and snuggled into Jana's free arm. She began rubbing Molly's soft, bald head and singing "Rock-a-Bye Baby" as sweet as a lark to put her to sleep.

Ma waited for Eliza to chirp her last note and Molly's eyelids to droop before opening up *The Last of the Mohicans* to her bookmarked page. She took up the tale from where she'd left off the night before.

For as long as Jana could recollect, Ma had read aloud every night. It was a habit she hadn't lost from her teaching days. She'd retired from the schoolhouse when she married Pa, not from teach-ing. She homeschooled her girls because she reckoned she could do it better than the public schools and private academies. She taught them mathematics and grammar and encouraged them to report on what they read about history, Greek and Roman mythology, astronomy, and philosophy from the scores of books crammed on the sitting room's shelves. They even got a dose of current events from the *Elmira Gazette*. Jana didn't mind being homeschooled; she never saw herself fitting in at recess. Jump-roping was too girlish, and the boys would never have let her climb trees with them.

While Ma narrated, Jana considered what might be irking Pa. Maybe her study habits of late had slacked off. Who could blame her for minding mostly current events with things heating up between the North and South ever since Abraham Lincoln had become president of the United States? She agreed with the president about preserving the Union at all costs, not with him refusing to abolish slavery where it already existed. Convinced Lincoln would break his promise soon enough, the seceded southern states couldn't be talked into rejoining the Union. Now, the Confederacy was threatening to seize Fort Sumter in South Carolina's harbor from Union control and make it their own. Jana knew any aggression against a federally owned property meant war. The South was wrong to goad the North, with its greater manpower and manufacturing of cannons and rifles, into war. They'd be crushed in a matter of days.

A heavy boot-stomping up the steps and across the front porch warned Jana something far worse than her studies ailed Pa right now.

Ma's recitation trailed off midsentence when the front door squealed open and slammed shut, setting the house's clapboards aquiver like a small earthquake might do.

With his large, calloused hands balled up and white-knuckled at his sides, Pa burst into the sitting room's archway.

Ma looked baffled by the ire that wrinkled the usually soft, jovial lines across Pa's forehead.

Unmindful of Pa's mood, Eliza skipped over and wriggled her small, pudgy fingers up at him, begging to be scooped up and swirled around—a nightly custom they had all enjoyed with Pa when they were young. But his gaze hardened on Jana.

Jana settled Molly in her crib under the pink and blue afghan, which Rachel and Rebecca had crocheted for her, and turned to face Pa.

Dropping their half-finished squares onto their laps with the needles still dangling from them, the twins leaned forward.

Pa started squealing worse than a hungry hog, "Damn it all, Jana! I know it was you who took that shot."

Eliza bolted to the safety of Ma's outstretched arms.

Jana knew she was truly in trouble when Pa's rare Irish temper flared enough for him to swear.

Molly whimpered, and a sternness in Ma's eyes warned Pa he'd be up all night coddling a crying baby.

Cutting his voice to a loud whisper, Pa said, "I know it was you because Commodore's still damp from a hard ride."

Jana had toweled and walked Commodore to cool him down for his own health, not to hide what she'd done.

Shaking her head, Ma appeared disgusted with herself for having left Jana and her rebellious nature alone in the barn.

The golden flecks in Pa's hazel eyes were like Indian spearheads, thrusting out in anger. Jana could almost feel them piercing her eyes as he said, "What were you thinking, young lady? I didn't teach you to run around half-loaded. John, the runaways, or I might've been hurt bad or—," Pa began, but Ma cut him off.

"John Jones was with you? I assumed he was afraid to show himself." Not giving Pa a chance to answer, Ma prattled on, "Why, Thomas Brady, you could talk the devil into shedding his evil ways. How on earth did you convince John to go along?" She could always calm Pa down by killing him with kind words or briefly rerouting his focus or both—like now.

"Told him twelve thousand Elmirans would revolt before we gave him up," Pa mumbled.

Gazing heavenward, Ma said, "The man's a saint. He's helped nearly a thousand slaves to freedom in the seventeen years he's been here."

"He sure is," Pa said and faced Jana with his scowl ironing out some. "You took good care of that bounty hunter, but his stray bullet passed between the mules and lodged in the wagon board. It missed my legs by inches." All gasped in horror while Pa continued, "Danger's got to be handled in a planned, not rash, way."

Marching up to Pa, Jana raised her chin to meet his stare. Now, the golden flecks in her hazel eyes felt like Indian spearheads. She often thought if she cut her hair like Pa's, she'd look just like him— though only in the face. His auburn hair had streaks of gray through it. And he was three inches taller at five feet nine and leaner than Jana; though, she wasn't plump. "I wouldn't have been rash if you'd let me go or at least told me why I couldn't."

"Jana's noticed you haven't been yourself around her lately, Pa. Because it has everything to do with your actions tonight, now is a good time to explain what's been on both of our minds," Ma said.

Pa pleaded Ma with his eyes to tell Jana whatever had his cheeks turning orange to match his hair.

Eyeing Rachel and Rebecca, Ma said, "Take Eliza up to bed, stoke up the chimney, and tell her a story. By then, you may return."

"No fair, Ma," Rachel said.

"We're always sent upstairs when the getting's not good," Rebecca added.

"They can stay," Jana said, not about to let her staunchest supporters get away.

"Very well," Ma said, and the twins mouthed their thanks to Jana.

Drawing her thumb from her mouth, Eliza asked in a hoarse whisper, "Can I stay, too, Jana?" She gave Pa a sidelong glance, making sure she hadn't turned him against her.

Ma kissed Eliza's forehead. "I'm sorry, little princess. It's your bedtime." To Pa she said, "That leaves you to tuck her in."

With a liberating exhale and a huge smile, Pa threw out his arms, and Eliza ran to him; he scooped her up and whisked her away.

Pa never backed down from a fight, making Jana fear she'd opened Pandora's Box by bringing up his quirky behavior of late.

Creaking floorboards upstairs cued Ma to say, "Please, sit down," which heightened Jana's anxiety. Ma only ordered her to do that whenever she had something unpleasant to say.

"I'll stand," Jana said, crossing her arms over her chest.

"And I'd rather you sit, so you're not staring me down," Ma said.

Plunking down into a worn sofa cushion, Jana braced herself for the unhappy news, probably the worst ever, always left in the wake of Ma's no-nonsense posture.

"I'll be forthright. Pa and I have awakened to your womanhood," Ma said.

Rachel blurted out, "Who hasn't? Why she's busting out all over the place," making herself and Rebecca giggle.

Jana shot her sisters a glare to show she'd chase them from the room with another such outburst. To Ma, she said, "So? I *am* a girl."

"That's precisely my point," Ma said. "You must start acting like one. Pa and I take full credit for allowing, even encouraging, your rough-and-tumble ways. It's time you put them away and embrace your femininity."

"But I know all about being a woman, Ma," Jana said.

As though trying to make it up to her older sister for mentioning her growth spurts, Rachel looked at Jana in particular when she said, "She dresses up real nice for church and makes the tastiest deer stew around."

"And she sews and keeps house and is a fun babysitter," Rebecca said.

Glimpsing Molly, Jana said, "I even know about birthing. I helped the midwife with Eliza, and if she wasn't here I could've turned Molly around to come out head first like I've done with our foals and calves."

"I admit you do all of those things … some of them very well. It's not about dressing and acting like a woman once in a while because you must; it's about doing it all of the time so you come to embrace it. Pa and I insist you put away your slingshot and rifle."

"How am I supposed to go hunting with Pa without a rifle?" Jana demanded.

"You won't be hunting any more; nevertheless, you may still ride Commodore. The exercise is good for you both," Ma said.

Jana gulped then squeaked out, "I'm not ready for marriage and babies if that's what you want."

"Pa and I aren't pushing for that; though, the only way you'll ever get there is by swapping men's britches for women's clothes and mixing with people your own age. These we do expect."

"But I have nothing in common with girls. And not one boy in Chemung County interests me," Jana said.

"Stop exaggerating. You'll find your love of reading in common with the other young ladies when you join Rachel, Rebecca, and me at quilting bees and teas," Ma said.

Jana's stomach turned queasy when she saw herself confined in a parlor quilting or sipping tea. She bet not one girl read about tomboys, like real-life heroine Joan of Arc or her favorite fictional character, Sarah Brewer, who cut off her hair and joined the marines in the war back in 1812.

Ma said, "The way Conor Bowan stares at you in church—"

"You mean ogles, Ma," Rebecca corrected.

Ma concluded, "I'd say he's very much interested in you. I'll bet he asks Pa to escort you to the Young Men's Christian Association ball, come Christmas."

"What would a wealthy merchant's son want with a poor, freckled, farm frump like me?" Jana asked.

Ma's face crumpled with hurt. "We might not be wealthy; however, our crops and animals produce enough to allow us material for a new dress every once in a while." With a dismissive wave of her hand, she said, "Not that I care a hoot about social standings. And, may I add, neither do the Bowans. I'm trying to say that your excuses don't justify you keeping on in your current way."

"I only meant my looks aren't favorable to his," Jana said.

"Well, embarrassingly enough, Conor's appreciation for your blossoming beauty awakened me and Pa to it. Take a good long look in the mirror, Jana. You too will see that who you've become requires a new way of dressing and acting," Ma said.

Jana had been noticing her physical changes in the mirror for some time now; she'd watched her button nose angle downward into a point and her chubby cheeks rise up and set high. Next time she ran into Conor Bowan, she'd thrash him for getting Ma and Pa to see these and her other growth spurts that she'd worked hard to hide beneath Ma's loose-fitting hand-me-downs. Growing up didn't bother her as long as she could keep on using her rifle and slingshot and hunt with Pa.

"And you'll stick to wearing a bonnet when you're in the sun. Then you'll have no more worries about freckles," Ma said.

"Rachel and I'll help you get your skin back to a milky shade," Rebecca said.

"We'll even have you ready in time for the Christmas dance," Rachel said, vying with her twin for the last word as usual.

Jana ran her fingers over each palms' scratchy calluses. *Such hands have no business in dainty gloves*, she silently lamented. Concluding she'd be forced to give up much more than her slingshot and rifle and hunting with Pa, she felt misery pressing her down deep into the sofa cushion. Donning womanhood wouldn't be as easy as Ma and the twins made it sound.

Military Camp
Elmira, New York
Mid-December 1861

Jana snatched a handful of flour from a ceramic canister. *Thwop*! She splattered it onto the oak tabletop and smeared it around, swathing herself and every inch of the kitchen in powder. She couldn't care less if she quadrupled her cleanup later. The doughy sweetness of bread rising first thing in the morning usually awakened all kinds of homey, happy feelings in her. Not today. She was furious with Pa. He'd gone off turkey hunting without her for the first time ever.

She seized some risen dough, hurled it onto her floured surface, and set her angry fists against it, punching it down and ripping it into four equal parts. Covering them over with a cloth while she greased their loaf pans, she stewed over the past nine months.

Ma and Pa had held fast to their word to try turning her from a tomboy into a lady. They'd made her push broom over plow, clean clothes over stalls, churn butter over chop wood, change diapers over groom horses, and pluck chicken feathers and boil off pig hair over their slaughter. When free of chores, they kept her busy with homework and attending quilting bees and teas with gossipy women and giggly girls. Just as she'd suspected, she felt caged like a traveling circus lion with Ma and Pa's changes.

Extracting one of the moist blobs from its resting place, Jana suddenly saw Pa's face in it. Instead of shaping it into the loaf pan for a second rising, she hoisted the dough over her head and prepared to lob it at the wall.

Ma breezed into the room. "I've never seen bread bake on a wall before. Be sure to let me know how it comes out," she said.

Jana lowered her projectile. Flushing with embarrassment, her cheeks felt as though they'd been put in the cast-iron stove to bake.

Sliding into one of twelve spindle-backed chairs tableside, Ma said, "Pa and I haven't done right by you. We let you run wild too long then force you to change overnight. We're to blame for your misery at home and rudeness to others."

"What? Rude to others?" Jana said, feigning innocence.

"Oh come, Jana. You've used every ridiculous reason for turning down invitations to picnics and parties with others your age. And every Sunday in church you've glared your way out of Conor Bowan ever asking you to the YMCA ball—such un-Christian-like behavior in the house of our Lord!"

"But I was behaving Christian-like. I'm not about to hurt his feelings by letting him think he can win my heart when he can't."

"How do you know he can't?"

"I just know it, Ma."

"I suppose you do." The black buds in Ma's coffee-colored irises stared off in a dreamy way as she said, "Pa and I knew we were right for each other the second we met." The memory wilted, and her eyes refocused on Jana. "You must accept your femininity. However, Pa and I won't spoon-feed it to you anymore. We'll not alienate you like the Perhams have their daughter."

"Leanne's run away?" Jana was surprised at first, until the memory of Mr. Perham always ordering his daughter about gruffly in his blacksmith shop, where Leanne worked and the Bradys took their horses and mules for shoeing, struck her. He never had a kind word for Leanne when she forged a perfect shoe or shod a horse's hoof without the slip of a nail. Pa complimented her within earshot of Mr. Perham every time. If life for Leanne was the same at home as it was at work, Jana would have run away too.

"Poor girl! Her pa made her dress and act like a boy from birth. I can't understand why her ma went along with it. Leanne's probably run off to find the woman inside of her." She reached across the table and patted Jana's hand. "Pa and I won't have you dressing and acting like a boy. Together, let's find a more agreeable path toward your womanhood." She withdrew her hand with globs of dough clinging to it. As she picked at them, she said in a casual manner, "We have a wagonload of jarred food and clothes for the soldiers. While we study your dilemma, why don't you take them into town? I'll finish baking and cleaning up."

Jana hugged Ma, and the flour from her apron dusted Ma's hair, aging her by twenty years. Then she skedaddled before Ma could change her mind.

Later that morning, Jana reached the city's western fringe within ten minutes of leaving the farm. *Boom!* She heard the cannons over on the northeastern hills where artillery practiced. But the nearer bugle blows and drum rolls, to which cavalry and infantry practiced respectively, lured her to the military camp. Mr. and Mrs. Brown could wait on the Brady offerings. Surely, they were overwhelmed sorting and divvying the heaps of donations for the volunteer soldiers from residents all over the county. The tailors prided themselves on making sure every soldier leaving for war, not just the local boys, got something. Jana giggled when she imagined the Browns lost in their shop under piles of blankets, pillows, hand-sewn clothing, and jars of jellies or preserved fruits and vegetables.

Pa had brought Jana to the military camp a few times when they came into town to pick up supplies. He loved to watch the soldiers drilling too. However, Ma and Pa would be real sore at her for coming here alone; she'd make her visit brief so they'd think she got hung up with the chatty tailors.

When New York State had announced the open thirty acres of elevated ground between Foster's Pond and Water Street near the Chemung Canal's basin would make perfect grounds for one of its three military rendezvous points, Jana was overjoyed. Pa, like other farmers and merchants, were tickled too. They'd all been profiting since Camp Rathbun was built, soon after the firing upon of Fort Sumter back on April 12, 1861. They'd sold plenty of their crops and wares with thousands of soldiers filtering through from the western part of the state to be organized into infantry, artillery, and cavalry.

Jana watched the infantrymen pour powder, drop ball, and pack both down their musket's muzzle with a ram rod and then aim and shoot at the burlap-stuffed enemies set up at the edge of the frozen pond. To her, the hundreds of muskets firing all at once rivaled the sound and ecstasy of a firework's grand finale. Most of the balls missed their target and either skidded across or stuck into the pond's icy surface. The cavalrymen grabbed her attention more. She could almost feel the cold steel of the hilt against her palm as she saw herself learning to brandish the saber alongside them. She bet she could learn to wield a saber faster, and she already knew how to fire a pistol and rifle better than the infantrymen she watched. Still, she envied them. Soon, they'd set their sights on glory in the fight for their country. She scoffed at Ma and Pa's attempts to settle her patriotic fervor by weaving words like "glamour" and "glory" into sewing for the volunteers. In her opinion, nothing women did to support the war could compare with the glory and glamour these soldiers would sow on a battlefield in putting down rebels. Her mood soured like the abounding smell of manure that the military manufactured ever since they moved in, swelling the horse and mule population.

A spirited jingle of metal drew Jana's attention toward a short, wiry soldier swaggering past. His saber rattled against the buckle of his waist belt from which it dangled. A fleeting glance of the brass, crossed sabers stamped on the rounded crown, sunken into the floppy sides of his forage cap, told Jana he belonged to the cavalry. She called out, "Hey, trooper, when's your regiment moving out?"

The cavalryman whirled around. Deepening his voice, he said, "Rumor is soon. Ain't sure where to, though." When he got a good look at Jana, he flung his face down toward the cuffs at the knees of his leather boots and started slinking backwards.

With her own eyes wider than the brass buttons down the trooper's greatcoat, Jana said, "Leanne Perham, I know it's you!" Neither her hair trimmed up to her ears nor the squared visor of her hat pulled low over her face disguised her from Jana. She'd studied Leanne's disgruntled face enough with every reaction to her pa's ill treatment. She recognized her pouty lips, her rare, steel-gray eyes, and the mole on her right cheek.

Leanne looked around to make sure no one had heard Jana. When she turned back, her fists were raised. "If ya tell on me, I'll gut-punch ya," she said.

Jana often thought if she and Leanne had attended the same school, they'd be playmates. Leanne was even more tomboyish than she. As far as she knew, Leanne worked every day in her pa's shop with no time to go to school. By her poor rhetoric, Jana doubted she got much schooling at home either. "From what I hear, you're better off… away from your ma and pa, that is."

"Away from my pa." Leanne's angry tongue whittled down to a sorrowful tone when she said, "Never my ma."

Jana hurried to change the obviously sore subject. "Did you really enlist?"

Puffing up with pride, Leanne said, "Call me Leander Perham of Company *D*, Tenth New York Volunteer Cavalry Regiment."

"Isn't it risky using pretty near your own name?"

"The men in my company ain't from these parts. So I picked a name I'd answer to right off."

"How're you getting away with your disguise around town when you look the same to me?" Jana stammered, "I-I-I didn't mean to suggest—"

"Don't worry. I know I ain't pretty, and I ain't ashamed of it," Leanne said.

Jana wanted to tell her that her plain looks as a girl made her handsome as a boy. Instead, she bit her tongue.

"To answer ya, I don't really care if anybody notices me. They won't tell my pa. Except for your pa, most everybody's left his shop 'cause they're afraid he'll bash 'em over the head with a hot iron one of these days when his temper gets the best of him. Besides, he doesn't give a hoot whether I'm dead or alive," Leanne said.

Noting Leanne's darkening mood, Jana pointed toward the thirty-five, two-story wooden barracks set up in neat rows and said, "You're living in close quarters with all those men, and they don't know you're a girl?"

"I tend to my private duties away from 'em. Nobody thinks anything of it 'cause a lot of boys, even men, are shy about relieving themselves or bathing in public." Leanne raised her fists again. "If ya call me a girl one more time, I'm gonna make good on that gut-punch."

Jana's instincts told her Leanne relished being a boy; she hadn't run off to find her womanhood as Ma had speculated. Brushing the notion aside, she said, "But you're not eighteen."

"Government can't prove I'm only sixteen." Leanne narrowed her eyes on Jana and said, "Unless somebody tells 'em."

"Not me. I admire your courage."

A bugle blared.

"That's my call to guard duty," Leanne said and turned to go.

"Wait! How'd you pass the doctor's examination? Didn't you have to strip bare for it?"

Leanne grinned. "I threw a fit about already having it at a recruitment office in Buffalo. I told 'em they must've lost my papers, and I wasn't gonna be shamed by stripping again. The regiment needed filling, so the surgeon passed me on account I didn't show any disease or deformity."

Sticking out her tongue to catch the large snowflakes, just beginning to float down from the black, bulging clouds, Jana mulled over Leanne's easy switch from girl to soldier with envy.

Leanne's grin broadened. "You're thinking about signing up, ain't ya?"

Jana jolted up to her revelation: disguised as a soldier she could go places and do things women couldn't. Better yet, she could join the fight for her country.

"Can I tell Colonel Lemmon I got us a new recruit?" Leanne asked.

Tasting sweet glory in the snowflakes, Jana said, "Yes, do that." She whipped the mules' fuzzy, gray rumps and turned for home. With any luck, she'd be with the Tenth New York Volunteer Cavalry Regiment when they moved out.

Brady Homestead
Elmira, New York
December 22, 1861

Without a peep from the hens, Jana groped around between their velvety, feathered bellies and scratchy straw beds to steal their eggs. Her mind churned like butter, hard-pressed to find a way to womanhood that would please Ma and Pa and free her to join the cavalry. She fretted over Leanne's regiment, almost filled up, being transferred soon to make room for other units to arrive and form up.

A sharp rap on the door incited a calamitous clucking from the hens and made Jana squish the egg in her hand.

The henhouse door screeched outward on its rusty hinges; Leanne stepped in, latching the door shut behind her. Eyeing the yolk oozing between Jana's fingers, she said, "Didn't mean to scare ya."

"How'd you know I was here?" Jana asked, wiping her slimy hand on the apron beneath her woolen cape.

"Watched from the woods all morning praying you'd come here before I froze to death." Leanne pulled her gloves off with her chattering teeth and clamped them between her bony knees. "Where're your ma and pa?" Her face disappeared behind a cloud of frosty air when she blew hard into her hands, cupped over her purpled nose and lips.

"Ma's in the kitchen cooking our noon meal. Pa might be in the parlor helping with the Christmas tree. Don't worry, they can't see the henhouse from either place."

"Have ya changed your mind about signing up?"

"I haven't figured a way yet."

"Run away like me."

"No. That'd worry Ma and Pa sick."

"Well, ya best fix on something right quick. Rumor is my regiment's leaving in three days."

"On Christmas Eve?" Jana asked, mistrusting she'd heard right.

"That's what they're saying. Listen, I'm on furlough 'til Monday, boarding at the Chemung House on my enlistment pay. If ya get there, my room's around back, first window on the right at ground level. I'll stick a handkerchief in the sash to mark my room. I keep my window unlocked to get in and out that way. The less I'm seen by the help in the lobby, who might turn me in to my ma, the better. Tap on the window before ya crawl in. I wouldn't want to shoot ya. And I'll scout a way to get ya into my company."

"I'd hate to trouble you for nothing."

Gawking at the eggs in the basket swinging on Jana's arm, Leanne said, "Ain't no trouble for a few of them. I can sell 'em to the men, still hungry after they eat their rations."

Jana offered her several, promising to bring more if she got to the hotel.

Leanne stuffed the eggs into her pockets. "I'm betting you'll get there," she said and opened the door, poked her head out to make sure no one lurked about, and gave a backhanded wave as she hurried off.

All the way to the house, Jana prayed for some scheme to jar loose from her brain. Ambling into the front hall, she hung up her coat and traded her boots for slippers then headed straight back through the hall to the kitchen. Her nose caught the aroma of rosemary-seasoned pork, and her watering taste buds stole her from her trance. She smiled when she recalled Grandpa Brady's boastings about Ma's cooking and how it could lead terrified men into the bloodiest of battles by their noses.

Ma was at the kitchen counter carving the roast while Pa had his nose buried in the *Elmira Gazette*.

"The hens were generous today, eh, Jana?" Pa said, peering over his newspaper at her eggs.

Nodding at Pa, Jana set down her basket, lifted dinner plates off a shelf, and began setting the table.

"Our Jana doesn't speak anymore, Ma. Is she mute?" Pa asked.

"She's just very pensive," Ma said, trading carving knife and fork for metal spatula. She went to the stove and began scraping the bottom of the cast-iron pan as she stirred the potatoes and onions hissing in hog lard.

Pa kept on, "What's she chewing on?"

"A way to womanhood that's agreeable to us but won't make her miserable," Ma said.

"Is that all?" Pa asked.

The devil tempted Jana to spit out that finding a way to womanhood as a means to join the cavalry was no light matter; the angel whispered for her to hold her sassy tongue—she needed Ma and Pa on her side.

When Jana set down Pa's dish next to him, her eyes feasted on a newspaper advertisement she'd seen many times before but had never given a thought until now. Her voice raised several octaves with excitement as she said, "But I've found a way!"

Ma and Pa cast curious eyes upon Jana.

"I'm going to join Miss Dorothea Dix's nursing corps," Jana said, relieved she'd finally hit upon a way to leave home without having to run away.

With an earsplitting clatter, Ma dropped her cooking utensil against the stovetop.

Pa looked as though Ma had just stunned him with a whack on his head from her spatula.

"Well, you want me to embrace womanhood, and I want to help my country in some grander way than sewing shirts and stuffing pillows. And you both always say to put God and country before self no matter what the cost to yourself," Jana said, feeling her cheeks baking with patriotic fervor.

Recovering from her surprise, Ma fetched a clean spatula and returned to stirring the hissing spuds. "In Washington … such a big city, so close to the fighting?" she said.

"Elmira's a big city, too. I've been getting around it all by myself since I was practically a baby. Besides, Washington's reported to be heavily fortified and guarded," Jana said.

"It seems Miss Dix'll send her nursing corps into the field," Pa said.

"And that means even closer to the fighting," Ma said.

"Surely, the federal government wouldn't put women in harm's way," Jana said.

"Perhaps not intentionally. Placing female nurses in the field is in its infancy. Who knows how it'll turn out," Ma said.

Tapping the ad with his index finger, Pa said, "Miss Dix wants women thirty years of age and plain-looking. You meet neither of those qualifications by a long shot, Jana."

"Where there's a will there's a way. And I have the will," Jana said.

"The will of a thousand people, I'd say," Pa said and chuckled.

Ma shot Pa a look of displeasure and returned to stirring. With her back to Jana, she said, "You're too young."

"Not too young to embrace womanhood, though," Jana murmured.

"And all you've done is mope around here without doing anything about it," Ma said.

Believing she had Ma cornered on this point, Jana said, "I won't be moping around any more when I'm off nursing. And nursing alongside other women is bound to make me a woman."

"Miss Dix just might be the one to turn our Jana into a lady," Pa said.

Ma swatted her spatula toward Pa, flinging grease everywhere. "Stop encouraging her, Thomas."

"You got to be a schoolteacher—," Jana began, but Ma interrupted her.

"Yes, and speaking of which, I'd like to see you attend the Female Seminary. Fortunate for us, we have a college right here in Elmira that grants degrees, formerly reserved for men only."

Jana crinkled up her nose. Maybe another time she'd find achieving a higher education thrilling ... not now when there were a whole lot more exciting things to do, such as soldiering. "That's not for me, Ma, but I know I'd love nursing," she said, feeling a stab of guilt for lying to them. The feeling evaporated when she sensed a greater glory in soldiering over nursing. And she knew Ma and Pa would forgive her when all ended well.

"Well, I was eighteen and, might I add, mature when I started teaching," Ma said.

"The war'll end long before I turn eighteen and get to try it. Great-Grandpa and Grandpa went off to war around my age and came home mature," Jana said.

"It's less dangerous for males, no matter what their age, to be traipsing about the country. Miss Dix's nursing corps is bound to succeed, making female nurses in demand after the war. Why not try it then?" Ma said.

"If you're worried about me being chaperoned, as Pa noted in the ad, Miss Dix has strict requirements to be one of her nurses. She seems the type who doesn't tolerate any fooling around and who'd keep a keen eye on me," Jana said.

"Sure does sound like a mother hen," Pa added.

Blowing at a tuft of her hair, freed from the netted bun at the nape of her neck and dangling in one eye, Ma showed her frustration with Pa for continuing to advance Jana's cause.

Jana wove her fingers together. "Please, let me go. I promise not to do anything to shame you," she said, hoping they'd realize she'd really never done anything to make them think she couldn't stand on her own.

"We know you wouldn't. We're real proud of you. You always do everything and more that Ma and I ask of you. We'd like to reward you for it. However, there's real danger in what you're asking to do," Pa said.

"*Real* danger," Ma echoed.

"If Great-Grandpa and Grandpa were alive, they'd shame you both into letting me help my country no matter what the danger." Jana was sure she'd said this to herself; a wince from both Ma and Pa told her otherwise. Now that the words were out, she wouldn't take them back.

Pa's look of anguish turned sympathetic. He nodded toward the cellar door and said, "Go put your eggs away, Jana."

Dashing from the room, Jana's hopes rose with every step down into the drafty cellar. Whenever Pa wanted a private word with Ma over her, it usually meant good things. She plopped down between the flour sack and barrel of pork preserving in brine, barely noticing the stones in the dirt floor jabbing her knees. And she didn't care that the preserving liquid of coarse salt and un-slacked lime splashed her face as she dumped the eggs into the pail. With her emptied basket swinging on her arm, she took the steps by twos to the top and pressed her ear against the door, just in time to hear most of the stove-side debate.

"We can't shelter her forever, Julia," Pa said.

"That close to the fighting she could be maimed or killed," Ma said.

"She could die from disease or an accident here at home. I'm sure Jana's right. The government wouldn't be foolish enough to put women in harm's way."

Ma fell silent for a minute. Then she said, "I must commend Jana for choosing a respectable profession. Perhaps she's starting to understand our bigger message that the most glorious fights happen without a gunshot."

Although overly anxious for their decision, Jana would sit tight a few seconds longer if only Ma would recite her usual list of glorious fights without a gunshot, which she did every time the subject arose. Ma needed to hear herself saying how she admired pioneers, such as former slave Harriett Tubman, who, armed with courage and disguise, had sneaked into the South to guide hundreds of slaves out. Or Susan B. Anthony, who, armed with eloquent words, was sure to one day gain equal rights for women. Or Elmira's very own John Jones, who, armed with empathy, had sent nearly a thousand slaves to freedom. Maybe then it would dawn on her how she was trying to stop Jana from being the very hero she heralded in others.

Surprisingly, Pa beat Ma to it, reciting those very examples. "Jana's right about us encouraging her to fight for her country no matter what the cost to herself. We'd be hypocrites to tell her she can't now. If we stand in her way, she'll run away like the Perham girl. If she falls in the fight for her country, I'd rather it be with our blessing. But I have faith she won't fall," he said.

Jana held her breath; the sugary aroma of Indian pudding, spiced with cinnamon and nutmeg, seeped through the cracks around the door's frame and dared her to take a loud sniff and give away her spying.

"I suppose we should reward her for finding a way to womanhood that's agreeable to us and, more importantly, seems to excite her. But—"

Not waiting for Ma to finish, Jana tossed her basket aside. She heard it thump all the way down the stairs as she flung open the door and whooped with victory. She flung her arms around Pa's neck, unbothered by the stubbles of his unshaven cheek scratching her lips as she kissed him. Next, she twirled Ma about the creaky floor in a clumsy waltz.

With Eliza on their heels, Rachel and Rebecca whisked into the kitchen, each holding an end of a half-threaded strand of cranberries. "What's happening?" they cried in unison.

"Our Jana's heading to Washington to be a nurse," Pa said, aglow with pride.

Jana detected a hint of envy in his voice. At forty-six, he was one year over President Lincoln's enlistment qualifications. She wasn't about to tell him age wouldn't stop her from signing up. Even if he could join, knowing Pa, he wouldn't leave behind a family dependent upon him.

Rachel dropped her end of the strand, and cranberries went rolling into every nook and cranny. Rebecca's chin dropped to her chest. For once, they were speechless.

When Jana released Ma from their dance, Eliza, understanding only that something good had happened to her big sister, dove at Jana's leg and hugged it.

Between gasps of breath, Ma said, "First, you must prove to us you won't be unsupervised."

Jana felt her hope extinguish. Ma was throwing up an obstacle next to impossible for her to hurdle by tomorrow. "When Miss Dix learns my age, she won't accept me. And by the time I write and get her reply, the war could be over. I have to sell myself in person and get started tomorrow," she said.

"It's our best offer," Ma said.

"Take it or leave it," Pa said.

Jana didn't reply, and Ma and Pa didn't press her. They probably took her silence to mean she'd agreed with their terms.

To Jana, Ma said, "Let's put the matter to rest for now." To all, she said, "Come sit, it's time to eat."

Jana knew she wouldn't be able to let the matter rest. She barely heard Pa's prayer of thanks for his family and their farm and food. Her mind was frantically reeling in search of another tactic to set on Ma and Pa.

Brady Homestead
Elmira, New York
December 23, 1861

Around midnight, Jana found herself still tossing and turning after she'd blown out her bedside candle a few hours before. She was mulling over Ma and Pa's terms about leaving home. She loved her parents and birthplace, but neither could offer the kind of glory and adventure that came with fighting for one's country up close and personal. If she stayed home, her misery would soar with each passing day of war, and Ma and Pa would grow despondent with her. She threw her goose-feather quilt aside, sat up, and swung her legs over the bed's edge. Her parents didn't deserve to be pained by her wretchedness. And she couldn't pass up on Leanne's help, her only chance of becoming a soldier.

Before she changed her mind, Jana hurried to gather two dresses, a bonnet, and undergarments from her wardrobe just for show. She couldn't have Ma and Pa puzzling over how she was off nursing without the proper attire. Starting out of the room, it dawned on her she'd need to hide her chest better, so she fetched her corset. She was glad she didn't share her bed chamber with anyone, especially Rachel or Rebecca.

Jana let the moonlight, peeping through the frosted windows, guide her down the staircase; she avoided the creakiest spots in the steps. At the front hall, she slipped into her wool coat and pants. She made one of her dresses into a sack and stuffed it with her still-warm nightgown and the rest of her clothes (except the corset, shoved down her coat) before tying it up. After tucking her auburn locks under her felt hat and lacing up her ankle-high brogans, she felt her way along the hall's wallpaper, with its raised leafy flowers, to the small secretary in the kitchen. On it was a candle that she lit; from one of its drawers, she retrieved a pencil and paper, which Ma kept handy for noting cooking supplies that she needed from town. Plunking down on the desk's matching chair, she kept her words to Ma and Pa vague because she hated to tell too much of a tall tale:

> December 23, 1861, Elmira, New York
> Dear Ma and Pa,
> Please forgive my impatience for wanting to see about helping my country sooner than later. I'll write as soon as I get set up and will keep you informed as to my whereabouts. Don't worry about me. I took my chore money for room and board and my pistol for protection. I'll send for more clothes if necessary. Take good care of Commodore for me.
> Your loving daughter,
> Jana

Jana used the candle to light her way down into the cellar, where she fulfilled her vow to bring Leanne eggs. Back in the kitchen, she tacked her letter down on the writing table with the candlestick and smothered the candle's flame with a brass snuffer. The smell of its burning wax tickled her nostrils, and she pinched her nose to squelch a sneeze as she crept outside.

The night pressed its crisp air against the nape of Jana's neck as though warning her to return to the warmth and safety of her bed. Determined not to let it get its way, Jana turned up her coat collar and slid on gloves, which she fetched from her coat pocket. She took refuge in her clothes and comfort in having gotten at least half a blessing from Ma and Pa about leaving home. It didn't feel right saying a proper goodbye to Commodore without one to the rest of her family, so she resisted the footpath's temptation to the barn.

At the top of the lane to the Brady homestead, Jana turned and stood riveted by a sweeping view of the farm under the moon's fullness and a star-crowded sky. The hens were fast asleep in their house. The corral encircling the barn was emptied of livestock, now sharing the barn with Commodore. The silo bulged with corn. And the barren fields of wheat and corn looked pretty under a thin, glittery layer of snow. She'd been outside at this time of night before, though only in the barn helping Pa with the births of their animals. From her perch now, she marveled at the quiet; not even a whistle in the wind could be heard. She'd miss the joy of togetherness, always extra special on Christmas Eve as her family chatted and sipped eggnog around the tree in the parlor. But she had a war to get to. Up to now she'd believed as most Northerners did: the war would be short. She stole a last glance of home and suddenly sensed her journey away would be long—maybe forever.

Turning her back to home, she began her trek into town. On the way, she found the hollowed-out log in the woods where she'd often played. She felt no remorse in shedding her old life as she stuffed her sack of women's clothes into it. Bursting with excitement, she jogged the remaining half hour to the Chemung House. She crept through the shadows of the hotel's walls to Leanne's window. As Leanne had promised, there was a red handkerchief dangling out from under the window's sash. She tapped on the window and waited.

Within seconds, a candle's flame swelled as it drew closer to the window. Finally, it framed Leanne's face in a square of the lower sash. Her features were recognizable, though somewhat distorted by the window's frosty patterns.

Leanne set down her candle. She raised the sash slowly with a small swooshing sound and waved Jana in.

Jana crawled in and stood up. Peering down at Leanne, a good three inches shorter than her five feet six inches, she was pleased to have found her without any trouble.

"By the hour, I'd say ya ran away like me," Leanne said.

Noticing Leanne's tousled hair and sleepy eyes, Jana ribbed her back. "And by the looks of you, I'd say I woke you up."

"Since I knew you'd come late, I reckoned I'd catch a little shut-eye. Nothing like cutting it close," Leanne said, pulling down the frilled, cloth shade and snatching up the candlestick to light a path to the bureau. From its top drawer she fetched scissors and then dragged a wooden chair away from its matching desk over to the bureau with an attached mirror. Cutting the air with the scissors and patting the back of the chair, she motioned for Jana to sit. "Ain't no time to waste. Regiment's pulling out first thing in the morning."

Jana removed her coat and hat and tossed them onto the bed. Plopping down onto the un-cushioned seat, she dropped her eyes toward the floor; she'd wait, though breathless, until Leanne was done to see her metamorphosis.

Click! Click! Click! Leanne worked the scissors to chop Jana's hair.

Again, Jana felt no remorse when she saw her auburn tresses landing all around her worn, black shoes.

When Leanne quieted her clippers, she said, "You can look now."

Jana had always thought she'd look like Pa with her hair trimmed like his. When she peered into the mirror, she had a hard time believing it was her, not Pa staring back.

"Amazing what a haircut can do. You're not as pretty a boy, but that's how we want it," Leanne said, looking satisfied with her job.

Before the new day dawned, Leanne set off to see about getting Jana into the regiment. When she returned, she was elated over having found the disbursing and mustering-in officer too busy preparing to muster in nearly seven hundred men to worry about one new recruit just as she'd figured it. She said he'd thrown the recruitment form at her and told her to get the new volunteer to complete it and to take him to the surgeon for examination. As she was leaving the military camp, as also ordered, she'd fetched a uniform for Jana from the regiment's quartermaster.

Jana stood before the mirror, feeling important in her cavalry uniform with the yellow stripes down the sides of her sky blue pants and the brass, crossed sabers with their regiment's number 10 stamped over them on her forage cap.

"Ain't no time to admire yourself. I've got to report back to my unit before they think I've deserted and I get punished for it." She hustled Jana from the hotel to the train depot.

Along the way, Jana kept her hat low over her face. She couldn't have anybody mistaking her for Pa and telling him and Ma about it later; though, not many people milled about on this chilly, drizzly morning.

As Jana and Leanne rounded the corner, they each sucked in a lungful of air, delighted to see both steam-powered engines of the Williamsport and Elmira Railroad pointing in a southerly direction. Up until now, Leanne claimed there'd been much speculation amongst the ranks over where they'd head from Elmira. Away from the war, some said.

Through the open doorway of one of the cars, Jana noticed a man she estimated to be in his early thirties directing soldiers to stack boxes labeled "Fragile" on top of unmarked boxes.

Leanne put her hand out to keep Jana at her heels. "That's Dr. Pease. Let me do the talking," she said and marched his way.

Dr. Pease jumped down from the car, almost on top of Leanne. When he got a good look at her, recognition flashed in his eyes. He waggled his index finger before her nose and said, "I don't have time for another one of your fits."

Leanne set her jaws, showing she meant to have it her way. "I reckon that's up to you, Doc. I got us a new recruit, and I've been ordered to bring him to ya for examination. But us volunteers are about to be mustered in and we ain't missing it. The way I see it you're busy and your tools are all packed up. And I've known"—Leanne paused for a split-second as though trying to recollect the name they'd penciled in on the recruitment form for Jana—"Johnnie Brodie here all my life. I can vouch there ain't nothing wrong with him."

Dr. Pease raked a harried hand through his thick mane of black hair while he chewed on it. With a roll of his eyes almost to the back of his head, he sped over to Jana and said, "Open your mouth." He mostly examined her teeth, making sure they were good enough to tear open a powder cartridge. Then he groped her neck for lumps and peeled back her coat sleeve to check for spots. Inspecting her hands, he noted, "These are some fine trigger fingers," which further supported Jana's theory that her hands were meant for more masculine work. "You appear healthy all right. Nevertheless, I'm ordering you to report to me when we get where we're going for a full examination."

"What about a certificate to show he's passed?" Leanne asked.

"Tell the disbursing officer I'll have to finish and file that with him later." Making a sweeping motion with his hands, he said to them, "Off with you, now. I've got tons to do before we move out."

When they'd put some distance between them and Dr. Pease, Leanne leaned over and whispered, "Stay out of his sight for a while, and he'll forget all about your examination."

Jana counted her blessings for having stumbled upon Leanne when she had, and she thanked Leanne a hundred times for helping her to enlist, with a name she'd answer to right off and without having to strip bare. The quartermaster had told Leanne, Jana would be acquiring the uniform of a deserter named Porter; he'd chosen not to follow in the footsteps of Colonel Peter Buel Porter of Niagara Falls, after whom the regiment was nicknamed the Porter Guards. Jana determined to serve her uniform well and make a fighting name for herself just like the colonel had in the war against Great Britain back in 1812.

Havre De Grace, Maryland

April 1862

Jana sat cross-legged on the western bank of the Susquehanna River where it met the Chesapeake Bay. She was preparing to write her second letter home since leaving Elmira on Christmas Eve with the Tenth New York Volunteer Cavalry Regiment. Neither the late-afternoon sun brightening her surroundings nor the fresh, salty air tickling her nostrils revived her from her grouchiness. Over the past three months, she'd been shuffled from Gettysburg, Pennsylvania, to Perryville, Maryland, and now to this place. And her regiment had yet to receive their arms, equipment, and horses—their only hopes of joining the fight. She'd take her newer station over the last one, where she reasoned not even a whole summer of sunshine could dry up its mud. There were comfortable barracks here; each man got his own bunk, and no one had to sleep in tents. So far, Jana had gotten lucky in drawing a comfortable sleeping arrangement everywhere she went. But this place especially represented one step closer to war in the East. That alone made it more appealing.

Compounding Jana's misery was her bodily woe. She scratched her midsection and looked around to see that none of the troopers throwing away their pay on poker or making bracelets out of horse-tail strands were within earshot when she said to Leanne, "I hate this itchy corset. You're lucky you don't have to wear one." Feeling sweat trickling down her back, she added, "And you're lucky you can take off your coat without anyone figuring out what you are." She was careful not to call Leanne a girl after she'd made it perfectly clear she wouldn't tolerate that.

Leanne stopped polishing her musket's barrel with an oiled rag and faced Jana. "Would you rather be wearing it here or at home, Johnnie?"

Jana knew she should be more grateful to her corset than her boyish haircut and uniform for thus far helping to fool everyone as to her gender. She and Leanne fit right in with the young boys who didn't have pronounced Adam's apples or facial hair yet and were shy about bathing or emptying themselves in public.

"I'll scout out a looser shirt and jacket for ya. Even if I find 'em, you'll probably still have to wear that darn corset. Maybe ya can loosen it a little. And if you'd like to take your coat off now for a spell, I'll shoot whoever comes poking around," Leanne said.

"I'd be mighty grateful to you," Jana said. She'd seen how Leanne acted tough to most everyone yet showed a soft side to those she liked. She was glad Leanne was in her corner. Feeling refreshed by the light breeze sifting through her shirt, Jana picked up her pencil, rested her stationery on the canvas-covered wood slats of the lap desk she'd bought in a Gettysburg book shop, and wrote:

April 5, 1862, Baltimore, Maryland
 Dear Ma and Pa,
  Things didn't develop as I had hoped in Washington. However, the regimental surgeons aren't as picky as Miss Dix and are grateful for any help they can get in the field hospitals. I'm glad for any chance to serve my country. I hope you're glad too. I've been transferred to Baltimore but will be moved whenever and wherever I'm needed. I'll write as often as I can. Please send my love to my sisters and Commodore.
  Your loving daughter,
  Jana

Again, Jana kept her words vague to avoid lying to Ma and Pa. She stuck a reddish-brown, three-cent stamp profiling George Washington to the envelope in which she sealed her letter. Then she stashed the mail in the tube of her lap desk—this she rolled up into its attached canvas-covered slats. Later she'd pass her note on to a courier to post from nearby Baltimore. While stationed in Gettysburg, Jana had seized the chance to make Ma and Pa think she was in Washington. A few of the regiment's officers had been sent to the Union capital to see the then Secretary of War Simon Cameron about building barracks for the men, housed in private homes, shops, and warehouses all over town. She had one of them post her letter from there.

Lying down in the grass, Jana felt its prickly spires stabbing the nape of her neck. She stared up at the cloudless, indigo sky and got to thinking about home. Right about now, Ma was taking down the laundry she'd hung outside to dry. Pa was sharpening his plow blades, readying for the planting season. Rachel and Rebecca were sewing new dresses, anxious to show them off at some spring picnic. Eliza may have given up dolls for slingshots by now. Molly was most likely taking a few steps on legs wobblier than a newborn foal's. She missed them all and was mulling over if they missed her when a duck's honk stole her away from her reflections. She sat up.

Quack! Quack! A mallard with its green neckband glistening in the sun flew overhead. With a splash, it skidded its webbed feet across the bay's glassy water.

Leanne grabbed her musket and shot to her feet. "I'm gonna get us a Rebel duck for supper tonight, Johnnie," she said, pouring powder and dropping ball and packing both down the musket's muzzle with a ramrod in quick time.

"About the only thing that rusty Revolutionary-War piece is good for," Jana said, thinking back on how she and the other troopers had almost mutinied when compelled to shoulder them. They were superstitious about President Lincoln turning them into foot soldiers if they took up these longer-barreled, infantrymen's muskets over the shorter-barreled carbines cavalrymen needed for maneuvering in the saddle. Since this was the fate of other units first formed as cavalry, the Tenth finally caved in to their use; they needed something for drilling and guarding. Now, she and the Porter Guards, as did all other cavalrymen who passed through here without their proper arms, grumbled about training these antique muskets on the president and his cabinet for continuing to relegate cavalry to sending messages between generals, scouting enemy positions, and guarding railroads and bridges. What blinded this administration to the cavalry's fighting importance, especially after Confederate cavalry had routed the Union army at Bull Run ten months before? She prayed for Rebels to try burning the bridges she guarded between here and Baltimore while on their way to capturing Washington so she'd get off at least one shot, even with her outdated musket, before the war ended.

Leanne pointed her musket and pulled its trigger. With the explosion, the musket's butt bucked like an angry mule, flinging her backward.

Drawn to the spray made by the musket ball's splash into the water, Jana began to squirm uncomfortably. It had hit wide of its mark, awfully close to those Porter Guards who were watching over the *Maryland*, a wooden ferry that carried the cars of the Philadelphia-Wilmington-Baltimore Railroad the short distance over the river between Perryville and here. She knew it was going to spell big trouble.

The mallard flew away, honking with fright.

The gunfire lured the attention of the guards, walking the ferryboat's deck and dock, and the gaggle of privates loafing about. They all howled with laughter when they saw Leanne laid out.

Someone hollered out, "Better to let a man give you a whipping than a gun, son."

Leanne scrambled to her feet. Her cheeks, already crimson with embarrassment, purpled with anger. "Come on out, and I'll show ya a real whipping," she said.

Jana sensed something fouler on the rise than the stale gunpowder wafting up from Leanne's gun barrel. Ironically, sick of being kept out of the fight brought the men to fighting each other almost every day. Jana detested such foolishness. She was especially disgusted with how, during their seventy-two-day encampment at Gettysburg, the regiment had recruited the lovely townsfolk into taking sides over which one of their officers was more competent to lead them. Leanne wound up in the middle of that squabble and a good many others. Though she only took on bullies, Jana was baffled as to why she went around picking fights when she lost every time. Maybe she needed to take her pa's bullying out on other bullies. So long as she didn't pick on anybody innocent or get badly hurt, Jana figured, why crush her spirit for the real fight. The really bad bullies deserved a licking, if only Leanne could give it to them.

Billy Martin, a towering mass of muscle and one of the regiment's biggest bullies, rose up from amongst the other troopers down by the river fishing for shad. He threw down his flimsy, hand-carved pole and came lumbering toward Leanne.

Jana feared for Leanne. She was bound to wind up with the rest of the rotting fish on the riverbank by the time Billy got through with her. Leanne was wiry and muscular for a girl, probably from all the pounding of hot metal she did in her pa's blacksmith shop. Still, her muscles were no match for Billy's. She'd have to find his weak spot to defeat him, just as mythology recounts Paris of Troy had done in the Trojan War when he shot a poisoned arrow into the Greek Achilles's heel (his only vulnerable part) and killed him.

The loafers formed a ring around the bickerers. The guards stayed where they were, shouting in favor of a brawl.

Unruffled by Billy's size and strength even as he flexed his huge biceps over her, Leanne stood her ground.

With a sneer, Billy said, "Why I can't fight a house mouse."

Leanne raised her fists. "And I ain't afraid of no big ugly louse!"

Holding Leanne and Billy apart at arm's length, a private gave everyone a chance to write their bets on torn pieces of paper. A second private finished collecting the chits before the first private dropped his arms and backed away. The crowd began cheering with Billy's backers outdoing Leanne's.

"Time to settle it, mouse," Billy said and threw a punch.

Preying upon his slowness, Leanne ducked. With lightning speed, she swung her leg, sweeping Billy off his feet. She pounced on his stomach and socked him good on the jaw.

A musket crack caught Leanne's fist midair and silenced the crowd.

Jana prayed the instigator of the shot came to end the scuffle before Billy could retaliate.

Parting the crowd like Moses to the Red Sea, Keeley Cassidy came marching in. He shouldered his musket, its barrel still smoking, and he carried his six-foot frame with confidence, giving the impression if you tussled with him, you'd lose.

Jana exhaled with relief—the fight was over. She'd once heard Keeley say he hated fighting amongst men who were supposed to stand together. And she'd seen him put stops to scraps with a mere scowl.

Scampering behind Keeley, twelve-year-old Charlie Watson struggled to hold up uniform trousers two sizes too big for his scrawny frame. He tripped on his pant cuffs, sailing past Keeley and into the inner circle. His spectacles and kepi flew off, both landing together but far away from where he himself came down face first with a thud.

The crowd hooted and hollered over Charlie's accident.

Keeley's cheeks flamed the same copper-red as his hair. He shot the crowd an angry look. It shamed the merriment from them for finding fun in another man's woes.

Jana brought Charlie his glasses and hat, with its rounded top set upon squatty sides, which were even more squashed now. "Are you hurt?" she asked him.

"Nah." Charlie squinted up at her through his sapphire eyes. "Just embarrassed." He settled his spectacles onto the bridge of his button nose and around his ears, which were elephant in size compared to his small head. Holding his oversized hat by its visor, he planted it back on his head and his ears stuck up over the rim to help pin it in place.

Aiding Charlie up, Jana brushed grass blades from his pants and tried to ease his embarrassment by saying, "We can't have you struggling to free your boots from your pant cuffs instead of fighting the Rebels all war. I'll tuck and hem them later."

"What would I do without you, Johnnie? You make sure my guns are spit-shined for inspection, share your rations with me when I'm still hungry, and sew my buttons. You're a true friend."

Jana was as overly protective of Charlie as she was her sisters. She considered it disgraceful that the army signed up young boys, barely able to push a plow, as soldiers, not just drummer boys.

Keeley dragged Leanne off her opponent and then gave Billy, rubbing his jaw, a hand up. He stepped between them and removed a roll of bills from his pocket. As he held it up for all to see, his lips turned up into a devilish grin. "I'll bet all of me money there's not a lad about meself who knows where I hail from," he said.

"If you'll shake on it, I'll bet my whole war's pay on it," someone called out.

Laughter rippled around the crowd; everyone knew Keeley came from Ireland.

Sobering, Keeley pocketed his money and said, "As a wee lad, I survived hunger from the potato blight in me homeland. But it took me mam, dad, and sisters."

The crowd released a collective moan.

"I'm not looking for sympathy, lads." Keeley paused before continuing, "In a rat-infested hull of a cargo ship, I fought dying from disease when I stole meself to this country. And on the streets of New York City, I fought dying at the hands of homelessness, gangs, and prejudice against Irishmen."

Jana observed not one trooper moving. They seemed to cling to Keeley's words like those of a minister's at a spiritual gathering. She wondered if the noncommissioned officers had secretly assigned Keeley their peacekeeper because they were too chicken to discipline their friends, neighbors, and kin who'd elected them to their posts.

"Now, I'm betting all of ye here can say ye've had to fight something to keep from dying." Keeley singled out an older private. "Tom, tell the lads what ye've fought."

"Mexicans for two years," he said loud and proud.

"Sam, what was your fight?"

"Cattle thieves."

"Your fight, Lyman?"

"A near drowning in Lake Erie."

Keeley turned to Billy. "Before Leander here, what was your fight?"

Everyone laughed.

Shamefaced, Billy mumbled, "Typhoid fever."

Keeley waved a hand around. "Share your fight with your fellow man." He waited for the chatter to wane before saying, "The point of this drill is to know your enemy, lads. Ours is Johnnie Reb."

Amidst a great hurrah, someone cried, "Keeley for colonel!" to which a greater hurrah erupted.

Keeley raised a hand to hush them. "I don't aspire to high places, but I believe in fighting to earn me pay."

Jana noted steadfast respect for Keeley etched onto the faces of every trooper. At twenty-one years old, his life's trials made him more battle hardened than the regiment's commissioned and noncommissioned officers combined, many of whom had no fighting experience. She bet if he countermanded an officer's order, the men would follow him. He had the kind of grit Ma and Pa would admire. Jana felt her own adoration for him beginning to bud.

Peering especially at Leanne and Billy in a scolding way, Keeley said, "We're a family, lads. We don't go around beating each other up."

Leanne winced hard at his words.

Jana sensed some deeper meaning behind her reaction than any humiliation she might feel over fighting other bullies.

Keeley continued, "As family, we watch each others' backs."
Another cheer.

"Ain't gonna have to worry a hoot about watching each others' backs 'cause we ain't ever gonna join the fight," Leanne said.

Reaching into another pocket, Keeley removed a paper that he waved about. "Our lads downriver wrote this petition, demanding the secretary of war mount or disband us. I'm to get your signatures."

Bands of worry streaked across Charlie's forehead. He tilted his soft, boyish face toward Jana. "Does this mean we'll join the fight for sure, Johnnie?"

"It's no guarantee," she said.

Charlie drew a long breath, expelling it hard. "How am I ever going to kill somebody when I can barely kill a chicken or pig?" Everyone knew he'd enlisted for the soldier's pay, caring nothing about any gripes with the South. Ever since his pa had died from a fall off a barn roof, Charlie was determined to provide for his ma and younger brother.

A gruff voice said, "With all the diseases, desertions, and discharges, won't rightly be enough of us left to make a regiment soon."

Crossing her arms over her chest, Leanne said, "I ain't signing it. Lincoln'll only use that paper to get rid of us as troublemakers."

Keeley nudged Leanne with his elbow. "Aye, now that's the pot calling the kettle black."

Leanne bowed her head, looking disgraced.

Keeley patted her back. "Let's stick together, lad."

Keeping her head bowed, Leanne nodded.

Jana was aghast. She'd never seen her friend concede anything to anyone before. Keeley seemed able to cast some kind of magical spell over everyone.

Turning back to the crowd, Keeley said, "We won't be getting a piece of the action sitting around talking. This appeal's some kind of action. If we're disbanded, we'll be getting a fighting chance elsewhere, even if as infantry. If ye enlisted just to ride around on horses, go back to your homesteads." He stared every man down. "I meself'll be signing the petition."

The crowd roared.

Jana wholeheartedly agreed with signing the plea. The Porter Guards had to act in some way, just like this country's forefathers had done when they signed the *Declaration of Independence* and risked their life. She unrolled her lap desk, onto which Keeley placed and smoothed out the crackly paper, wrinkled by water marks, and then she offered him her pencil.

Keeley autographed it, followed by Charlie and all else present, including Leanne. Finally, he turned to Jana and traded pencil for lap desk to give her a chance to sign. He wore a great big smile, which showed perfectly chiseled front teeth, until his expression abruptly changed to one that appeared lost in a maze of confusion. Leaning in close to Jana, his eyes raked over her face.

Fixing her gaze toward the parchment to avoid his intense scrutiny, Jana could still see Keeley shaking his head as though trying to expel some ridiculous notion. When she got the courage to look up, he was smiling again. She couldn't tell if it was because he was pleased to have his petition signed or because he'd found her out. Either way, she couldn't help being drawn to his smile. It produced the most dazzling dimples and sparkling emerald eyes she'd ever seen. It sent butterflies fluttering all through her as nothing had ever done before. She believed Keeley could lure her into the bloodiest of battles by his radiant features.

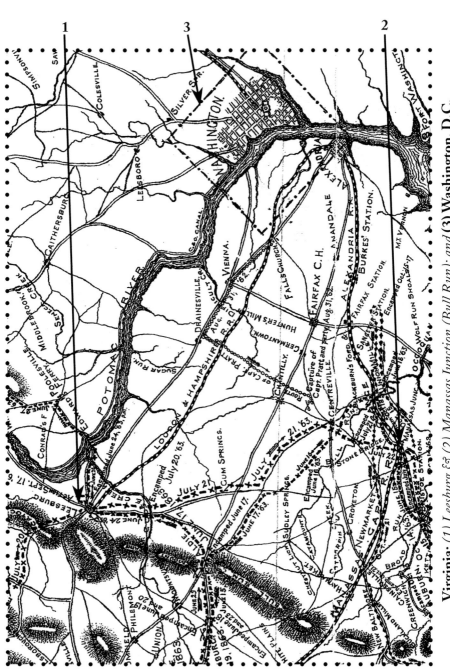

Virginia: *(1) Leesburg & (2) Manassas Junction (Bull Run); and (3)* **Washington, D.C.**

Bladensburg, Maryland

Early August 1862

Just before dawn, Jana slipped out of the two-man tent that she shared with Leanne at their new, remote encampment, five miles northeast of Washington. She and her regiment had marched here last night, arriving around midnight, with the promise that they'd receive the rest of their cavalry arms and equipment and horses today. With everyone still in their tents, Jana hurried toward the woods, hoping to catch a private moment to satisfy her morning necessary. The chilly air soothed her puffy eyes. Exhaustion had weighed heavy upon her by the time she and Leanne had pitched their tent last night. Though, after she'd crawled in between her blankets, she grew dizzier with the anticipation of breaking in her horse come morning. She'd lain awake all night long, listening to a cacophony of critters chirping, burping, and croaking.

Looking back to make sure no one tailed her before entering the woods, she caught a glimpse of the regiment's sleeping quarters through the predawn light. She marveled at it; somehow, in the black of night, hundreds of men had managed to arrange their tents in almost perfect rows with pastured avenues in between.

In the woods, Jana hid behind a grand old cherry tree before dropping her pants and squatting. In the midst of emptying her bladder, she heard twigs snapping underfoot. She no longer flinched—any trooper who came to the woods for private duty was just as modest as her and would about-face when they saw her. Besides, in a squat, nobody could tell her from male or female. Still, she was tired of others showing up during her sacred time. On the march, she'd found it much easier to slip away to tend to herself. Contrary to what she'd thought, bathing was easier inside when it was too cold to do in the rivers or streams. She'd either sponge herself off in her tent or hide behind a curtain when in a tub in the barracks. Even men comfortable with relieving themselves in public cherished a private bath in close quarters.

"Top o' the morning to ye, Johnnie," Keeley said as he trudged through a screen of mist, rubbing his sleepy eyes.

Though taken off guard by his appearance, Jana stayed in her squat. He had no trouble watering himself in the public sinks and was always asking her why she avoided them. She wondered, *Why does he badger me so much about it when he doesn't object to Leanne or any of the other boys or grown men who are just as modest?* He must've discovered something in her when he got that close-up of her face back in Havre De Grace. He was probably here now trying to gather proof of his suspicions. Not about to get kicked out of the army after how far she'd come to get here, she'd watch everything she said and did around him from now on.

"Don't worry, Johnnie. We're all men around here, right?"

"Some of us are," Jana said, purposely baiting him to probe her meaning.

"Aye? Is there something ye'd like to tell me, lad?"

Jana silently rejoiced; he'd swallowed the worm. Now, she'd reel him in and release him only after she repeated to him what she'd heard other bashful boys say. "I only meant you're a grown man, and I'm still growing. Try to step back into my shoes when as a yearling you too were shy about parading around in plain view."

As though her words had hit their mark in making him think she just might be a male with this kind of insight, he said, "Forgive me thoughtlessness, Johnnie."

With a huff, Jana chortled, "Can I have some privacy now?"

Keeley turned his back to her while she pulled up her trousers.

Hoping to add to his confusion, Jana mimicked the way men sometimes behave. As she passed him, she slapped him hard on the back and said, "I'm famished. Let's go get some grub."

Keeley whiffed the air as she walked by. "Good Lord, lad, might ye be needing a bath?"

Jana had sweated very little since her last bath before their march yesterday. She knew it was another attempt by him to crawl under her skin like a chigger and get her to make some girlish show of shame for stinking. She smelled her underarm and then leaned into his space and sniffed. She mimicked his Irish brogue when she retorted, "Aye, and I meself think it's ye who might be needing a bath, lad."

All the way back to camp, Keeley kept quiet. His knitted-together eyebrows told Jana he was probably summing her up. Why was he intent on proving whether or not she was a boy? It suddenly dawned on her: maybe he cared about her more than she realized and he needed solid proof that she was a girl before he'd let his feelings cut any deeper. Her sympathy for his anguish almost squeezed the truth from her, but until she was sure he'd keep her secret, she'd remain silent. Distracted by a thick burning in the air, Jana looked up to see if their tent city was afire. A curtain of smoke was drawn around their sleeping quarters. While in the woods, the sun had popped over the horizon, and seven hundred hungry privates had crawled out of their tents before the bugler could blow reveille. Messes of six to eight men hovered around their campfires; they clinked and clanked their pots and pans as they cooked their breakfasts and compared strategies for breaking in their horses today. The sleep-deprived eyes of all she passed proved nobody had slept a wink last night. Advancing to her mess, Jana's taste buds watered for the eggs and bacon she could hear sizzling in their griddles.

Leanne poured and handed Keeley and Jana a mug of coffee while Charlie dropped an egg and two slices of bacon onto everyone's tin plates.

Before biting into the salty and fatty yet tasty piece of fried pork, Jana slurped her freshly ground coffee. She thanked her messmates for their part in slaying the growling monster in her stomach.

After breakfast and roll and sick calls, Jana lined up by her friends and the other Porter Guards along the paddock fence far away from their sleeping quarters. Leaning her hands on the top rail, she barely noticed the splinters jabbing her palms as she stared in wonderment across the vast field. It fenced in over seven hundred snorting, nickering, and whinnying horses from which to choose. She didn't think it possible to top the thrill she got that Christmas morning when Ma and Pa had sent her to the barn to find Commodore with a red bow around his neck. But, here, there was a sweeter glory. Breaking in her horse meant getting into the fight real soon—their officers had promised.

A satiny, black gelding kicked at a mare for biting his rump. That got other horses rearing, kicking, and neighing.

"Fighting horses for fighting men," Charlie said.

"Hopefully, our fighting days amongst ourselves are behind us, lad," Keeley said.

Jana recalled how Keeley's words about family sticking together had cut the regiment's fighting by more than half. "We have you to thank for that, Keeley."

"And the secretary of war for giving us our horses and equipment and making us too happy to fight any more," Charlie said.

Clearing her throat, Leanne said, "You mean Saint Stanton." She called President Lincoln's latest secretary of war that in honor of Saint Nicholas for his generosity.

Jana wondered if the regiment's petition to Edwin M. Stanton had anything to do with him making them official cavalrymen. She wouldn't dwell on it; it only mattered that they'd gotten their wish. And it wasn't likely to be rescinded with recruiters heading back to New York State to raise four more companies of Porter Guards.

Charlie scanned the land. "I'm going to write Ma and Little Billy all about our new cavalry station. Do you really think it sits on sacred fighting grounds like the officers claimed this morning?"

Jana replied, "I don't think they'd lie about things we could easily confirm. Besides, they don't need sacred fighting grounds to motivate us Porter Guards into putting up a good fight." Their fight today would be against beast, risking only a bruise or bite mark as opposed to death. Nevertheless, she too hoped to one day tell her family, especially Rachel and Rebecca, she'd fought where the British had defeated the Americans on their way to sacking and burning Washington in 1814. And where many duels had taken place: the most famous in 1820 between two high-ranking officers in the United States Navy in which Commodore James Barron shot and killed Commodore Stephen Decatur, Jr., one of the greatest naval heroes for his escapades in both wars against the Barbary States in North Africa earlier in this century.

"I ain't gonna stand around chitchatting and get the spoils of the herd," Leanne said. Armed with halter and lariat in one hand, she hurdled over the fence and headed toward the black gelding that was slurping from a spring-fed stream flowing down from the hills at the ground's southern edge.

Knowing how Leanne liked a good fight, Jana called to her, "Be gentle or he'll be breaking you in."

Leanne waved the back of her hand to signal she knew what she was doing and trudged onward.

Charlie's face scrunched up with concern. "What did you mean by that, Johnnie? I've ridden lots of horses but have never broken one in before."

"An unbroken horse doesn't know right off he's stronger than you unless you pull him hard by a rope. He'll pull back and learn he can pull back harder. Then he gets stubborn to what you want him to do," Jana explained.

Charlie's look of worry doubled. "I won't hurt the horse, will I?" he asked as he mined a louse from beneath his hair. Pinching it between his thumb and forefinger, he set it on the ground.

A nearby trooper, who'd seen Charlie set the tiny parasite free, began stomping the ground where the creature might have squiggled off to. With gruffness, he said, "For the last time, Charlie, don't set those nasty graybacks free. They'll only go looking for someone else to feast on. With my luck, it'll be me."

Jana feared for Charlie. Besides setting lice free, he was always saying how he hated to hurt anything or anyone. *Would he ever be able to shoot down a Rebel aiming a gun at his head?* She didn't embrace killing either, but she'd do what it took to survive. She had to make Charlie see it that way too before he got his head blown off. Patting Charlie's back, she felt his bony shoulder blade poking through his short coat. It wasn't from lack of nourishment. He ate like a pig. "You won't hurt the horse." She winked at him and said, "Thank goodness my pa's slow, gentle approach to horse taming doesn't require a whole lot of muscles."

"So even ye've broken in horses before, Johnnie?" Keeley asked.

The way he asked that made Jana think he was trying to incense her into saying something like, "Yes, even we lassies tame horses." Instead, she said, "I helped my pa with some of ours, and I broke in my own stallion."

"I've not ridden many a horse and nary broken one in. Might ye show me too, Johnnie?" Keeley asked.

Jana scolded herself for looking too deeply into his words. Come to think of it, most boys she knew would never admit to not knowing something a boy ought to know. Keeley wasn't like other boys; that's why she admired him very much. "I'd be glad to, but first we need horses to break in." She pressed her hand against her forehead to shield the glaring pink rays of the early morning sun from her eyes and returned to inspecting the herd.

"Is there a horse that tickles your fancy, Johnnie?" Keeley asked as a dapple-gray mare lifted her head and nickered.

Keeley, Charlie, and Jana shared a laugh.

"I think you tickle her fancy, Johnnie," Charlie said.

"Aye, what are ye waiting for? Go claim her, lad," Keeley said.

Before Jana did, she chose a chestnut mare for Charlie and a butternut gelding for Keeley. "The key is getting the horse to trust you." She pointed to the other troopers, running around like chickens with their heads cut off trying to catch a horse, and said, "You definitely don't want to do that. It makes the horse afraid of you. Contrary to what most everyone thinks, horse-taming is slow and gentle." With Keeley and Charlie still looking perplexed, she said, "Just follow whatever I do." Flinging the soft, leather halter and lariat with its fraying strands over her shoulder, she clambered over the fence. She felt a little clumsy in the bigger short coat Leanne had traded away for her smaller one while back in Havre De Grace; she wouldn't gripe about it because it allowed her to tie her corset looser, making it a lot less scratchy. Jana stationed herself near the dapple-gray and waited for Keeley and Charlie to do the same with their horses. She held out a carrot and started taking baby steps toward the horse.

The mare grazed on the dewy grass, keeping an eye trained on Jana. She shied away with a whinny when she sensed Jana's approach.

"I'm not going to hurt you, girl," Jana said in a soft voice while continuing to advance. When she stepped up close enough for the untamed animal to see and smell the earthy-smelling vegetable in her outstretched palm, she stopped and waited.

After what seemed like forever, the horse's curiosity got the better of her, and she ambled over. Her whiskered muzzle tickled Jana's palm as she scooped the carrot into her mouth and smacked it down. With her last swallow, the mare's big brown eyes gazed upon Jana as though querying what she had to do to get another.

"You're a good girl," Jana said and began rubbing all around the mare's head, first with her hands to get her used to her touch, later with the halter to get her to willingly accept it when she fitted it on her head. With each step's progress, Jana fed the mare a carrot and allowed herself a silent whoop of victory. In the meantime, after Charlie had gotten his horse haltered, Jana saw him divvy a carrot and feed half to himself, half to his mare. She called out, "What are you doing, Charlie?"

"I'm showing her nobody's boss in our new relationship," Charlie responded.

Jana's awe over Charlie's inventiveness was cut short by Keeley's struggles to approach his horse. When Keeley turned his back on the gelding and started away, she called to him, "Giving up are you?"

Keeley said, "I'm hoping he'll see I mean him no harm."

Jana recollected Pa saying the greatest horse-tamers turn their backs on a belligerent horse to let it think it's the boss. Even so, she was surprised when the horse finally followed and accepted Keeley's carrot. She found his gut instincts not to force his way with an animal and his gentle nature quite agreeable.

By mid-afternoon, Jana, Keeley, and Charlie succeeded in leading their horses around in all directions by light tugs on the ropes clipped to their halters. On their way to the stable, they met the exasperated looks of those still trying to catch or halter a horse.

Jana praised Keeley and Charlie's handiwork. "We'll use the same slow, gentle steps to get our horses to take bits in their mouths and saddles on their backs. That shouldn't take long. Getting them to accept our weight in the stirrup then the saddle will take greater time and patience."

Just then, their Company-*D* commander darted into the stable ahead of the trio and sped toward a lone trooper, the first to have his horse tamed and stalled. They pulled up their mounts sharply and shared looks of disbelief. The lone trooper was the rough-and-tumble Leanne.

Jana was even more flabbergasted by Leanne's rare show of tenderness in the way she ran a curry comb through her gelding's forelock while humming in his ear.

With his back to the arriving trio, Captain Purdy said, "Tell me, man, how you've tamed your horse swiftly without any bumps, bruises, or bites. Are you a miracle worker?"

Leanne faced the floorboards to hide her blushing cheeks.

"Well?" Captain Purdy demanded.

Pushing around some straw with the tip of her boot, Leanne stammered, "I-I-I been around horses enough to know they ain't gonna do what they don't wanna do." When she lifted her head, she spied Jana over the captain's shoulder and pointed toward her. "Ask Johnnie. He knows all about it, probably better than me 'cause he can teach it." She bowed her head, again hiding her blushing cheeks.

Prickles of delight danced up Jana's spine. She'd never heard Leanne compliment anyone before, and she was honored to be the recipient of it. At the same time, she felt sorry for her. Giving and receiving kind words obviously came hard for her. Who could blame her? She didn't have a kind pa to lead by example. Jana imagined Leanne's world at home (no doubt more of the same gripes and groans she got from her pa in his blacksmith shop) to be darker than the underworld. She vowed to make Leanne feel good about herself every chance she got.

Their leader turned, and his bushy eyebrows furled with surprise when he saw three more troopers leading obedient horses into the barn.

"Aye, Johnnie taught me and Charlie here to tame our horses," Keeley said.

Captain Purdy removed his hat and scratched his head, ruffling his lush, dark hair as he thought aloud, "By the looks of things in the paddock, it's going to take forever to get our horses tamed." A lightning bolt of an idea flashed across his face. He pointed outward and said, "I'm ordering you boys back there to show the others how to do it."

"It'll take time to get the fright out of those horses before they can even be haltered, sir," Jana said.

"I'm confident you boys can do it," Captain Purdy retorted. "Meet me out there, and I'll make your introduction as paddock instructors. The sooner it gets done the sooner we start mounted drill. And that'll take even longer than taming horses." He wheeled about and left the barn.

Keeley, Leanne, and Charlie stood like statues with their mouths sculpted wide open, no doubt at the enormity of the task.

Jana felt her disdain festering. She'd expected to be detained from the war only until the horses got tamed. Not for more drill—especially mounted. What could be so hard about maneuvering guns or sabers in a saddle or a horse into battle formation? Shy of selling her soul to the devil, she'd give anything to tell her superiors they were being plain-old chicken to join the fight.

Bladensburg, Maryland

Mid-August 1862

When the bugle blasted the boots-and-saddle call, Jana and the sixty other men of her company saddled up their horses and trotted them from the stable to the drill grounds. They waited for Captain Purdy to come show them how to maneuver their arms in the saddle, first at a standstill and then in a gallop.

Jana reined in her dapple-gray mare alongside her friends on the vast field, which was growing muddier by the minute under a mere mist that had lingered for many hours since dawn. Beyond today's instruction, she could think of nothing else they had yet to learn to keep them from joining the fight. The horses were all tamed, and man and horse knew how to form up in different ways for battle.

Scanning the field of horses, Keeley said, "It's hard to believe, lads, we've had a hand in breaking in every one of these steeds."

With the back of her gloved hand, Jana swiped away the beads of mist clinging to her eyelashes and then gazed at all of the tamed horses. She too absorbed the magnitude of their feat.

"I love all the gifts the men gave us for helping them. I don't have any use for chewing tobacco, but I'll keep the stamps and soap," Charlie said.

"I'll take your tobacco," Leanne said. Before any of them could admonish her again about her new, filthy habit, she said, "I ain't much for reading; whoever wants the books and newspapers I got can have them."

With fondness, Jana reminisced about their day's furlough around Washington, awarded to them by the officers for their huge role in taming the horses. While there, the four of them had posed for a photograph together. She patted the lump beneath her corset that was the tintype of their likenesses. She'd tucked the small iron plate there for good luck.

Leanne looked toward the bleak skies and said, "I'm betting the officers turn yella and cancel the drill."

Shivering, Jana turned up her collar to keep out the cold wind and drizzle and her sudden ominous feeling. She hoped nothing more than the dreary weather gave her this gut reaction. Twitching her feet in her stirrups, she wished to get on with their training and then to the battlefield.

Jana's mare began to prance around as though she too was impatient with the delay and for her next challenge.

While stroking his gelding's neck, Keeley said, "No horse was born for war like yours, Johnnie."

Jana loved Keeley's name for her mare. He'd christened her Maiti (Irish for strong battle maid) because she'd learned to form up to the bugle calls faster than the other horses and, for that matter, many of the men. And she held her head proud when she pranced into formation and burst to the lead during a charge. Seeing Leanne's shoulders slumping with dejection, Jana remembered her promise to make Leanne feel good about herself every chance she got. Even though she doubted any horse could outdo hers in any way, she said, "Maiti's lust for battle might put us in a fix, whereas, Leander's horse is too smart for that."

Leanne nodded at Jana's kind words, and raindrops shook free of her fatigue cap's visor.

"What about my horse?" Charlie asked.

Leanne quickly said, "She's got heart and listens to ya, Charlie."

Jana, Keeley, and Charlie shared winks unseen by Leanne. Over the past couple of weeks, they'd subtly taught Leanne to give and receive kind words by praising even her small successes. This, in turn, got her praising others.

Finally, Captain Purdy came galloping over and got right down to instruction, straight from Cooke's *Tactics*, the cavalry's trusty manual.

Jana swept aside her bad feeling, chalking it up to the gloomy weather, and turned to practicing. She drew her pistol and saber from their waist-belt holsters and her carbine from its saddle boot. Except for the saber, handling a pistol or rifle in the saddle at a standstill was nothing new to her from her hunting days. She felt sweat trickling down her back as she worked to draw one while holstering the other, given only seconds to do it. When Captain Purdy had his men follow this same procedure in a trot and then a gallop, Jana and everyone else fumbled their sabers into the mud dozens of times before they could finally draw it every time without dropping it.

Once the men had passed the mounted arms maneuvers with flying colors, Captain Purdy divided his company into columns of four. He readied them to draw pistols and charge the straw-filled burlap targets set up at the edge of the woods. And he ordered pistols not to be fired.

Jana silently scoffed at his last command. *When would he and his superiors cease babying men eager to fight?* One battle could end the war, and she might never get off a shot at a Rebel. She deserved at least one chance for all of her troubles in getting this far, even if only at a Rebel dummy.

While Jana, Keeley, Leanne, and Charlie lined up in that order in their column of four, Jana leaned over and felt the fluffy hairs of Maiti's ear brush across her lips as she whispered into her ear, "Let's show them what you're made of, girl."

Bouncing her head, Maiti acknowledged Jana's confidence in her, which she came to know through her mistress's tone of voice.

Jana felt her forehead break out in a euphoric sweat as she awaited the signal to charge. She determined to make this drill feel real.

Captain Purdy motioned to the bugler.

Over the din of a steady rain now tap-dancing on her oilcloth hat's leather visor, Jana heard Captain Purdy bellow, "Charge!" simultaneously with the bugler's blare.

Maiti sprang from her prance into a full gallop.

Jana felt her mare's unbridled spirit in her churning muscles. Sweat dripped off Jana's forehead and dropped onto her lips; its salty grit dared her to give the Rebel dummies a taste of her grit by shooting at them. Caught up in the moment, she forgot the order not to fire. She aimed her pistol, cocked its hammer, and pulled the trigger.

Maiti faltered to the pistol's pop close to her ears. Her hindquarter slammed into the shoulder of Keeley's gelding.

Jana's pistol and reins sailed from her clutches. Her right foot dislodged from its stirrup, and she was dethroned so that she lay with her ribs banging against her horse. Supporting herself by her left foot in its stirrup, she grabbed for the curved ridge of her McClellan saddle to try and right herself. Her hands slipped off the pommel, slickened by the rain and saddle grease. As she tumbled backwards, she found and clung to the cinch, binding the stirrup boot to the saddle.

Meanwhile, Maiti seemed to have sensed Jana's plight and she slowed to an amble.

Jana freed her left foot, dropped both feet, and dug her heels into the grass as she glided across it. A searing pain shot through her strained biceps, and she released the strap from her grip. She landed hard on her right buttock and then slid down onto her back. Squeezing her eyelids tight, she prayed not to be trampled under the stampede of hoofs all around her.

Over the clamor of receding horses came a concerned snort. It was followed by a warm, moist gust of oat-scented breath against Jana's cheeks. Jana opened her eyes to find her battle maid straddling and shielding her from harm.

Maiti dropped her head low; her whiskers tickled Jana's chin as her brown eyes gazed apologetically into Jana's. She snorted with relief when Jana rubbed her nose and uttered, "Good girl," plenty enough for her to know she was blameless.

To the sound of galloping hoofs, Jana lifted her head.

Captain Purdy, followed by Keeley, pulled up and dismounted. Their boots sloshed through the puddles as they took long strides toward her.

Though she felt heartened to see Keeley unharmed, Jana smarted with humiliation. Laying her head back down into the muddied grass, she pleaded with it to turn into quicksand and suck her in.

Keeley slapped Maiti's hindquarter, commanding her to move aside and make room for him and their captain to kneel beside Jana.

Sheepishly, Jana caught her captain's eyes.

"Might we interrupt your tender moment with your horse to inquire as to your health, Johnnie?" Keeley said, trying to ease the tension.

Laugh lines, bursting from the corners of Captain Purdy's dark eyes to his temples, evidenced his usual, good-humored nature. "Are you hurt, son?" he asked.

Jana wasn't about to tell him her right buttock throbbed. One drop of her pants and Surgeon Pease would have her booted out of the army. "No, sir, just embarrassed," she said.

Captain Purdy twisted his goatee. "I reckon you now understand why I ordered pistols not to be fired."

"Yes, sir." Her impatience had gotten the better of her. She knew all horses had to be weaned into the sound of a gun; she'd done it with Commodore before taking him hunting. And Maiti was no exception, even if she was a horse born for battle.

"I'm glad you did it; it's best the men learn all about following orders now rather than in battle. If I'm to protect my men, I must keep order. Danger's got to be handled in a planned, not rash, way," Captain Purdy said.

Jana winced at his words—the same ones Pa had used after she'd almost gotten him shot. With genuine remorse, she said, "I'll take whatever punishment I deserve, Captain."

Captain Purdy misunderstood the significance of her wince, attributing it to the bruises he must figure she'd gotten from such a fall because he said, "For now, tend to your sores. Next time, I'll go much harder on you." He rose to leave. "I'm just as anxious as you, son, to get to the fighting. But we'll make our move only when man and mount are ready." Astride his horse again, he addressed Keeley. "Give Private Brodie another minute to recuperate, then assist him from the field before he's trampled by our next exercise and back to the barracks for some rest."

"Aye, aye, sir," Keeley responded with a salute.

Captain Purdy wheeled his horse about, clicked his tongue, and galloped away.

Facing Jana, Keeley said, "Don't be ashamed, Johnnie. Ye did what every lad was itching to do. I meself had me gun cocked and ready to shoot." He chuckled. "Only I didn't do it because it wouldn't be a fair fight; dummies can't return the favor."

Under more favorable circumstances, Jana would've found humor in his joke. Instead, she said, "Captain let me off easy."

"He'd be a fool to crush ye. If I were him, I'd wish every one of me men had a smidgeon of your fighting spirit."

"Really?" Jana said, groaning at the soreness in her arms when she pushed herself up into a sitting position.

Keeley bobbed his head in assurance. In mid-motion, he abruptly halted and stared wide-eyed at Jana's stomach.

Looking down, Jana wanted to scream in horror when she saw she'd popped some of her buttons and her corset was poking through her blouse and short coat.

When Jana reacquainted her eyes with Keeley's expression, she swore she read in it the satisfaction of a barn cat that had just cornered a mouse.

Still uncertain if he'd give her away, Jana's mind spun faster than a top for some explanation to maintain her disguise. Aha! Her brain settled on not just one but two ruses. She was grateful to Ma for having the family act out *Romeo and Juliet* and other plays by William Shakespeare on blustery days when there was scarce else to do. She'd have to call on those skills now. First she grimaced and said, "Though I see how it could look that way, I hope you don't think I like dressing as a girl." Before Keeley could respond she got down to her second ruse. With care not to expose her chest, she reached down into her corset. She banked on him believing no female, even one disguised as a boy, would ever reach down into her shirt in front of a male. She retrieved their picture, holding it up for him to see. "I know this is going to sound strange, but we've all heard how one of these," she said, running her fingers across the tintype's glossy surface, "got between a bullet and a soldier's chest. Since belly wounds are death sentences, I thought if I put our picture up against it, I'd have luck on my side and no trouble with bullets. The only way I could think to keep it in place was with this corset." She set her pleading eyes upon Keeley. "Please don't tell anyone you found me in it. I'd be shamed into deserting. And I want to stay and fight."

"Who am I to judge ye, Johnnie?" Keeley asked, sounding flustered.

What did he mean by that—he won't judge me for being a boy dressing as a girl or just the opposite? Jana inwardly questioned. Either way, she felt sorry for him; he'd stumbled upon the truth but had gotten no closer to it without her admission.

"Don't worry, lad, your secret's safe with me." Though his voice held a trace of dejection, he said, "I've heard corsets shield bullets even better than tintypes. I just might put one on meself."

Jana felt relief soothe her stomach spasms. Whether Keeley surmised she was a girl or a boy didn't matter to her; she only cared he'd vowed to keep her secret.

Reaching out to help her up, Keeley wrapped his hand around hers.

Jana's heart fluttered when she felt how his hand fit hers as snug as a glove tailored just for it. In fact, they felt as though they belonged together as a pair.

Keeley pulled Jana to her feet. "We might want to clear the field before Captain Purdy trains his gun on us instead of the dummies. Speaking of which, Charlie found your pistol. He'll give it to ye later," he said.

Jana's head turned woozy and her legs wobbly when she stood up too fast. She fell into Keeley, who caught and held her in his strong, but gentle arms. The brush of his sweet-smelling breath across her cheek when he asked, "Can ye mount your horse, Johnnie?" sent a warm tingle down her spine and tongue-tied her.

Upon her silence, Keeley bent over, tossed her over his shoulder as though she was no heavier than a rag doll, and carried her to his horse. On the way, he gathered up Maiti's reins. He helped her up onto his horse's rump before he swung into his saddle. "Hold on to me tight." With a nervous clearing of his throat, he said, "Just so ye don't fall off." He set off at a slow pace, towing Maiti behind them.

Jana wished the ride would never end. She felt warm and cozy this close to him. She liked how he made her feel good about herself even when she'd done wrong, how he made her laugh, and how he made her heart sing every time he looked at her.

When they reached the barracks, Keeley dismounted. "Can ye swing your leg over, Johnnie?" he asked.

"I think so," Jana said, feeling a stabbing pain in her right buttock. She slid down the horse and into Keeley's outstretched hands. Her eyes met his just before her feet hit the ground. In their fleeting glance was affection. She dropped her eyes to hide her deep fondness for him.

Keeley turned away from her. Sounding a bit flustered, he said, "I'll be feeding and watering Maiti for ye. And I'll bring ye some supper later." He mounted his horse and trotted off toward the stables.

Inside the wooden barracks lined on each side with bunk beds that disappeared to the eye after a point, Jana stoked up a fire in the woodstove. She hung her jacket over it to dry and stood before it, rubbing her hands together to get rid of the tingling in her cold fingertips. It felt good to have a quiet moment to herself, the first since she'd joined the army. Her mind reeled back to Keeley's tender gaze and his fussing over her. Those delights warmed her insides long before the heat from the fire took away her damp and chill. And when she imagined him fussing over her forever, she felt a fear stoke up inside of her. She was in love with him, and this disturbed her. He could be a distraction that got her shot or killed in battle.

Skirmish at Leesburg, Virginia

September 17, 1862

Amidst a thousand other men, mostly troopers backed by can-nonneers, Jana sat astride Maiti on the Leesburg-Alexandria Pike. Chewing on the inside of her mouth, she was anxious to know who'd be sent in to take Leesburg, a small town in the Loudon and Shenandoah valleys, away from the Rebels. She didn't care about its being desired by both armies because of its location along the Washington-to-Winchester Railroad and its bountiful crops; she cared only that it represented her chance to finally take part in this war. She grew despondent, thinking their commander, Lieutenant-Colonel Hugh Judson Kilpatrick, might assign the day's task to his Harris Light Volunteer Cavalry Regiment, its men all present today as opposed to only half of the Porter Guards. And they had more fighting experience.

Major Avery, the most senior Porter-Guard officer present and second in command overall for today, came galloping ahead of a red-clay dust cloud churned up by his mount. He reined in, calling for Captain Bliss and Lieutenant Weed of the Porter Guards to join him for their orders.

A cheer rippled on down through the ranks of the Porter Guards, now assured they'd be carrying the day.

Eager for a fight, Jana shifted in her saddle and felt the slow-healing bruise on her buttock. It reminded her about her humiliating lesson back in Bladensburg. She clamped her jaw, determined not to let her impatience get the best of her.

Major Avery finished giving his orders, wheeled his horse about, and galloped off to rejoin Kilpatrick at the head of the column.

Lieutenant Weed left to give his troopers orders while Captain Bliss yelled in his loud, deep voice, "Companies *B* and *D*, attention!" He readied his squadron to ride into town and draw out the enemy for Union artillery to fire upon and then for Lieutenant Weed's party to charge and finish off. With his thick horseshoe mustache bristling, he shouted, "By fours, forward march!"

As Jana wheeled Maiti out of single-line formation and into a four-man column, she experienced the thrill before a battle in the horses' sweet-smelling sweat, jingling spurs, creaking saddle leather, and flash of brass buttons and metal arms against the sun's glare. Even the wind whistled a lively tune as it rushed through the trees of the gently sloping wooded hills.

Leanne took the lead of their four-man column followed by Keeley. They'd set the pace with their slower horses and stop Jana and Maiti from getting ahead of them. Keeley and Leanne seemed to share Jana's inclination about shielding Charlie from harm when they lined him up last.

The Porter Guards' color-bearer led the way with the regiment's hand-sewn, yellow-fringed flag raised almost to the sky for all to see. Its bright, red-white-and-blue tassels bumping around in the breeze beckoned all to be aware of the Latin motto that it bore "E Pluribus Unum."

From her history lessons, Jana knew these words translated into "Out of many one." They were adopted by the first Great Seal Committee in 1776 to inspire the thirteen independent colonies to unite as one country against the British. Today, she was proud to unite with the Porter Guards to preserve that union. She and every trooper around her swelled with patriotic pride as they followed their waving flag and passed Kilpatrick's troopers, pumping their fists with encouragement.

Captain Bliss halted his outfit at the crest of the knoll, waiting for the cannons to move into position.

Below them, Buell's Battery began hustling about. The artillerymen whipped the draft horses. They, in turn, bowed their heads against the strain of hauling the big guns to the top of the hill while forcing the wagon wheels to grind around their axles with a commotion that in less exuberant times would be grating on the nerves.

As the cannons were unlimbered and the work horses cleared from the way, Captain Bliss held up a hand to silence his men. "Our day to meet the enemy is here! Let's show Kilpatrick and his veteran troopers we aren't green." Softening his voice, he said, "And may God be with you as we preserve our country."

Jana turned to check on Charlie; his head was bowed and his lips moved in silent prayer. She fretted over him freezing up when it came time to shooting a Rebel.

Lifting his head, Charlie met Jana's stare. He looked neither scared nor eager as he pointed heavenward and whispered, "Don't worry, Johnnie. My pa's watching over me. He won't let anything happen to me because Ma and Little Billy need me."

Jana prayed that was true. Still, she wished she could tuck him in her saddlebag. "Stick to my flank, Charlie, you hear?"

"You're always fussing over me like my ma. I hope you meet her some day."

"I'd love that. For now, don't let your trigger finger freeze up when it comes time to shoot. Those Rebels'll pick you off faster than a burlap dummy."

"I know. Just as you've been sticking it to my brain, those Rebs aren't any more defenseless than a nasty grayback," Charlie said and then stared past her, fixing on what was to come.

Turning forward, Jana peeked around Keeley to check on Leanne; she displayed a rare childlike giddiness since they'd broken base camp yesterday morning at Upton Hill, near Arlington Station. And she'd vowed to find a way to wield her saber, Smith carbine, and Colt revolver all at once against the Rebs and still fiddled with them now. "Psst," Jana whispered, catching both hers and Keeley's attention. "If you keep on with those weapons, Leander, Johnnie Reb'll get the best of you."

Leanne's cheek twitched as though it had been slapped by Jana's words. When she straightened around in her saddle, she finally sat stiff like the tree stump parallel to her roadside.

Keeley mouthed to Jana, "Be safe, lad."

Jana melted under his regard for her well being. As soon as she realized she loved him, she'd tried avoiding him—she couldn't have him distracting her during battle. Instead, she wound up spending nearly every waking moment with him after he'd asked her to teach him to read and write. How could she turn her back on him? In return, he'd taught her Gaelic (the ancient language of his Celtic homeland). Not that she needed anything in return; he made her laugh and feel good about herself. That was payment enough.

Without a bat of her eyelashes or blush of her cheeks, Jana said, "You too." She'd learned not to show her heart to him. She yearned to fight for her country now more than ever, just to stay close to her friends.

After a wink and a nod, Keeley turned around.

Jana angled her face skyward to let the sun's warm rays filter in and inspire her. She prayed for her friends and the Porter Guards to come through unscathed. Her lips curled upward into a smile. Wouldn't Ma and Pa be tickled to death, hearing her fret over others like a mother hen did her chicks? She said another prayer, asking for strength enough not to be preoccupied with her friends that she caused them or herself harm.

Captain Bliss severed Jana's entreaties with the call, "Draw pistols!"

Jana shuddered with excitement at the sound of all hands, including her own, uniting in chafing metal across buffed leather to unholster their pistols.

Pointing his pistol skyward, Captain Bliss jabbed his spurs into his horse's sides and bellowed, "Forward gallop!"

Maiti needed no more coaxing than a light squeeze of Jana's knees to be away with the rest of the thundering herd of hoofs, stirring up a tornado of dust.

When they reached Leesburg's outskirts, not a Rebel was spotted. Hoping to drive them out, Captain Bliss halted his unit, halved it, and sent them down separate streets. He went with the southward party, putting Company *D's* Sergeant Robb in charge of the half Jana and her friends were in.

Sergeant Robb's party put light spur to horse and marched in, keeping a keen eye to window, door, roof, and alleyway. They'd covered much ground through town when they heard gunfire—Captain Bliss's troop had met the enemy.

Pop! Pop! Pop! Crack! Crack! Crack! Now, Jana and her comrades were under siege. They spurred their mounts into a gallop. Lead rained down on them as they raced through the town, firing back at the Rebels.

With bullets whizzing all around her, Jana sighted a Rebel in a second-story window. His rifle was pointed toward Leanne. She aimed her six-shooter. Her fingers froze on the trigger.

A pistol exploded close behind Jana.

The Rebel tumbled out of the window and came to rest on a small balcony below.

Numbed by her own confusion and dizzy from the racket of gunfire and troopers whooping, Jana didn't react to the bugler's call to retreat.

Disciplined to the call, Maiti tried to angle around but was penned in by the lead and rear ranks, still engaging the enemy.

The feisty Sergeant Robb spurred his horse through the rank and file. He brandished his pistol, threatening to shoot any trooper who lingered another second.

Finally, Maiti maneuvered free to sweep Jana away amidst the other retreating horses. They retraced their trampled path to the top of the knoll with Rebel cavalrymen only lukewarm on their tails.

As both decoy parties reached the top of the knoll, Buell's Battery ignited their cannons, hurling shot and shell amongst the Rebels. The deep, echoing booms of the big guns put to shame the grandest Fourth of July firework show Jana had ever heard; though, she failed to appreciate that right now.

Cannonballs blasted the Rebels who reined back hard and sideways. Their rearing horses twisted about and galloped away in retreat.

The cannons quieted followed by a bugle blaring the second charge.

Kilpatrick took the lead to the crest of the knoll. He stood in his stirrups, pointed his saber, and yelled, "See the rascals! Go for 'em, boys!"

Lieutenant Weed and his squadron sped down the hill and chased the Rebel cavalry through and out of town. Rebel infantry, hidden behind fences, opened fire and tried to no avail to pick off the Yankees as they sped by.

With the sights and sounds of the fight receding, Jana trotted Maiti down the backside of the knoll to reunite with Companies *B* and *D*, now in reserve. She was disillusioned with her actions. *Had anyone else frozen up when it came time to shoot?* she wondered. Maybe this was commonplace with green soldiers and why Kilpatrick had assigned Company *A*, the most seasoned of the Porter Guards, the more dangerous charge? Back in April, when guarding the railroad bridge over Back Creek off Chesapeake Bay, they'd captured a schooner loaded with Confederate recruits. And, in August, they'd scraped with the enemy near Centreville, Virginia. Whatever the case, Kilpatrick had upheld his reputation for fairness, giving the Porter Guards, even if Jana hadn't seized the chance, the bulk of the day's fighting over his own veterans.

Maiti snorted multiple times as though vying for Jana's attention.

Patting her mare's neck in silent appreciation for her gallant charge and disciplined retreat, Jana felt glory in Maiti's lather all over her palm. At least one of them had served their country admirably today.

Maiti bobbed her head, welcoming Jana's approving touch.

Jana reined in beside her friends, relieved to see them all unharmed.

"Are ye well, Johnnie?" Keeley asked.

"Just fine," Jana said, bloated with sarcasm that Keeley failed to detect. "And you?"

"Aye, meself too," he replied.

With her cheeks polished red with Herculean valor, Leanne said, "I felled two Rebels."

Guilt slashed up her insides, and Jana had to look away from Leanne, who had been nearly killed because of her. "I froze up when it came time to kill," she muttered.

"I didn't get off a shot either," Keeley said. "Picking off Rebels'll have to wait 'til the morrow."

Jana snapped her head up. "Picking off Rebels? Do you like killing?" She was shocked at his sudden disregard for her concern and coldness toward killing.

"Only to pick off prejudice," Keeley said, giving Jana her first taste of his fixation with discrimination. He turned to Leanne and inquired, "With such entanglement of man and horse, how're ye sure it was your gun picking off those Rebels?"

Looking to Charlie for sympathy, Jana noticed his ashen face and his teeth chattering as though he'd dallied in an icehouse too long. "What's wrong, Charlie?"

Leanne turned cross eyes on Charlie. "I got a score to settle with ya for pretty near shooting my head off."

Charlie stared off into nowhere, his teeth chattering worse now.

"Well, Charlie. What do ya have to say?" Leanne demanded.

Stammering, Charlie uttered, "I-I-I killed a Rebel about to k-k-kill you." His eyelids fluttered shut. He sagged and began sliding from his saddle.

Leanne jerked back in surprise as though she'd just been gut-punched.

Leaping from his saddle, Keeley caught Charlie just in time and lowered him to the ground.

Jana dismounted, grabbed her canteen, and kneeled next to Charlie. She soaked her handkerchief with the cool water from her canteen, wrung it out, and used it for dabbing Charlie's clammy forehead.

Before long, Charlie revived.

Keeley patted his arm and stared down Jana when he said, "Ye did fine, lad."

Jana was glad to know he wasn't as callous as she'd feared.

When a victorious cheer echoed around the foothills of the Blue Ridge Mountains, Charlie tried to sit up but was still too weak.

Dismounting, Leanne raced to Charlie's side. She nudged Jana and Keeley aside with her bony elbows. As though she was under the spell of her newfound hero, she helped Charlie to his feet.

Lieutenant Weed's charging party marched over the knoll. In the lead, a corporal waved a large Confederate flag that they'd captured. The rest of Company *A* prodded along a good number of Rebel prisoners with their gun barrels.

"We Porter Guards are a family after all, lads," Keeley said, puffing up with pride.

Jana felt forlorn and more like the cousin who never gets invited to a family shindig. Surprisingly, Charlie had succeeded where she'd failed, and she began to think she should start worrying more about herself.

With Leesburg in Union hands, Kilpatrick turned his men toward home.

Later that evening, in a field somewhere miles south of Leesburg, Jana sat around the campfire, chewing on salted pork, softened a little by heating it, and bland wafers—the soldiers had nicknamed hardtack. It was pretty much fact by now that only their Company *A* had losses today: Three wounded. One bugler along with the slaughtered wild turkey he had strapped to his saddle captured. One horse killed. Conversely, the Rebel infantry and cavalry had suffered considerable losses.

A trooper visited every one of his fellow Porter Guards' campfires, spreading the news that Kilpatrick planned to emphasize their two gallant charges in his report to Union headquarters. Everyone around Jana cheered. And they praised their leaders for their incessant drilling and discipline, both of which they now realized had given them the best chance for survival.

Jana rallied around that, but she couldn't celebrate the Tenth's success today. Her hesitation to kill and Leanne's near death sobered her to war. The killing part of soldiering wouldn't be easy for her— she saw this now. It didn't make her want to give up and go home. Instead, she brightened to think maybe she just needed weaning into it like Maiti had needed weaning into gunfire so near her ears. She was craving another fight and chance to redeem herself. Next time, she'd heed her own advice to Charlie and see the enemy as burlap dummies.

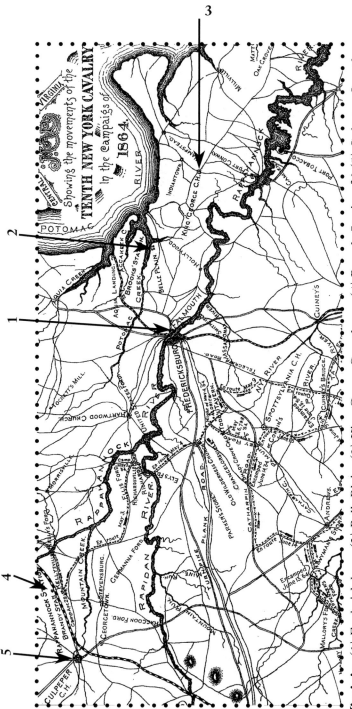

Virginia: *(1) Fredericksburg; (2) Belle Plain, (3) King George Courthouse, (4) Brandy Station, & (5) Culpeper Courthouse*

Fredericksburg, Virginia

December 13, 1862

Jana and her friends bumped around on the cold, hard bench inside the covered ambulance. It rumbled with urgency over the southernmost pontoon bridge below Fredericksburg to get to the wounded. The bridge had been laid by engineers two days earlier for the Union army to cross over the still-swollen Rappahannock River. Jana bet if Union General Ambrose Burnside had known he was sending his men to their slaughter, he would have rushed the bridge's construction before Confederate General Robert E. Lee could gain all of the high ground. Though, in her opinion, he should've delayed its construction until the situation was more wisely assessed. The ambulance jouncing to a stop awakened Jana from her silent preparation for the carnage that lay ahead.

During the raging battle, the Ambulance Corps had only been able to evacuate a few wounded. As soon as the fighting had stalled around noon, both sides called a truce to bury the dead and care for the wounded.

"If we didn't fight, why do we get to tend to the wounded?" Leanne asked, twirling the button on her greatcoat between her gloved thumb and forefinger.

Jana stopped herself from scolding Leanne, who fully understood the unwritten code: soldiers held in reserve owed it to their battle-fatigued brothers to clean up after them. Any tongue lashing right now would only heighten all the unease Jana already felt hovering between the canvas walls. She left Leanne to prattle on if that calmed her nerves.

"It's the end of the tour, folks," the driver said, pulling the wagon's brake with an agonizing screech.

"The smell won't be bad in these frigid temperatures," his assistant said.

Another wagon filled with wounded clattered past. Their cries for help wrenched Jana's heart. Many screamed for relief or water. Some whimpered like babies for their mothers. Others pleaded to live or to be left to die. She wished she could wave a magic wand to ease all of their suffering; all she could do was pray for them.

The driver and his assistant vacated their wagon seat, allowing a clear view through the archway and over the mules' ears.

Jana saw thousands of bodies, many more clad in blue than gray, littering the open plain, and many more lifeless ones being heaved into a massive grave.

Keeley and Charlie looked away in revulsion.

Leanne moaned, "It ain't right," her eyes glued to the scene.

Saliva swirled around Jana's mouth, giving her just enough warning to reach the back of the wagon. She leaned her head over the hatch and spewed up her breakfast. A sourness, as much from her vomit as the sight of the slaughter, pasted her tongue. It was unspeakable for the brave to be denied proper burials—their families beside them sending them off into the hereafter with prayers and songs of praise. *Interred far away from home, could they ever rest in peace?* Jana wondered.

Crawling up alongside her, looking as green as she felt, Keeley passed her his handkerchief. "Y'are lucky, Johnnie, to be getting that over now. I pray not to get sick on these sacred grounds and disrespect the dead and wounded," he said.

Jana wiped her mouth on the soft, flannel rag, grateful for his offering and encouraging words. If she were to die in this war, she hoped her three best friends, who she now considered family, were by her side to see her off.

Leanne intruded upon Jana's misery, saying, "Those dang Rebs are picking through our deads' pockets!"

Jana and Keeley turned to witness it for themselves.

"Aye, and I see Yanks picking through their deads' pockets too," Keeley retorted.

Bang! The wagon hatch dropped open, making Jana and Keeley—closest to it—jump. The driver poked his head in. He was sincerely apologetic when he said, "Didn't mean to make it sound as though the cannons were heating up all over again ... we better get a move on, else the wounded'll be dead."

"Mind you, leave the near dead behind, especially belly wounds," the assistant added.

Continuing to gaze across the battlefield, Leanne mumbled, "Wasn't a fair fight being marched out into the open toward a bunch of cowards hiding behind trees."

The assistant pointed upriver toward Fredericksburg. "Our right had it far worse. They were picked off by Rebs crouched on a sunken road behind a stone wall. And flanking them were lots more entrenched on the heights." He spat tobacco the color of blood and said, "It might've been worse if our generals hadn't talked Burnside out of going it again."

The driver said, "We can debate it 'round the campfire later. Right now, we've got lives to save." He removed a litter and waited for his assistant to grab the opposite end. Then they hurried away.

To a crescendo of pleas, Keeley said, "Come on, lads, we've got to give our boys a nigh fighting chance like they gave their country."

Charlie added, "My ma always says, 'Whatsoever ye would that men should do to you, do ye even so to them.' We might need those men we save here to save us some day." He leaped down from the wagon and began shifting in his cavalry boots, showing his eagerness to be off.

Keeley followed him. They drew out a stretcher and sped off.

Jana took the lead on their litter, forcing Leanne to a fast pace to keep up with Keeley and Charlie. She wanted all of her friends, especially Keeley, around her to draw from their courage.

As the foursome wound their way toward the battlefield, Jana's eyes devoured a far greater bloodbath than she'd ever imagined from her grandpa's war stories.

Leanne's mutterings about the unfair fight grew more disgruntled with each dead and every body part they stepped over.

Jana tried hard to pretend the dead were like the many pigs and chickens she'd helped Pa slaughter. She couldn't help seeing them for what they really were—someone's sweetheart, father, son, brother, or, maybe like her, a daughter.

The final postures and expressions of the dead made Jana cringe with horror. Most lay in the throes of agony with twisted or severed appendages or their insides dangling out. Many lay clutching their wounds with eyes bulging in surprise. Others lay holding their rifles with determination or anger still clamping their jaws.

Stepping over a young soldier with wide-open eyes, an overwhelming urge to shut his eyelids forever to the devil's mark struck Jana. She reached down, and frostbitten fingers reached up and clasped her coat sleeve. Shrieking, Jana stumbled backwards and dropped her end of the litter. She landed atop another body and heard its ribs crack as they broke beneath her forced weight.

The youthful soldier, his uniform saturated crimson all around a bullet hole in his belly, made a feeble appeal.

Jana recovered from her distress and made sure the soldier beneath her was really dead before abandoning him. As she crawled over to the injured man, she swore she felt the blood on the battlefield seeping through her wool trousers and feeling sticky and sickening against her skin. It never bothered her to have the blood of slaughtered livestock on her hands; they were put on this earth as food for man. She grew ill all over again to think she might one day soon have to kill a person.

Would she be able to live with the stain of human blood on her hands as Shakespeare's Lady Macbeth could not?

Click! A cocking pistol hammer snared Jana away from her torments, and she looked up.

Leanne aimed her gun at two Rebel privates, marching toward them in their tattered and filthy uniforms.

The Confederates halted and reached for their revolvers.

"Do it and you're dead!" Leanne said.

The privates held up their hands and pistols in surrender. The lankier of the two men said, "We've just come to make sure y'all don't intend any ill toward our own."

Jana then noticed the gray of the wounded man's uniform, easily mistaken for a shade of Union blue beneath the blood and soot. With a harrumph, she said, "We'd never harm anyone in a compromised state, no matter what side they're on."

"Well, we've seen many of you Billy Yanks robbing our men's pockets even as they're dying. Right, Henry?" he asked his shorter, stockier friend.

Behind a frosty huff, Henry remarked, "You know darn well, Silas, our fellows do that to Billy Yank too."

"Either way, nobody's shooting anybody, right?" Jana said, her stern eyes demanding reassurance from Silas, Henry, and Leanne.

Keeley and Charlie came up behind Jana and Leanne.

Silas said, "We're under strict orders not to," and holstered his revolver.

Holstering his firearm too, Henry shrugged and said, "We're plum out of ammunition anyway."

Jana turned to Leanne. "Put your gun away."

Leanne did, but she kept a firm hand on it.

A throat gurgling drew everyone's attention toward the soldier, clearly dying.

Henry fell to his knees next to his comrade and opposite Jana.

Desperation gripped the blood-webbed whites of the failing private's eyes as he clawed at his breast pocket with his bloodied fingernails. "W-w-w," he uttered.

"Come on, Henry. We've got orders to leave belly wounds behind," Silas said softly.

"I know," Henry said, making no effort to move away.

Yanking Jana's arm, Leanne said, "Come on. We got the same orders. And we ain't tending no Rebel."

Jana tore her arm away from Leanne's hold and said, "I'm not leaving yet."

Charlie kneeled beside Jana.

With great persistence, the mortally wounded warrior uttered, "W-w-w."

Peering over Jana's shoulder, Keeley's warm breath felt comforting against Jana's cold cheek as he asked, "Might he be needing water, Johnnie?"

Jana lifted and cradled his head in her arm while Henry unscrewed the top from his canteen and pressed its mouth against his lips.

The dying soldier pinched his lips together in protest and continued to scratch at his pocket.

When Jana reached to help him, Leanne pulled her arm back, more gently this time. She nodded her head at Henry and said, "Let him do it. Ain't no friend of mine gonna be accused of robbing no Rebel."

Jana knew Leanne was right. They didn't know these Southerners or what they might pull. She smiled her gratitude at Leanne and motioned for Henry to search the pocket.

Silas and Henry shrugged as though to say they wouldn't make a fuss over a Yankee for helping one of their own.

Henry fumbled around in the pocket and fished out a tintype. He stole a glance at it before passing it on to Jana.

Jana noted a depiction of the dying soldier and his bride, clad in their wedding garb and gazing lovingly upon each other. Their joined hands wore matching wedding bands. She noticed how the tintype still retained its shine. The newness of it made her think the matrimonial bond was recent too. Most married couples she knew had their wedding likenesses captured within days of the ceremony. Thinking the groom wanted his fate known to his bride, Jana asked Henry and Silas if they knew him.

With gloominess, they shook their heads no.

The dying soldier pointed his index finger past Henry. "Wife," he said in a forced whisper.

Henry moved aside for all to witness his hand clutching that of a dead soldier.

Jana caught her breath, stunned. The dead soldier was the bride! The sight of her exposed hands, soft and dainty, proved to Jana she'd enlisted for love rather than for glory and adventure, like her. She admired this woman who'd chosen to fight, knowing full well she could lose everything, her country and her husband—the ultimate sacrifices.

"Sweet Lord! It's his wife!" Henry said.

The others followed with their own startled exclamations.

Traumatized by the scene before them, no one noticed the approach of a Rebel, sporting on his greatcoat sleeves a chevron of three stripes shaped into a *V* that ranked him as a sergeant. He pushed Silas aside and grabbed the bride's ankles, preparing to drag her away.

Silas shoved him to the ground.

With lightning speed, Henry drew his empty pistol and pressed its barrel against the sergeant's forehead. "You aren't taking her anywhere."

The sergeant looked baffled by the reference to the perished combatant as a female, but he said, "Let me remind you, I outrank you and can and will have you imprisoned if you accost or disobey me. Now, I intend to do my job, so move aside."

Overhead, Jana again heard the click of a pistol hammer.

Leanne was aiming her pistol, this time at the Rebel sergeant. "Not before we drag ya off to some rat-infested federal prison, truce or not," she exclaimed.

Outnumbered under the glares of twelve vengeful eyes, the sergeant scurried backwards like a spider on his hands and feet.

Leanne called after him, "And if you make good on your word to imprison these boys, we'll come after ya with our best sharpshooter and pick ya off."

Springing to his feet, the sergeant scampered away like a dog with its tail between its legs.

Leanne, Silas, and Henry shared looks of respect, cut short by the groom's strained efforts to get into his pocket again.

Henry came to his aid; this time he found matching wedding bands in the pocket.

The groom released his bride's hand, signaling for the rings to be returned to their hands. With that done, he groped around until he clasped his wife's hand again, and then he began pushing with his feet. Jana and Henry helped him to roll over and once more, as in the tintype, behold his bride in his eyes. Eternal love uprooted misery's vice-like grip from his expression. He drew a long, last, peaceful-sounding breath before his eyelids closed, his face relaxed, and his body fell limp.

Jana's tears warmed her cheeks as they rolled down and dissolved between her lips. They tasted bitter to match her mood. As she brooded over these young lovers, whose blissful bond had been cut short by such nonsense between countrymen, she felt the cold tintype sliding from her hand; Henry was returning it to its rightful owner.

Sniffling, Charlie said, "I only know one prayer by heart."

Leanne patted his back. "Something's better than nothing, Charlie," she said with a sniffle too.

Charlie closed his eyes, bowed his head, and prayed, "'The Lord *is* my shepherd; I shall not want.'" When he reached the part, "'He maketh me to lie down in green pastures: he leadeth me beside the still waters,'" his sobs garbled his words.

Over quivering voices, all chimed in to help Charlie through the remaining scripture and to conclude with "Amen."

Keeley broke the somber silence. "They're in far greener pastures together now, lads."

Rising, Jana turned her watery eyes toward the battlefield and said, "Let's see how many of the brave we can send home to their loved ones."

All that day the six combed the battlefield, rescuing the wounded until the skies darkened. At dusk, they parted as friends, knowing tomorrow they'd be rivals once more.

Jana prayed never to line up on a battlefield against Silas and Henry. She'd heard plenty of stories about Yankees and Rebels in a moment of peace trading coffee for tobacco, singing ballads to each other, and comparing their thoughts and dreams across picket lines. Now, she had her own story to tell, only hers would end on a note of irony: today, the battle ground had become common ground where enemies had put down their guns to unite in the greater cause of brotherhood.

Chatham Manor
Fredericksburg, Virginia
December 14, 1862

Fuzzyheaded with exhaustion, Jana stumbled from the outbuilding into the morning's grim light. Her eyes needed little adjustment to it since it closely mimicked the dusky-shaded room where all through the night she and Leanne had administered chloroform to tranquilize those soldiers about to have one or more of their limbs amputated. She gazed toward the back of the makeshift hospital, a brick Georgian-style house built on the bluffs overlooking the Rappahannock River and Fredericksburg beyond. She saw movement in a second-story window and hoped either Keeley or Charlie waved to her. To see them would raise her spirits right now. The shadow left as quickly as it had come.

She inhaled a heavy dose of purifying air to expel the harsh smells of blood, cut flesh, and sawed bone clinging to the hairs of her nostrils. She slid her back down the wall until she was sitting on the ground. The cold crept through her wool uniform pants like a giant ice pack against her aching legs, which had held her up for more consecutive hours than they had ever before. Closing her weary eyes, she tried to forget all of the cruelty she'd heard and seen. Staged against the black backdrop of her eyelids, a surgeon hacked through flesh and bone to sever a shot-up limb with blood spurting everywhere; against the shores of her eardrums crashed a tidal wave of agonizing screams from the victims of this barbaric procedure. She whipped open her eyelids only to meet more ugliness. Bloody trails snaked their way toward a heap of amputated limbs almost as high as the stable's roof, and the dead rested beneath their woolen blankets or uniform coats in a flowerless garden.

James Lacy would be appalled if he were to come home today to find bountiful stumps in place of his trees; muddy, rutted roadways across his manicured lawns; trampled paths through his gardens; and permanent blood stains in his walls and floors everywhere, Jana mused. He was a Confederate staff officer, and, as such, he should especially understand the beast of destruction wrought by war with two great armies tramping all over his home and state.

Followed by Dr. Mary Walker, Leanne exited the surgical quarters in a uniform just as spattered with blood and filth as Jana's.

Casting Leanne a weary smile, Jana said, "Thanks for taking the last patient."

"You looked like you were gonna drop, and I got a second wind," Leanne said.

Dr. Walker stretched, and her loose-fitting blouse drooped off her arms. "You fellows deserve a medal, coming through your first amputations without getting squeamish or fainting."

In the light, Jana got a good look at Dr. Walker. She was pleasant looking with a small face, which angled sharply down from a wide forehead to a rounded chin. Her oversized ears, bushy eyebrows, and flared nostrils gave her more of a masculine appearance. Although she was a petite woman, there was nothing small about her. She stood out in the way she dressed—half like a man in trousers beneath a skirt but cussed worse than one if you got her mad—and in her determination to blaze a path, alongside a handful of other women in this country, through the male-dominated profession of doctoring.

Jana had never seen Leanne take to anyone as quickly as she had to Dr. Walker, probably because of her masculine peculiarities. Dr. Walker had told them that her pa, a country doctor, had never forced her into boy's clothes. He'd just forbidden her to wear corsets or other tight-fitting women's clothes, which he claimed squished the internal organs, especially the lungs to hamper their breathing. So she'd chosen to wear men's clothes because of their loose fit. Jana knew women who'd fainted from corsets strung too tight and had always worn hers looser, especially now. She wasn't about to be discovered because she'd fainted from a suffocating corset.

A good three inches taller than Dr. Walker's five feet, Leanne gazed down upon her with great admiration. "You should get a medal for putting up with those bossy surgeons. I came close to socking 'em for brushing you aside and telling ya to hand over their saws like you weren't a doctor."

"But, Dr. Walker—," Jana began before the doctor interjected.

"Please, both of you boys, call me Mary."

Jana concluded, "Well, Mary, the other surgeons sure sucked in their pride when they got overrun with cases and needed your help."

Leanne whistled. "The tongue-lashing ya gave them to get 'em to back away from your cases with their bad advice was sure something."

With a rebellious flip of her dark curls, Mary said, "They fear us women invading their territory and showing them up. They better get used to it because we're here to stay."

"They sure didn't like it when you went ahead and removed bullets and shrapnel instead of amputating; we soldiers did. It renewed our faith that not all surgeons are butchers," Jana said.

"Unfortunately, army doctors follow orders to amputate everything. The government claims my kind of doctoring costs them too much time and money to help these soldiers heal. But surgery and rehabilitation could get a limb working again. The men who benefit from that will be independent of the government's help and productive to their families and society again. Why can't they see that?" Mary said through clamped teeth.

Jana too admired Mary. What woman wouldn't? Only thirty, she already had two medical degrees, both from colleges in New York. And she could easily pass as a man to pioneer her way into his world. Jana decided she had more courage than both the Union and Confederate armies combined. It made her seem a whole lot bigger than the short, petite woman she was.

Pointing toward the big house's back portico, Mary said, "Now there's someone who really deserves a medal. Have you met her yet, boys?"

Jana and Leanne's eyes followed her pointing finger. They shook their heads and watched with curiosity as a matronly woman, about the same height as Dr. Walker, took the last step down.

"Her name's Clara Barton. She puts herself in peril bringing supplies that she's gathered herself to our army and nursing the wounded on the battlefields with bullets zipping all around her," Mary said.

As Miss Barton came their way with a tray of steaming rations, Jana observed a bounce in her step that hinted to feistiness.

Miss Barton halted before them, holding out her tray. When Jana started to rise, she said in a soft voice, "Please, stay where you are," and leaned over to put the food within Jana's reach.

Jana judged her to be about forty years of age. She was a pretty woman. Her face was ovular with a hearty complexion and gentle lines. Her dark eyes were rimmed with red, and the skin around them was puffy from the many hours she'd been on her feet. She looked more exhausted than Jana felt. "Thank you, Miss Barton. My name's Johnnie. And my friend here is Leander," she said, taking a mug of hot coffee and a warm biscuit.

Looking from Jana to Leanne with a kind expression, she said, "I'm glad to know you boys. You must call me Clara."

Jana nodded and bit into the yeasty biscuit and washed it down with the robust coffee. Both sent a homey feeling sifting through her and warmed her inside and out. She shivered as she felt herself beginning to thaw out.

Mary slurped her coffee. "Ahh. You're an angel, Clara." She invited Clara to join them. "You ought to be resting instead of serving us. I bet you haven't sat in days."

"There's a method in my madness, Mary," Clara said with a devilish twinkle in her eye. "I've heard all about Johnnie and Leander's diligence in the surgical quarters, and I could use their kind of help inside. I came to bribe them with food. If it works its magic, then I'll rest a spell." Dark brown strands of her hair hung down from the braid along the crown of her head, clipped back by a barrette with the rest of her thick hair.

Leanne pointed to a bullet hole in Clara's skirt. "How'd ya get that?" she asked.

Gesturing across the river toward Fredericksburg, Clara replied, "Crossing a pontoon bridge to get to wounded soldiers holed up in a church."

"I'd keep it as a reminder if I were you," Leanne said, her eyes finding Clara as another target for her admiration.

"I'll have to. In my haste to get here, I didn't pack another," Clara said.

The sound of hoofs smacking through the mud and wagon planks groaning under the weight of more shrieking wounded reached their ears. Two mules, straining to lug a four-wheeled ambulance up the deeply rutted road bluff-side, turned the corner.

Jana shivered again, this time with apprehension. She was drowning in war and hated to see any more suffering. She'd have to swim up and out of her lamenting and loathing right away because only those cases needing more complicated surgeries were brought here. To the contrary, however, war had given her something to love. Over the past twenty-four hours, she'd found great pleasure in making others feel better, even if only in some small way.

Tucking the emptied tray beneath her arm, Clara pressed on with her fast-swaying hips and loud-swishing skirt even though she had to be just as weary of war as the wounded.

Jana jumped to her feet and trotted after her.

Clara reached the ambulance as it bumped to a stop. "Would you kindly hold my tray while I have a look at the wounded?" she asked the steward just jumping down from the back of it.

"I ain't no woman's slave," he said and started away.

Jana was dumbfounded by his reaction. He wore the green half-chevrons with yellow piping that designated his belonging to the medical department. Of all people, she expected him to be compassionate and to welcome any gender willing to nurse the wounded with the shortage of help.

Leanne threw her mug to the ground and swallowed the sip she had swirling around in her mouth. She marched up to the steward. Not caring that he ranked above her, she pinched and twisted his earlobe until he begged her to stop. "And when you're bleeding all over the battlefield, she ain't gonna help ya." She shoved him away and said, "I met Rebels who act better than you."

Under the glowers of all around him, the steward slunk a good distance away.

Clara wrapped her hand around Leanne's in a tight squeeze, with the whites of her knuckles showing. "I've had to use those same words more than once. Thank the sweet Lord, for everyone like him, there's a whole lot more like you."

Leanne left her hand in Clara's and said, "And us soldiers hope there are lots more like you and Mary watching our backs."

With a smile, Clara took her hand away and returned to tending the wounded.

Inwardly, Jana praised Leanne's aggression. She'd put it to good use fighting prejudice against a woman who risked her life for the soldiers and gave her all to this bloody war. In the presence of Mary and Clara, who hadn't turned their backs on their gender to fight in this war, Jana suddenly felt her loose-fitting men's clothes growing small around her and suffocating her like a tightly tied corset.

Chatham Manor

Fredericksburg, Virginia

December 14, 1862

Jana and Leanne leapt into the wagon, straining to move the wounded onto stretchers. The steward, now apologetic for what he'd said to Clara, came over to help draw the wounded out. Mary assessed each case for surgical priority, and Clara decided their placement.

With all eight of the patients settled, Mary turned to Jana and Leanne and said, "One of you boys come with me, the other help Clara inside."

Leanne volunteered to assist Mary and was right on her heels when they disappeared into the surgical quarters.

Jana was glad. She'd rather go inside and hold a hand than go back into surgery and help take one off.

"Feel free to finish your breakfast and rest a spell, Johnnie," Clara said, blowing a wisp of her fallen hair away from her face.

Jana gobbled up the rest of her biscuit and gulped down her coffee. "I'm at your disposal. And as soon as you show me what to do, you must rest a spell," she said and hustled after Clara.

Inside, Clara armed Jana with instructions, soap, salve, cloth bandages, and wash pans to treat the wounded. Away she went, never resting that day as far as Jana saw.

The hours melted away fast for Jana as she cleaned and wrapped wounds. At first, she nearly fainted from the smell of pus-oozing wounds, made more rancid by the heat of the fires blazing away in each of the rooms she worked. She was able to quickly smother it beneath the rewards of her work. The wounded showed their appreciation with a wink, grateful nod, or kind word. Even so, with each pitiful whimper or gut-wrenching cry from the sufferers, she grew more spiteful of war.

Around mid-afternoon, Keeley ambled into the dining room, emptied of its table and chairs, where Jana bustled about. He whistled an Irish tune as he transferred the cherry logs stacked in his arms to the grate and then stoked up a blaze. On his way out, he collected the soiled bandages Jana had heaped in a basket by the door and returned minutes later with a mop and bucket of sudsy water. "Ye look dead, Johnnie," he looked around with a grimace and said, "I hope no one heard me say that."

"They didn't. Even if they did, they'd understand. We're all tired and bound to say whatever pops into our heads. And I doubt anyone would take issue with you with all of your hard work. Is there anything you haven't done?" Pointing at his mop and bucket, she said, "Besides that, you've stoked up the chimneys with the wood you've chopped, collected bandages, and delivered trays of broth and biscuits all around. And when did you learn how to bake bread?"

"Clara taught me. I suppose the best comes out in a person when they know they have others depending upon them." With playful eyes, he said, "Although I've come to regard meself a good kneader, ye better taste me biscuits before ye judge me baking." He sobered. "I've seen too how the wounded respond to your womanly touch." He slapped his head. "I did it again—said the first idiotic thing come to me mind. I didn't mean to call ye a woman, Johnnie; I only meant ye were born for nursing."

"Don't worry, Keeley. I took your meaning as a compliment," Jana said, truly believing this time he wasn't trying to bait her into giving up her secret.

Gazing at the floor spattered with mud and blood, Keeley said, "I better get back to minding me task."

Laughter erupted from the room opposite.

"Let's go see what that's all about. We could use some cheer," Jana said.

They hurried over to the former sitting room where the healthiest of amputees were kept. Crowded around Charlie, soldiers were crying with glee, and Charlie was giggling.

"What's funny, lads?" Keeley asked.

With a painful grunt behind his hoot, the soldier closest to Charlie rubbed his leg stump and said, "'Cause I can't write, Charlie here was writin' a letter home to my folks to tell 'em I lost a leg. I was actin' real down about it when he asks me what chore back home I hate the worse. I told him plowin.' He says, 'I reckon you won't have to worry about that anymore, will you?'"

Jana and Keeley shared in the hysterics erupting all over again.

It felt good to laugh, no matter how short-lived, Jana thought. She should've known she'd find Charlie at the heart of the joy. He'd never before shown a witty, humorous side. Yet, all day long, he could be heard lifting the spirits of the sick and encouraging them to use their weak hand in the absence of their dominant one or to walk again with a wooden leg.

When the merriment waned, Charlie went off to feed a soldier who'd had one arm amputated all the way up to the shoulder, the other to the elbow.

As Jana and Keeley were leaving, they heard Charlie tell him there were wooden legs; surely they'd come up with something for arms too.

What Keeley had said minutes ago hit the nail square on its head: knowing others depended upon you brought out the best in you. Jana decided Charlie's kind of medicine was better than any soothing salve or morphine.

Later that evening, Jana tended to a boy she recalled from the night before. She'd held him down while a surgeon amputated his left leg from the knee down. Without a balk, he said goodbye to his leg before bravely accepting the chloroform. She judged him to be no older than twelve. Although he'd walk again with a wooden leg, he'd never climb a tree or run the bases in baseball or ice skate or do whatever else he liked to do that needed two legs. Jana did her best to suppress her pessimism as she dropped down beside him on the hardwood floor. "I've got to change your bandage," she said.

Too weak to lift his head, the boy groped around with his icy hand until he found Jana's and gave it a frail squeeze. In a feeble voice, he begged, "Write me a letter instead?"

Jana recollected that same desperate expression on the dying groom's face. She gulped back hard, knowing what was coming for him too.

Sensing her concern, the boy summoned enough strength to give Jana's hand a heartier squeeze while he said in a voice growing feebler, "I'm not scared of dying, only of my ma and pa never knowing what happened to me."

"I'll go fetch a paper and pen," she said, scooting off in search of Mr. Walt Whitman, a poet sure to have writing implements. Ma had bought his *Leaves of Grass* when it was first published in 1855; she loved all of his poems within it. Jana wished she had that copy with her now. Wouldn't Ma be tickled to have his autograph on it? She found Mr. Whitman in one of the upstairs bedrooms. All the soldiers around him were under the spell of his deep, melodic voice as he read a poem she recognized from his earlier work. His soft, white hair and beard and ruddy cheeks reminded her of Saint Nick. He spread his own brand of joy, listening to the soldiers' talk of home, reading some of his own poetry, writing notes home for them, or just sitting quietly by their sides. He'd come to Chatham

Manor in search of his wounded brother. When he'd discovered him elsewhere and not seriously wounded, he returned here to help.

As Jana moved deeper into the room, she eclipsed the sun's glow through the window behind her, and her shadow embraced the poet.

Mr. Whitman must have noticed the sudden darkness cast over him. He lifted his head and looked Jana's way. Her eyes must have telegraphed her urgency because he asked, "What's the matter, son?" After she explained, he drew a pencil and stationery from his knapsack faster than she could draw her pistol.

Jana thanked him with the promise to return his pencil, and then she hurried back to the boy's side to honor his last request. Quietly, she asked his name and where to send his missive.

Isaac told her and then dictated the details of his enlistment, major battles, wound, and amputation for his note.

Jana wrote quickly and neatly, stumbling only once when she heard a gurgling in the boy's throat that garbled his speech and signaled his nearing death. She choked back her tears, trying to be as brave as him.

In a whisper, Isaac uttered his last words. He begged his parents not to mourn him because he didn't regret serving his country. Then his eyes fluttered shut, his chest heaved and settled, and his face grew peaceful.

As Jana felt the heartache she'd been holding back for Isaac's sake come surging up from deep within her, she turned toward the wall. She tried to hide her crying, but her body tremors would easily give her away. Isaac's story had moved her because it paralleled hers; both had run away and enlisted with only a paper goodbye. He'd never see his family again, whereas that hope for her was still alive. Even if she secured a furlough right now, she couldn't go home looking like a boy. Ma and Pa would know her ruse and never let her return to her friends. In the midst of her sorrow, she felt a tap on her arm. She used a clean bandage she had tucked over her belt to wipe her soggy face before circling around to greet her intruder.

A soldier, who appeared much older than her pa by the crackly skin on his face and who wore a different uniform than Isaac's, propped himself up off the floor on the arm he had left. Nodding at the paper in Jana's hand, he said, "Tell his ma and pa he died with honor, making a charge with his regiment's colors." He lay back down and stared up at the ceiling; his tears streamed back across his temple and into the hairline above his ear.

Jana agreed. Any young boy brave enough to serve his country deserved to be memorialized with honor. Penning in the older soldier's suggestion, she added her own entreaty for Isaac's parents to be proud of their heroic son who had matured well beyond his years. She folded the letter and tucked it into her pocket to mail as soon as possible. Then she went to find Keeley, who was in the kitchen scrubbing cloth bandages for reuse, and recruited him to help her carry Isaac outside to his temporary resting place in the garden.

Jana draped Isaac's woolen blanket over him. She gazed upon the rows of dead and prayed for the dying and destruction to end. If they were to go on, though, she'd rather heal than kill. The glory in women's work had touched her soul. And she'd seen how men, such as Keeley, Charlie, and Mr. Whitman, had found glory in it too. Ma and Pa were right—glory could be had without a single gunshot and in being a woman.

Near King George Courthouse, Virginia

March 1863

To break up the boredom of winter in camp and avoid paying the sutler the thieving prices he set on goods in his traveling tent store, Jana and her friends secured permission to forage for fresh eggs, milk, and cheese for themselves and corn and oats for their horses. As they left the camp, they took care not to trot their horses through the muddy avenues between the crudely built log huts. They weren't about to be the recipients of a united bark by their comrades to "walk that horse!" with their mounts' hoofs flinging clay everywhere.

Leaning over her saddle's pommel, Jana was rubbing Maiti's neck and whispering tender words in her ear when a great calamity arose from behind. She turned to see about it and a squealing pig raced by. On its tail were six troopers hooting and hollering as they kicked up mud from their boots to chase it down.

Leanne yelled out, "Walk that pig!"

Jana, Keeley, and Charlie snickered. Leanne joined their merriment when a trooper sailed through the air and slid off the pig's hindquarters and into the muck facedown. They'd seen the contest a hundred times. The rules were simple: the first man to capture the greased pig won a pot of money. It sometimes took hours to do. Jana didn't care to gamble herself, but at least the men were finding ways to have fun instead of brawling.

The hind contender yelled out, "Johnnie girl and her horse, isn't that precious? I might've guessed she'd be escaping camp to keep from playing in the mud."

Jana didn't want to resort to violence, but she felt it was necessary to react as any man would to preserve his dignity while protecting her cover. She tugged the reins right and pulled Maiti to a stop, blocking her heckler's path. Leaping from the saddle, she came eye to eye with him. She recalled Leanne's move back in Havre De Grace and swung her leg, swiping the bully off his feet. Grabbing his hand, she dragged him over onto his stomach, hopped on his back, and shoved his face in the mud. "Care to call me a girl again?" she asked, making her voice brusque.

He stayed silent.

Jana raised his head by his hair and said, "What? I can't hear you." No reply.

She pushed his face back into the muck, permitting him to lift it when he began squirming. "I still can't hear you. Care to call me a girl?" she repeated.

"No," he muttered.

"You don't seem sure," she said, nudging his head downward.

"I'm sure, I'm sure," he cried.

"Next time, you'll get worse," Jana said and stood up.

He turned over. With his face dripping grunge, he looked her square in the eye and said, "Guess I was wrong about you."

Whether he was really convinced of that or was saving himself a ribbing from his friends for being battered by a girl didn't matter to Jana. He'd said it loud enough for the many onlookers who'd gathered around to hear. "No hard feelings," she said, offering her gloved hand and helping him to his feet.

While Jana's critic ambled away in a slumped posture, Keeley and Charlie shared stunned looks and Leanne shouted, "That's the way to give it to 'em, Johnnie. He won't be botherin' ya no more."

Jana shrugged and remounted. "We better get moving," she said, wishing Keeley hadn't seen her acting like this. It would probably ruin any chance of him ever falling in love with her once he learned her true gender. She lamented to herself, *How could he ever be attracted to a girl who'd use her fists to teach a lesson?*

They'd ridden a good distance before Charlie broke their awkward silence. Glancing back at Camp Bayard, he said, "It's an awful sight—only one for sore eyes after some long, hard picketing."

Without looking, Jana knew he referred to the jumble of log huts: some had nicely thatched roofs while others were fashioned from tents or logs; all had lopsided chimneys. Her mind regressed to the way the area had looked when the Porter Guards first arrived here nearly four months ago. Their soon-to-be military city was a forest of dense bushes and scrub oaks. She'd branded the regiment insane then for wanting to christen such an ugly place after their honorable general, mortally wounded at Fredericksburg. Now, as she circled around to gaze upon the clutter, she suddenly saw beauty in the forested hills and valleys here before they'd scarred them with their saws and axes.

Over the next ten miles, they trotted their horses over country roads just as muddy as their camp's lanes. The sun intermittently peeping through the clouds did nothing to dry up the soggy earth. And the moderate temperatures kept it from freezing over.

Snowflakes swirled down around them, sprinkling the molasses-covered ground like powdered sugar over chocolate cake.

"I'd give anything to sink my teeth into Ma's moist chocolate cake with vanilla icing and a tall glass of milk to go along," Jana said. Instead, she stuck out her tongue to taste the sweet, swirling snowflakes, which tickled her tongue as they landed and melted. Pondering Ma's baking led Jana to wonder about her last mailing home. What fun it would've been to see Ma's shock when she opened the envelope to find two letters inside; one from Jana, the other from Walt Whitman, thanking Ma for appreciating his poetry.

Charlie interrupted her thoughts. "My ma wins first prize at the County Fair every year for her chocolate cake." He and Leanne were riding far enough ahead so as not to splatter Jana and Keeley with mud from their horses' hoofs, but not too far ahead to be excluded from conversation.

"I'm praying we get ourselves a twelve-point buck. Our Johnnie here makes a great deer stew, for a lad, that is," Keeley said.

When would he give up? Jana wondered. "My brothers always tease me about that too," she said, pleased with her quick wit.

From her saddlebag, Leanne retrieved a pouch that she'd stitched from a pig's bladder. She drew a pinch of tobacco out of it. "All this talk's got me hungry. I'm gonna rein in my appetite," she said and packed some into her cheek.

"Keep your eyes peeled, lads, for wild game. We'll load up on other rations when we head back. Then we won't weigh down and slow up the horses the whole trip," Keeley said, restating a pact that they'd made before starting out.

"I'm gonna get us a Rebel turkey for supper," Leanne said, her words garbled somewhat from the plug in her mouth.

Jana looked toward the woods for a hog to come ambling out onto the rolling, snow-covered fields. "I'd love some fresh ham." She kept guard for a while until she became hypnotized by Maiti's sways to her own rhythmic steps and by the smacking sounds of sixteen hoofs plunging up mud.

Leanne barged in on Jana's trance. "Why do we got to share our spoils with a bunch of murderous scoundrels? Ain't one officer deserving of a lick of milk."

"We don't have to, lad. We might better, though, if we're to expect any more favors," Keeley said.

Jana shared Leanne's sentiment, echoed by most Union soldiers, who also felt demoralized by one defeat after another due to the incompetence of their army generals. First, George McClellan had been slow to take the offensive against Confederate General Robert E. Lee at Sharpsburg. This cost the Union over twelve thousand soldiers, killed, captured, and wounded to about ten thousand for the Confederates. Then McClellan's replacement, Ambrose Burnside, had delayed in gaining the offensive position at Fredericksburg, making it impossible to penetrate Lee's stronghold over all the hills. The Union paid for it with another twelve thousand Union casualties, more than twice that for Confederates. Still, Jana deemed Leanne overly harsh to aim her strife at those officers who'd tried to dissuade their superiors' debacles and deserved at least a glass of milk.

"I'd rather be foraging for food than fighting," Charlie said.

Sniffing the air with contempt, Leanne said, "Why don't ya just desert, Charlie?"

"And be paraded around for all to see my head half-shaved and branded with a permanent letter *D* like Kilpatrick did to those two deserters in our brigade? Or, worse yet, be executed for it? I won't dishonor my pa's good name." Charlie's shoulders slumped in resignation. "Besides, I don't have a skill that could bring in anywhere near the thirteen dollars a month a cavalryman makes to take good care of my ma and brother."

Jana had noticed how Charlie's face had lost much of its boyish luster. She knew he'd been hardened by Leanne's near death back at Leesburg and since then the sight of many other deaths. He looked eighteen instead of thirteen; though, he still couldn't sprout a whisker if his life depended upon it—good news for Jana and Leanne, who were trying to hide that they never would.

"I meself don't pretend to relish fighting either," Keeley said.

Reining in abruptly, Leanne caused Maiti and Keeley's gelding to rear up. Her saddle leather squeaked when she circled around to face Keeley. "Why'd you sign up if ya feared fighting?" she asked, leaning to one side to spit tobacco.

Jana caught a whiff of Leanne's chewed-up spat, not an unpleasant smell, but it was a filthy habit by the way it stained the fresh, glittery snow the reddish-brown color of dried blood. It reminded her too much of all the gore she'd seen back in Fredericksburg. Why did Leanne have to keep proving she was a man? Nobody questioned it.

"I've been in many a fight, and I only fear the unfair ones. I'd like to live nigh long enough to build me hearth and home on me soldier's pay," Keeley said.

Leanne pressed her lips together. She knew Keeley had the right to fear death, having faced it before.

"And why might ye have enlisted, Leander?" Keeley asked.

Leanne stiffened, and her eyes began to smolder with hatred. "To get the fear of fighting out of me," she said, spitting this time with a heap of anger behind it.

"I don't understand, lad," Keeley said.

Leanne balled up her gloved hands around her horse's reins. "Next time my pa gets liquored up and beats on my ma, I'm gonna be man enough to stand up to him."

Slapping a gloved hand over her mouth to suppress her horror, Jana reopened a split in her chapped upper lip. She'd witnessed Leanne's pa's mental abuse but never gave it a thought that he'd gotten physically violent with her or her ma. Not that one behavior was any better than the other; both were unpardonable.

Keeley and Charlie looked just as shocked as when they'd all stumbled upon the dead soldier-bride back at Fredericksburg.

With her tongue, Jana put pressure on her bleeding lip. The blood tasted bitter, sweet, salty, and sour—a combination as complex as Leanne. But then Jana put it all together: Leanne's glares at the back of her pa's head in his blacksmith shop, her oft-instigated fights against bullies, her wince to Keeley's words about family beating up on each other, and her shocking news. She understood Leanne more fully now. Only a man could stand up to another man in the way she had to stand up to her pa.

Leanne broke their numbed silence. "I ain't ever again gonna bully like my pa just to get the fear of fighting out of me," she said and hung her head in shame.

Charlie reached over to pat Leanne's back. "It's what you reckoned you had to do." He drew a long breath and said, "My ma always says to turn the other cheek. Instead of fighting your pa, take your ma away from him for good."

"I could write my ma and pa. They'd take your ma in," Jana said.

"Or my ma would love another woman her own age around. And Buffalo's a good distance from Elmira and your pa," Charlie said.

Leanne's head whipped up. Her steel-gray eyes flashed disbelief. "You'd both do that for my ma when ya don't even know her?"

"If your ma's anything like you, our kin will love her, right, Charlie?" Jana said.

"They sure will," Charlie said.

Leanne dropped her chin to her chest. Her shoulders quaked as she sobbed.

Jana's heart crumbled as she witnessed Leanne's lifetime of suffering come spewing out. She looked toward Keeley and Charlie who seemed accepting of Leanne's emotions. Why shouldn't they be? Just because a boy cried didn't make him a girl. Any boy who'd had to endure such hardship deserved a good cry. Besides, they'd both cried over the dead soldier-bride, and tears were streaming down their cherry-frosted cheeks now. She let go of hers too before they completely crystallized in their ducts.

"We're sorry your kin is the enemy." With a sniffle, Keeley gestured toward himself, Jana, and Charlie and said, "Consider us your family, lad. And now ye have three good apples to replace the rotten one."

"And we're watching you and your ma's back," Jana said, dabbing her tears with her gloved knuckle.

Leanne nodded her gratitude. She swiped her runny nose across her uniform sleeve and dabbed her tears with a rag. Looking embarrassed, she spurred her horse on away from them.

Jana was glad when Charlie sped off after her. He'd make her feel good again, and it wasn't long before she heard them laughing. She warmed all over to hear Leanne happy. It was as though she'd become a different person now that she'd shared her secret and found people who cared enough to shoulder her burden.

When a sudden snow squall whipped up, Charlie called back, "We better get somewhere fast or we'll be lost in a blizzard."

"Don't fret, lad. We've been over these roads nigh enough scouting Rebels to know where there's shelter," Keeley said.

They put light spur to horse to keep the pace slow and make it less painful to go against the biting wind and blinding snow slapping their faces. They tied scarves around their faces to ward off frostbite.

Keeley's voice was slightly muffled behind his scarf when he asked, "So why'd ye enlist, Johnnie?"

"To preserve the Union my great-grandpa and grandpa fought hard to build." Jana still wanted that, but she no longer wanted to kill or be killed for it. She prayed her grandpas could see neither their nation divided nor its savage fighting.

"Aye, a patriot."

"And to free the slaves," Jana said, cowering behind the rubberized cover over her hat that draped down to her shoulders to protect her head, ears, and back of the neck from the cold. She knew Irishmen loathed freed slaves who took jobs away from them by working for cheaper wages. "I hope that doesn't make you mad at me."

Keeley peeked at her from around his own fatigue cap's curtain when he said, "I like how ye speak your mind, Johnnie. But I'm not like most Irishmen. I believe it's every man for himself no matter what his situation." He shrugged. "I've been prejudiced against enough to know I don't like it, and I'm not about to do it meself. Besides, me issue's with this country, not the freed black man."

"Huh?"

"This country thinks of us Irishmen as no better than a hog and keeps us in the barnyard class. Me fight for this country goes no deeper than to collect the soldier's pay on which to build me dream hearth and home."

Jana shifted uncomfortably in her saddle. Protective of her home and country, his words ignited a fire within her. She didn't want to argue with Keeley; she only wished to understand him better. Maybe he wasn't her prince after all. "Why stay here then?" she asked.

"Like the freed slave, we Irishmen are stuck here. We're kept in poverty by wages barely enough to feed ourselves and none left over to better ourselves."

"What about women? We—" Jana began and quickly coughed to cover up her mistake, which Keeley didn't seem to catch.

He jumped to reply. "Women deserve equal rights and opportunity too. They have more sense than men, and we men ask their opinion on just about everything. Why shouldn't they have a say for themselves?"

"They should. But in reaching for that, they don't turn their backs on their country and give up the fight to make it better."

"This isn't me country, and I don't intend to give up me own fights," Keeley said.

"By accepting a soldier's pay, aren't you accepting this country has something to offer? And in a way making it your country?"

Keeley paused for a long minute before saying, "I'll save me answer until I've lived me dream."

Disheartened, Jana sank into her saddle. She could never embrace a man who'd fight only for himself.

As though reading Jana's mind, Keeley said, "I hope I haven't ruined our friendship, Johnnie."

Jana debated Keeley's viewpoint, trying to step into his boots. Before she'd donned men's clothes, she'd had nothing to do with the fight for equal rights. And she'd never been where a woman wasn't tolerated. She'd only lately witnessed prejudice against Mary

Walker and Clara Barton as they pioneered their way into the male-dominated professions of doctoring and nursing. Still, it hadn't been aimed directly at her, so she hadn't felt its full force. She'd grasped enough of it, though, to know she'd hate it and be angry with a country that didn't tolerate her as a certain people—especially when that country was founded by pilgrims escaping discrimination from their homeland. Keeley's anger with this country for putting him down was one thing; it was another to take from a country and make it home, yet refuse to call it home without fighting to make it better. Neither made Keeley a bad person. His gentle, caring ways made him a good person. Jana decided right then not to give up on him and not to let him give up on this country. She answered Keeley in a firm, friendly way, "I'm not that shallow, Keeley." Before he could retort, she changed the subject. "Is there any place special where you'd want to build your hearth and home?" she asked, trying not to sound too interested.

"Aye." He got a faraway look as though picturing the place. "Elmira, New York," he said.

Jana choked on her spittle and began coughing.

"Are ye all right, Johnnie?"

"Yes," she said and cleared her throat.

"Are ye acquainted with the city more than as our regiment's place of organization?"

Half-recovered from her surprise, Jana said, "Yes, I have kin who live there." With most of her regiment recruited from western New York, she'd told everyone who asked she came from the eastern part of the state, making it unlikely for anyone to know or think they knew her. "How'd you find your way to Elmira to begin with?"

"When I labored to ship oysters upriver there from New York City, I fell in love with its surroundings and learned I could enlist at its military camp."

"Why didn't you join one of the Irish regiments formed up in New York City?"

"So ye'd have me sticking with me own kind too, is that it?"

"And, now, you're lumping me in with people who don't tolerate anyone unlike themselves, is that it? You see how it works both ways, Keeley?"

Keeley's eyes probed deep into hers, which they did too often of late for Jana's comfort. He seemed to be looking for her to slip up and show some emotion or do something to give herself away. "Don't get your feathers ruffled over me, lad. I'm a hopeless case."

Jana put up her guard to his words; they were the kind a man and woman would say to each other. He might trust she was a girl, but she wouldn't be baited into telling him until she was ready. Avoiding his trap, she laughed and said, "Again, tell me why you aren't serving in an Irish regiment from New York City?"

With a sigh that billowed his handkerchief, Keeley said, "All of the Irish regiments raised there were infantry. I wanted the better pay a cavalryman gets. And I was thinking if I got meself in with the local lads, they might show me around Elmira after the war."

"I could do that," Jana said, careful not to sound too eager.

"I was hoping ye weren't too mad at me to offer since I don't think Leander will be sticking around her home long enough after the war to do that."

Stifling her excitement, Jana realized the answer to Keeley's problem: her hometown and its people, especially her family, were great cures for anyone ailed by prejudice. Smitten with them all, Keeley would be proud to fight for this country and call it his own. Only, with this war, his arrival there might be a long time away. She grew hopeful of him again but prayed nothing made his attitude worsen between now and then.

Near King George Courthouse, Virginia

March 1863

Jana squinted through the dark and the sleet pelting her eyes and spied a flicker of light between the bouncing tree limbs. Come to think of it, she'd seen a farm right about here on their previous outings; she led her friends to a small, two-story frame house.

Noticing smoke curling up from the house's central chimney, Leanne whiffed the air and said, "Ain't no cake baking here, only hickory burning."

"Right now, I'd settle for a hunk of hickory," Charlie said, rubbing his stomach.

Jana shivered. If she had to choose right now, she'd take a warm seat in front of the fire over a piece of cake.

"Before we pay the homesteaders a visit, we might want to scout the property for Rebel cavalry. If we're riding on a night like this, they're sure to be too. Why don't we pair up, lads, and make a wide sweep around the house in opposite directions?" Keeley said. "Keep your pistols handy to fire a warning shot if ye run into trouble."

"Look for fresh tracks in the snow too," Jana said.

"You come with me, Charlie," Leanne said and reined her horse to the right.

Spurring his mare on, Charlie kept close behind the swinging tail of Leanne's horse.

"Stick to me flank, Johnnie," Keeley said, urging his horse to the left. "Ye mind the property and buildings. I'll look for tracks in the snow."

They found a barn, big enough to hold about twenty animals, not too far from the house. Keeley reported no tracks leading up to it, and Jana saw no sign of light seeping through the crack between the latched door panels. Except for the sleet bouncing off the barn's roof and the bleat of a sheep inside, all was quiet. They pressed on, passing a corral, which enclosed about two acres of flat land behind the barn.

Jana admired the small farms dotting Virginia's countryside. They reminded her of home with their charm and coziness that the sprawling, flamboyant plantations lacked. And most of them got along without slaves. This confirmed for her the rich, Southern man had instigated the war, using the argument of states' rights to decide on matters over the federal government just so he could keep his slaves. If you erased the issue of slavery from the equation, Jana trusted no other issue hot enough existed to bring brothers to war against each other. She did, however, realize the North couldn't be held blameless. They wanted to force the abolition of slavery without a plan to help their brothers continue their way of life without it.

Halfway around the property, Jana and Keeley met up with Leanne and Charlie, who reported all was quiet around the barren crop fields, chicken coop, and smokehouse. Together they retraced Jana and Keeley's tracks back around to the front of the house.

Charlie started out of his saddle to go knock on the door while the others covered his back with their drawn pistols. His foot never escaped its stirrup before the front door thrust open and sledge-hammered the outside wall.

Light from inside formed a halo around a man as lanky as President Lincoln; he stepped out onto a roofed porch that spanned the front of the house. With his hunting rifle aimed their way, he inched forward and stationed himself between the roughhewn pillars before the steps. "I'll drop the next to move," he said.

"If one of our Colts don't drop ya first," Leanne sneered.

"Who are you and what do you want?" the farmer asked.

"We're Yanks. Our commander sent us to gather whatever food ye might spare. We can pay ye in greenbacks," Keeley said.

The farmer said nothing.

Jana found his lack of interest incredulous. Most Virginians they'd offered Yankee currency to practically threw smoked hams at them. Who could blame them with one federal dollar equaling at least seven of theirs? Confederate money scarcely held any value. It was all because Union ships blocked most of the South's ports and prevented their trade with Europe. Their money couldn't even be backed by cotton, let alone gold or silver, most of which had been in the federal government's hands when the South seceded.

Over the whipping wind, a loud, guttural wail, which could've shattered the glass-paned windows from the inside out, pierced the air.

Leanne shot up in her saddle. "If you've hurt somebody in there, I'm gonna shoot ya down right quick!" she said and clicked back her pistol hammer.

Familiar with the sound of a woman in labor from the births of her four sisters, Jana told Leanne this to calm her.

Worry crept into the farmer's voice when he said, "My wife went into labor early. With just the two of us here, I couldn't leave for help."

Jana waved her hand around. "We'd fetch help for you if we could find our way in the dark or this blizzard. We barely saw your light."

"It's too late, anyhow. My wife's water broke a while back. It seems the baby should've arrived by now."

"We could trade our help, even if only to boil water, if ye'll allow us to hole up here for the night and some milk from your cow if ye have one," Keeley said.

Waving her revolver Jana's way, Leanne said, "He probably knows something about babies with four younger brothers."

The farmer lowered his rifle, seemingly disarmed by their genuine concern and desire to help.

Jana shrugged. "I've done more with assisting my pa to birth our calves and foals; though, I have delivered some tough cases with Pa guiding me."

"I've had to help my animals some in giving birth. But I don't think I have the guts to help with my own child." His voice cracked as he said, "I'd never forgive myself if—"

Another gut-wrenching scream.

The farmer raked a trembling hand through his light hair. "I'd be mighty grateful for any help y'all can give."

Jana remembered that when their cows still labored some time after their water had broken, something was wrong with the calf. It was either in the womb backwards or the umbilical cord was wrapped around its neck. Whichever the case, the calf could live if it got help down the birth canal in time. To maintain her disguise to Keeley and Charlie, she said, "I can help, but I'm no doctor or midwife. Probably, the best your wife's going to let me do is guide you from behind a door." Sensing urgency in the situation, she didn't wait for a reply. She holstered her revolver, untied her cavalry-issued, rubber blanket from the back of her saddle, and dismounted. She motioned for Leanne to follow her.

The farmer yelled to Keeley and Charlie, "Help yourselves to my cow. She's in the barn. There are empty stalls enough for all four horses. When you're settled, come up to the house for something to eat and a chair fireside."

Keeley gathered up Maiti's reins while Charlie did the same for Leanne's horse. As they towed the horses to the barn, the storm swallowed them up along with the sound of hoofs crunching through the snow.

On the porch, Jana and Leanne stomped their boots, slapped their kepis against their thighs, and brushed off the arm-length capes over their greatcoats to rid of as much of the crusty flakes as possible.

The farmer welcomed them into an entrance hall that led to a kitchen on the left and parlor on the right, the only rooms on the first floor. A large double-sided brick fireplace made the wall between the two rooms. A hissing, crackling fire gave both rooms a warm glow.

When the farmer closed the door, Jana turned to him. He appeared to be about Keeley's age; though, on closer inspection, it was hard to tell with the many worry wrinkles maturing his looks. She handed Leanne her rubber blanket to hold and then took off her coat and vest, stuck out her chest, and said, "I'm not what I appear to be." A mere glance her bust's way would prove her womanhood. She had no problem with him seeing that for himself. Ironically, she lost her modesty being modest every time she'd sneaked into the woods to relieve herself and either stumbled upon or was stumbled upon by men equally as modest as her. She felt immensely lifted of the burden of playing the part of a male with most of her uniform shed. If someone presented her with a petticoat and skirt right now, she'd leap into them. She loved the camaraderie in the army but hated all that came with hiding who she was.

With a bob of her head, Leanne verified for the farmer what she presumed Jana was about to unbridle.

The farmer drew his eyebrows together, perplexed.

"I'm really a female, fighting to preserve our country," Jana said.

The farmer staggered backward, astonished.

"She ain't lying," Leanne said.

As Jana hung up her clothes on wooden pegs near the door, she rushed to say, "My real name's Jana. Please call me Johnnie, just so you don't slip later in front of the others who think I'm a boy and have four brothers. I really have four younger sisters. Besides calves and foals, I've watched and helped some with their births. If you and your wife want, I can do more than just guide you from outside the bedroom. I claimed I couldn't earlier just to keep up my disguise."

A scream snatched the farmer from his surprise. "I must see to my wife," he said and vanished up some stairs on the kitchen side.

Nodding toward the ceiling, Leanne asked, "If they need you up there, will you be all right by yourself?"

Jana smiled. "I won't be alone. You'll be close by if I need you, right?"

"You can count on me. I'll stand guard on the front porch and warn ya when Keeley and Charlie head this way."

"If I'm upstairs when they come, do what you can to keep them from knowing I'm actually in the bedroom. I'd rather tell Keeley and Charlie I'm a girl than have them discover that for themselves." To the sound of sleet tapping against the windowpanes, Jana said, "And you can watch just as easily through either of the front windows. I'd be happier knowing you covered my back here inside where it's warm and dry."

Leanne took up guard, seating herself in front of the parlor window.

Rolling up her shirt sleeves, Jana headed into the kitchen, more brightly lit by lanterns burning hog lard. She fumbled around and found a cake of lye soap, scrub brush, and small basin into which she ladled hot water from a kettle hanging fireside. Catching sight of her hands, she thought with dismay how they had no business handling a baby. It was easy to shed a man's clothes to become a woman again, but it would take forever to scrub away the grime embedded under her nails and in the cracks all over her palms. As her rough fingers snagged on the soft, cotton towel she used to dry her hands, she found herself desiring the softness and delicacy of a woman's hands. Creaking stairs disrupted her wishful thinking.

The farmer appeared on the bottom step and requested Jana follow him. On their way up the narrow staircase, he introduced himself as Marcus.

As they entered a large bedchamber, flames burst high in the fireplace's grate. The warmth of the room heightened the perfume of frantic sweat that loitered in the air.

The mistress of the house lay in her bed in damp clothes, hands clutching her abdomen, a strained expression evidencing the painfulness of her labor.

With his fingers, Marcus combed his wife's matted straw-tinged strands away from her green eyes and forehead to reveal her lightly tanned and youthful complexion. He started his hand away, and she latched onto it tightly, obviously wanting him by her side. "Anna, meet Johnnie, our Yankee midwife," he said.

Anna smiled at Jana. Although it was small and weak, it showed a heap of relief and gratitude behind it.

Keeping her voice calm, Jana said to the expectant mother, "Marcus says your water broke some time ago. He thinks the baby should've been born by now. Do you agree?"

"Yes," Anna said, her voice quivering with fear.

"I'll give it to you straight. You probably need someone to put a hand up inside of you to coax your baby out. I've done it before with our calves and foals and have seen it done to one of my sisters. I can tell Marcus how to do it or I can do it. Either way, we should get to it. My hands are scrubbed and ready to go."

Husband and wife held a silent conversation with their eyes the way Ma and Pa always did. Then Anna nodded for Jana to proceed.

"I'll do my best and pray I don't let you down," Jana said.

"We're thankful for your help. Do what you can. God will decide the rest," Anna said.

Beads of sweat blotted Jana's upper lip. Her hands turned clammy. It was one thing to have an animal dependent upon you, another for a human.

When Anna doubled over in pain and wailed, Jana pushed aside her own fears. She waited for Anna's cramps to subside, and then she recruited Marcus to help her slide Anna diagonally in the bed and onto the rubber blanket. She never dreamed she'd use it for anything other than repelling rain, sleet, and snow. Now, she'd use it to collect the blood and clots of afterbirth; it would clean up faster and easier than scrubbing cotton sheets against a washboard later.

Marcus propped Anna up onto two pillows.

With care, Jana slipped Anna's nightgown up past her abdomen and bent her legs up, exposing her dilated birth canal. She explained to Anna what she was about to do.

Anna braced herself.

Jana took a deep breath and then forged a path up Anna's warm, moist canal with her fist so as not to scratch up her patient's insides with her chipped fingernails.

Crying through clenched teeth, Anna crumpled the sheets up into her fists.

Marcus dampened a towel in a wash basin on a bedside table and mopped Anna's forehead and face, trying to distract her from the pain.

Jana found a tiny foot at the head of the birth canal. By the heel, she pushed the baby up and around until its head pointed outward. She felt great relief when she didn't feel the cord around the baby's neck, and she withdrew her hand. "Now, Anna, push!" she said. She'd often seen the Brady's calves and foals, trapped in the womb too long, come out stillborn after suffocating to death. She prayed hard for this not to be the case.

Anna rose up slightly onto her elbows; her eyes blazed with determination to suffer through the pain and deliver a healthy baby. She huffed and puffed and then pushed hard enough to bulge her neck veins. When a head finally popped through the birth canal, Anna dropped back onto her pillow, sapped of all her energy.

Clamping her hands gently around the baby's head, Jana guided it the rest of the way. She was elated that the baby's coloring was not blue from a lack of oxygen. Wrestling to hold the slimy newborn, Jana slapped its bottom the way she'd seen the midwife do with her sisters.

They all held their breaths until the baby belted out a good, strong cry.

Jana heaved a sigh of relief. "It's a girl!" she announced, and Anna and Marcus laughed until they cried.

As Marcus took his girl and held her up for Anna to see, Jana cut the umbilical cord. Making clicking noises with his tongue, the father calmed his crying infant.

The newborn's anger over being plucked from the safety of the womb gave way to curiosity as her tiny, birdlike eyes roved over the face staring back at her.

Marcus and Anna gazed upon each other with joy and their baby with pride, reminiscent of Ma and Pa's shared look after the births of Jana's sisters.

With a wink at Anna, Marcus said, "Since we haven't settled on a name for her yet, what do you say we call her Jana?"

Anna caught her breath with delight and said, "It's a fine idea."

"I'm honored. Thank you," Jana said, with tears welling up.

After holding their little Jana for some time, Anna's eyelids began to droop. Marcus took the baby away just as Anna's eyelids fluttered shut; she gave in to her exhaustion, wearing a relaxed and contented countenance.

In a whisper, Marcus asked if Jana would tend to his child while he tidied up Anna and the room and then watched over his wife for a while. Before he did, he hurried away to draw a bath for the infant.

When he returned, Jana carried her namesake down to the kitchen and was weaning her into the basin of soapy, lukewarm water when Leanne appeared.

At the sight of the baby, Leanne skidded to a stop. Pumping her fist in the air, she said, "You did it, Johnnie. I knew ya would."

"Do you know what they named her?" Jana asked, feeling proud.

"By the looks of you, I bet I can guess." Smiling, she said, "You earned it, Johnnie. I'm proud of ya."

To Leanne's kind words, Jana felt doubly honored tonight. "I'm proud of you too, Leanne. You've come a long way in giving and receiving compliments." Jana couldn't wait to write and tell Ma and Pa about her accomplishment; she knew they'd be proud of her too.

When the infant spit and sputtered, Leanne looked frightened. She held her hands up in surrender and said, "If ya don't mind, I'm gonna see if Keeley and Charlie need my help milking the cow."

Jana giggled to herself as Leanne scooted out through the back door. She finished bathing, diapering, and dressing the newborn in the hand-sewn, cotton nightdress that Marcus had left folded tubside. Tucking the extra cloth around the cooing tot's toes, she carried her to a chair fireside and began rocking her. Besides the heat shed by the burning logs, Jana felt warmed by the glory of having helped bring into the world a small, perfect life—all in the midst of a war where thousands had already died and thousands more would probably meet the same fate. She leaned her head back against the rocker's cane slats and closed her war-weary eyes. She was tired of death and dying, of lying, of sneaking around, and of dressing in men's clothes.

Cuddling with Little Jana awakened a sudden and agreeable maternal feeling in Jana. She tried to imagine what her child might look like, and when she saw dazzling little dimples and sparkling emerald eyes, her eyes popped wide open. For Keeley to consider building a hearth and home with her and sharing the joy of children between them, he had to know her as a woman. She wanted that badly and for him to love her as she loved him. What good would it do for her to trade uniform for skirt if he were to die in this war? She couldn't and wouldn't desert him or Leanne and Charlie either. She wished for some honorable way for them all to be discharged without another gunshot. She'd have to hurry. The spring campaign would open in a month, maybe less.

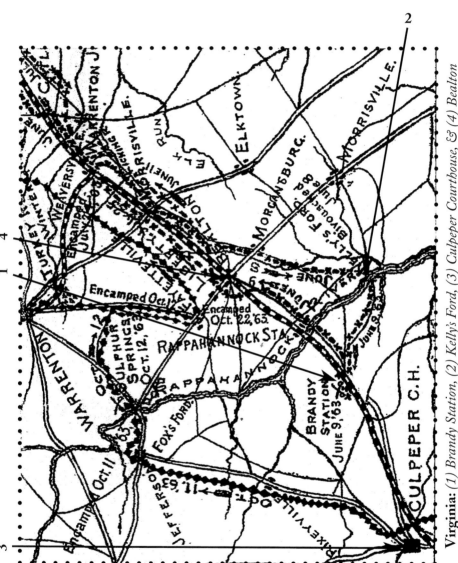

Virginia: *(1) Brandy Station, (2) Kelly's Ford, (3) Culpeper Courthouse, & (4) Bealton*

Battle of Brandy Station, Virginia

Afternoon, June 9, 1863

To the sound of heavy artillery booming upriver, Jana and the left wing of the Union Cavalry Corps splashed across the Rappahannock River at Kelly's Ford. She knew their right wing had collided with the enemy hours before planned. The two wings were slated to have converged at Brandy Station and make a westward sweep toward J.E.B. Stuart and his Confederate cavalry, amassed at Culpeper Courthouse.

Jana began despairing because she'd failed in her quest to find an honorable way out of the line of fire for herself and her friends before some heated battle. She'd been trying hard since March, finding only jobs, including hospital steward, that required some sort of promotion. Keeley's popularity might get him elected to a higher post. Leanne could become a blacksmith with a portable forge to keep the horses shod. And Jana could shed her men's clothes to become a nurse. That left Charlie out in the cold all alone. She wasn't going anywhere until she saw them all safe. Just as the Union cavalry had to refocus their attack this morning, she had to adjust and start dwelling on her immediate situation as opposed to what could've been.

With the left wing further divided, Colonel Hugh Judson Kilpatrick led his unit from the woods into a grassy field. He began readying them for a charge up a sprawling hill.

Jana felt the scorching sun frying her insides as she maneuvered beside the rest of her brigade into step-like formation. When her regiment was positioned at the top of the staircase, followed downward to the right by the Second New York and First Maine cavalry regiments, she knew it would take the lead into battle.

An enemy shell shrieked across the blue sky, streaked with wispy clouds. It struck the ground behind the Porter Guards with a horrific blast and rumble of the earth.

Maiti snorted and pawed the grass, raring to go while every horse around her squealed and reared in fright.

Like all of the other troopers around her, Jana crouched against her horse's neck to avoid being maimed or killed by flying shards of metal. Luckily, only plowed-up clumps of earth rained down on them as all brought their horses under control.

Jana tried to cough up the knob of panic, making her already parched throat feel more choked. It had gotten this way from a morning's hard ride over roads made dustier by a sun that blazed away soon after it had popped up over the horizon.

"Are ye all right, Johnnie?" Keeley asked.

Jana nodded. With a shaky hand, she drew her canteen, uncorked it, and pressed its pewter mouth against her lips. She let the river water, kept cool by the wetted cotton and wool covering around her flask, moisten her dry throat. Up to now, she'd been lucky. The Porter Guards had only nibbled around the edges of war. They'd never been in a battle where the enemy launched their cannon fire on them with such ferocity. She pondered how many Rebel vultures waited behind their grayish-blue sulfur cloud of cannon smoke to swoop down upon them.

With his pencil-thin lips spread wide in demented glee, Kilpatrick galloped his horse across the front of the brigade. He held his sword up high to rally his men.

"It's gonna be another unfair fight. And us Porter Guards are gonna be the guinea pigs. He'll kill us all," Leanne sputtered.

Jana understood Leanne's meaning. They were about to get their first real taste of Kilpatrick's reputation for sending his men into battle with reckless disregard, the reason he was called Kill-Cavalry. Although terrified to go up the hill first, she put her finger to her lips to hush Leanne. There was nothing they could do to avoid the charge. And it did no good to unravel anyone's courage by reminding them of past Yankee slaughters by Rebels on heavily fortified grounds. Jana patted her breast pocket to make sure the letter to Ma and Pa was still there. In it she divulged her whole truth. She'd made Leanne promise to mail it home if she were killed today. If Leanne was kept from the task, she hoped some other kind soul would find and forward it.

A Porter Guard hollered out, "Let's show them Southern horsemen who's superior," to which a great cheer erupted.

Only a few besides Jana and her friends sat quiet in their saddles, unable to share in the euphoria; though, like the eager, Jana was confident about the Union cavalry's capabilities, especially after they'd run circles around the Confederate cavalry on their Southern soil back in the spring. They'd crippled a good amount of Rebel lines of supply, communication, and transportation. As far as she was concerned, what they were about to undertake required more luck than skill to escape unharmed.

Directing his somber eyes at Jana in particular, Keeley said, "Be safe, lads."

Jana presumed he was experiencing the same numbness many soldiers claimed to have had minutes before they were sent into their first heated engagement. Why couldn't she be that way too? Instead, she was far too aware of her own fears. She was terrified of herself or her friends dying, of never setting eyes on her family again, and of never knowing life as a woman—especially with Keeley.

While waiting for the order to charge, Jana frantically called upon her surroundings for help out of this fight. To her front, the enemy's guns bore down on them like a mountain lion with its razor-sharp incisors ready to rip them apart. With her saddle leather creaking, she turned to her left. The sun's evil rays skimmed off sabers as superior numbers of Rebels thrashed Yankees in a mostly hand-to-hand fight near Brandy Station. She flinched with every saber blow that sent a trooper, Yankee or Rebel, reeling to the ground, or with every horse that was mowed down, disemboweled, or torn in half by cannon fire. Only the dense forest from which they'd just emerged offered shelter in the shadows and embraces of its outstretched tree limbs. She'd never reach it, let alone get Keeley, Leanne, and Charlie to follow her, before being spotted and branded a deserter or worse, a coward. There was no way out.

The flag-bearers trotted to the lead of their respective regiments. Though the silks lay limp against their staffs on this breezeless day, each regiment's flag had distinguishing features to follow should the troopers, who all looked alike in their army-issued short coats and hats, become entangled in battle. Jana and the Tenth New York would serve under their yellow-fringed flag with its red, white, and blue cords and tassels. The Second New York would follow its swallow-tailed guidon in the stars-and-stripes pattern. And, for now, the First Maine would stand in reserve behind their standard with its bright blue background.

Lieutenant-Colonel Irvine of the Porter Guards shouted, "Trot! March! Guide left!"

With their spurs jingling, Jana and hundreds of troopers urged on their mounts. Her forehead speckled with a crazed sweat. Hemmed in amidst the rear ranks, Jana felt like a fox in a foot trap; it could see where to run and hide but couldn't shake loose to do it. The landscape rolled by her in a blur, and the wooded sanctuary behind her faded away.

Lieutenant-Colonel Irvine ordered, "Column, walk! Draw sabers! Trot!"

Hundreds of men reined in their mounts, holstered their pistols, drew their sabers with a great clank of steel, and urged their horses forward.

Jana took a deep breath to calm her nerves, strung much tighter than the Union's telegraph lines. She fixed her eyes straight ahead and dared not even a sidelong glance her friends' way for fear she'd fall to pieces fretting over them. She willed her mind to be as sharp as her saber blade.

"Charge!" Irvine bellowed, followed by the bugle's blare.

Jana and the Porter Guards surged forward. As they neared the tracks of the Orange and Alexandria Railroad in an earth-quaking gallop, a large column of cavalry advanced toward them. The tornado of dust around them made it hard to tell which uniform they wore. On the other hand, the legendary bloodcurdling yell, initially heard at the first battle of Bull Run and everywhere since, betrayed the combatants as Rebels.

A staff officer of a Union cavalry general dashed by on his roan. Pointing at the enemy's flag, just poking through the head of the advancing column, he challenged every trooper within earshot to go capture it.

Troopers from Company *D* swerved to the right, and Maiti followed.

Jana felt her dapple-gray's muscles rippling beneath her calves as she galloped after the Rebel colors. Her detachment didn't get far when a greater number of the enemy slammed into their rear and cut them off from the rest of their command.

Someone shouted, "Retreat! Retreat!"

Jana wholeheartedly agreed with the warning; if they took a stand, they'd be slaughtered. With every beat of her heart crashing up against her chest, Jana wheeled Maiti around and sped off toward the woods with the rest of her company.

Maiti glided over a deep, dry ditch about ten feet wide and landed on the opposite bank with the grace of a horse bred for the steeplechase.

Jana looked back to see Charlie's horse clear it too. Many other horses fell into it, including Keeley and Leanne's. Reining in Maiti and wheeling her around, Jana recoiled with horror at the scene in the ditch: horses thrashed about, crushing or striking down unsaddled troopers with their hoofs as they tried to get their legs under them or claw their way up and out of the gully. Yankees and Rebels, saddled and unsaddled, lunged at one another with angry thrusts of their sabers; the clash of metal against metal rang above the chaos.

Flinging dirt everywhere, Lieutenant Robb's horse pawed its way up the embankment. It cleared the ditch too late to save its master, killed by a Rebel sword thrust into his right shoulder and out through his breast. The lieutenant clung to his mount for a few yards before falling to the ground dead.

Leanne spurred her horse away from the melee, missing a beheading by a hair.

As Keeley grabbed his gelding's mane to haul himself back up into the saddle, three Rebels swarmed around him like angry bees. He let go of the mane, dropped his saber, and held up his hands in surrender.

Enraged over Lieutenant Robb's death and Keeley's capture, Jana dug her heels into Maiti's side, spurring her back toward the chaos. She ignored Leanne and Charlie's pleas for her to stop. She'd slash up and shoot down every Rebel who got in her way of saving Keeley.

As Rebels gained the high ground and charged toward Jana, Keeley flailed his arms like a madman, signaling for her to retreat.

Pistols popped and rifles cracked behind Jana. Some of the charging Rebels jerked up and then fell from their saddles.

Jana knew full well they'd been picked off by Leanne and Charlie, trying to save her. She wouldn't linger another second and sacrifice their lives. There was nothing more she could do for Lieutenant Robb or Keeley right now—maybe never. She'd just felt a mighty blow to her left bicep and looked down to see blood saturating her coat sleeve. Frantically holstering her pistol, she shifted the reins to her right hand, wheeled Maiti around, and hightailed it after Leanne and Charlie. As they fled through the woods, Jana felt herself growing weaker with each spurt of blood. The forest began to blur into a mishmash of green and brown. She slumped over Maiti's neck, and the light turned to dark.

Late Evening, June 9, 1863

Jana felt herself choking and coughing on burning oil and wax. Her eyes shot open. She felt lightheaded and thirsty as she squinted through the dull light, shed by both a lantern, hung from a tall pole that held up a large, cone-shaped tent, and a tallow candle on a bedside table.

Moving into Jana's sight, Charlie lifted her head with care and put a tin cup to her lips.

Jana let the cool, sweet water soothe her pasty tongue. She swirled it around in her mouth before letting it trickle down her dry throat. After a few greedy gulps, she pushed the canteen aside, not wanting to get sick from too much of it all at once (something the officers had warned against on hot, sticky days).

Charlie's forehead creased with concern. "How do you feel, Johnnie?"

"I don't know," she replied, trying to shake off the fuzziness in her head.

"You've lost a lot of blood and probably need lots of water, but the doctor says you'll be fine."

"Where am I?"

"Our division's field hospital, only"—Charlie looked mortified, and he lowered his voice to finish saying—"in a tent for female nurses to separate you from the men."

The memory of her wound came flooding back. Jana feared an amputated arm. All of the amputees she'd tended at Chatham Manor swore their severed extremities still felt painfully attached. She too felt her arm attached and a great soreness there. With deliberate slowness, she glanced down. Her uniform blouse was ripped up to her shoulder. Relief rushed through her when she saw her whole arm intact with her bicep wrapped in a blood-soaked bandage.

As though reading her mind, Charlie said, "Don't worry, Johnnie. The surgeon got the bullet out. He said it bled something fierce. You were lucky it hit the muscle instead of shattering a bone. It'll heal up good, but"—he grew fidgety—"you'll have a bad scar."

Grateful to be alive, Jana could care less about a scar, no matter how bad it looked. She cared more about Charlie's words. It just dawned on her how he'd said she was separated from the men. Her eyes probed his face for disappointment and hurt. Finding neither, she asked him, "Do you hate me for lying to you?"

Charlie shook his head with a passionate no. "I lied about my age to join up. Why can't you lie about being a boy?" He shrugged. "Anyway, I suspected you were a girl. After we found the dead bride, I got to wondering who around me could be a girl. It struck me how you and Leander always sneaked off to do your private business. And I came to the conclusion you fussed over me more like a mother hen than a rooster. Actually, it was Keeley who got me paying closer attention to you. We both noticed the way you moved your hands and hips; it seemed more feminine. And your modesty kind of added to the whole picture." He giggled. "We thought you sewed too good for a boy, especially when you don't have kin in the tailoring business."

"I didn't lie to just anyone . . . I lied to *you*, Charlie."

Charlie started unraveling Jana's bandage. His voice broke when he said, "I only care you're alive, Johnnie." He soaked a cloth in a bedside basin, wrung it out, rubbed soap into it, and with tenderness dabbed at Jana's wound. "Now, I'm going to make sure you don't get an infection." He applied salve and rewrapped her wound.

Tears pooled in Jana's eyes, and her voice broke too when she said, "You're a true friend, Charlie. And if you'll have me, I'd be honored to be yours forever."

Charlie removed his glasses, wiped his teary eyes on his uniform sleeve, and settled his spectacles back where they belonged. He leaned in close and whispered, "Leander told me her story too. I never would've suspected she was a girl; Keeley and I assumed she was just someone you trusted enough to stand as your guard."

At the mention of her name, the tent flaps swished open, and Leanne stepped in. "How's our patient?" she asked, her expression knotted up, obviously from worrying.

Not thinking, Jana pushed up off her bad arm to try sitting up. She barely got anywhere when pain sliced through it and forced her to lie back down. Through gritted teeth, she said, "I'm fine now that I see you are too."

"And I'm mighty glad you ain't in the Rebs' hands." Leanne whistled in awe. "Don't know how you clung to that warrior horse of yours long enough to escape those devils."

The memory of Keeley surrounded by the enemy struck Jana. This time she ignored the excruciating pain when she raised on her bad arm and sat up. "Where's Keeley?" she asked.

Leanne grunted. "Last we saw, corralled like a wild horse. Probably in some rat-infested prison in Richmond where he'll rot 'cause prisoners ain't being exchanged or paroled now."

Charlie's face sunk in gloom. "It was a bad day for us Porter Guards. We lost about a hundred men—only a few killed, but just as many wounded as captured. Lieutenant-Colonel Irvine is our only officer missing."

"Keeley will die of starvation. We've got to help him!" Jana said.

"I don't see no way we can," Leanne said.

Sinking back into her feathery pillow, Jana ruminated over what she could do for Keeley. Suddenly, she recalled a newspaper account of Rose O'Neal Greenhow who got caught spying for the

Confederacy in Washington, D.C., and was imprisoned there at the Old Capitol Prison. "I think I know a way. I've got to speak with the colonel," she said.

"Kilpatrick ain't gonna talk to you. He's booting ya out of the army," Leanne said, biting her lower lip. She stared down Charlie as though seeking his permission to tell Jana whatever she was chewing on.

"It's all right. Tell her, Leander," he said.

Leanne burst out, "I'm going home with ya, Johnnie, but I ain't going unless Charlie comes with us."

Dazed by her words, Jana raised her eyes to the ceiling, expecting to see the tent falling down on her. There was a greater chance of that happening than Leanne's abandoning a fight.

"I told you a hundred times, Leander. I'm staying. I need the pay and I won't desert," Charlie said.

To Jana's continued amazement and silence, Leanne said, "I joined up to get the fear of fighting out of me. It's gone. Now, I'm afraid of dying 'cause I'm all my ma has. I got to get home to her. I don't care if anybody calls me a coward for deserting. Leander Perham doesn't exist anyway."

"I agree your bigger fight is at home. It's time you saddled up and rode home to your ma. And you're no coward, Leander ... I am." Jana felt her guilt spill off her tongue when she said, "I tried looking for ways to run from the fight."

"Any man would be lying if he said he didn't think about that too. We all shed our yella by making a stand and hightailing it only when we had to. You shed your yella by taking a bullet trying to save Keeley. I'd call ya brave, not a coward," Leanne said.

Leanne's kind and understanding words peeled away Jana's shame. "Thank you, Leander. That means a whole lot coming from you."

With a twinkle in his eye, Charlie said, "You like Keeley as more than just a friend, don't you, Johnnie?"

Jana flushed with embarrassment. "No more lying, Charlie. Yes," she said.

"Keeley's going to be happier than a pig wallowing in mud to finally know for sure you're a girl, Johnnie." Charlie giggled. "It's awkward calling a girl Johnnie." He cleared his throat. "I mean woman. It's plain to see that now, and you *are* eighteen years old," he said.

"Do you know what gave me away right off to Keeley?" Jana asked.

"He decided you were way too pretty to be a boy. He claims he tried getting you to admit you were a girl a few times."

"A few?" Jana snorted. "More like a hundred times. Why didn't he just come right out and ask me?"

"He respected whatever reason you had for keeping your secret, even from us. And what if there was the slim chance he was wrong? He didn't want to insult you." Charlie saddened when he said, "Now, he might never know the truth."

"That's why I've got to see Kilpatrick," Jana said, throwing her legs over the side of the cot, sending her head into a spin from too fast a move.

Easing her back onto her pillow and then rewetting his cloth in the bedside basin, Charlie cooled Jana's clammy forehead and face with it.

Charlie's gentle touch gave Jana a whim about his future in the army that she'd address with the colonel. "Please, Leander, would you bring Colonel Kilpatrick here? It's urgent."

"I'll drag him here by his bushy sideburns if I got to," Leanne said and scampered out of the tent.

The momentary parting of the tent flaps brought in the night's pure, cool air and the chirp of tree crickets. Both refreshed Jana and settled her mind in time for her conference with Kilpatrick.

After a short wait, Leanne ushered the colonel into the tent. She motioned for Charlie to follow her outside to give Jana and Kilpatrick their privacy.

Kilpatrick pulled up an empty crate beside her cot. It groaned under his weight as he sat down; he ignored its threat to break in two. With a sigh, he said, "I regret having to send you home, son, uh,

I mean, miss. I admire your sacrifices and courage … far greater than some men who fight for their country. If you'd come to my attention only, I would've seriously considered keeping you on. Now that the truth's evident, I have no recourse. I must discharge you."

"I understand, Colonel." Jana put intrigue in her voice to bait Kilpatrick's lust for a good challenge when she said, "With your help, though, I could still serve my country, just in a different way."

Kilpatrick leaned in closer to her on his creaky crate. The candle's flame accentuated the inquisitiveness in his eyes.

"If you'd send me to Richmond as a female spy, I could gather information about the Confederacy's military plans and try to bust our men out of the prisons," Jana said.

"Hmmm," the colonel uttered as he leaned back and scratched his stubbly chin, deep in thought.

Jana preyed upon why he was called Kill-Cavalry to coax his consent. "Washington's got spies. And, if we don't already, we ought to have spies in the Confederate capital. I'm sure you have contacts in Richmond who'd get me a pass there, then claim I was a relative, or something like that, come to visit. I'm a pretty good actor. After all, I've been playing the role of a male for well over a year now." She looked at her wound. "If it hadn't been for this, I'd be in uniform still. Please consider it, sir. I know I'd make a great spy."

"I do regret the loss of your Lieutenant-Colonel Irvine and would love to have him back," he said. "And I reckon the army owes you for your bravery."

"Huh?"

"I heard all about your charge back to the ditch to save some of our men. And, now, you want to sacrifice yourself again for the good of our country."

Jana knew someone had given her far more credit than she deserved since she'd only gone back to the ditch for one man. That someone was probably Leanne, trying to give her an extra boost to help her get her way with Kilpatrick. "But I—"

"I love your spirit and will do my best to reward you," Kilpatrick said, standing quickly to leave.

Before he got away, Jana traded arguing over her bravery in favor of discussing two more important issues. She hated to tell another lie, but Charlie was determined to stay and neither she nor Leanne could leave him behind in harm's way. "The bespectacled boy who just left here shot me, not the enemy," she said.

Kilpatrick blinked to this, even though nothing ever seemed to surprise him.

"He's clumsy with a gun. And he can't always tell whom he's shooting at when his glasses fog up. We can't have him picking off our own men." With his full attention, Jana prattled on about Charlie's popularity with the wounded at Chatham Manor. She showed him her bandage to prove Charlie's nursing skills. By the time the colonel left, Jana had him talked into promoting Charlie to hospital steward for the duration of the war. And she made him promise to keep Charlie's shooting a secret even from Charlie and to investigate the cost of her buying Maiti from the federal government. Jana would ask Marcus and Anna to stable her horse until she could take her home.

As Kilpatrick passed Leanne and Charlie on his way out, he gave Charlie a sidelong glance. His cheek muscle twitched in a fleeting acknowledgement when he saw Charlie's glasses fogging up after he'd traded the cool of the night for the warmth of the tent.

Only Jana had noticed the colonel's reaction, and she was pleased he'd witnessed the occurrence.

Leanne and Charlie nearly tripped over each other to get to Jana's side and hear her news.

First, Jana told Charlie about his new assignment in the medical corps.

"You mean I'm going to be ranked above a company sergeant and get a pay raise?" Charlie asked.

"Yes, you are," Jana said.

Since Charlie couldn't hug Jana because of her bad arm, he turned and twirled Leanne around the tent. The candle's flame fluttered, threatening to extinguish under the merry breeze the two of them created. When they finally fell to the grassy floor, huffing and puffing with exhaustion, Jana told them about her own potential assignment.

Charlie jolted up into a sitting position; a lightning bolt of concern struck his face. "Oh no, I won't let you go! The Rebels already hung that Timothy Webster as a spy," he said.

Leanne said, "And he was s'posed to be the best detective the Pinkerton Agency had."

"The Richmond papers say the Confederacy will hang even females caught spying," Charlie said, growing more and more agitated.

Seeming to sense Jana's silent determination, Leanne said, "If ya got to go, I ain't letting you go it alone."

"It'll be hard enough to get one of us past the Rebel pickets without raising too much suspicion." To Leanne's opening her mouth in protest, Jana gave her a stern look and said, "You belong with your ma. Don't force me to turn you in to get you to go home."

Leanne held her hands up in surrender. "I get it, but I ain't got to like it." Lowering her arms, she said with firmness, "You watch your back. Don't trust nobody." Her voice softened. "And you definitely ain't a coward, Johnnie."

Jana nodded at her kind words and turned to face Charlie, trampling the grass as he walked off his anxiety. Disguising her own apprehension behind a confident tone, she said, "Don't fret, Charlie. I'll be fine. Just like you always say your pa is watching over you, my grandpa and great-grandpa are watching over me. They won't let anything happen to me because Keeley needs me."

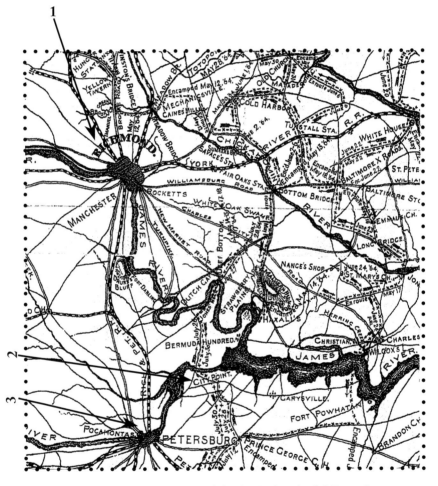

Virginia: *(1) Richmond, (2) City Point, & (3) Petersburg*

Jana felt the crackling fire blanketing her in warmth as she swallowed a spoonful of buttered grits. She looked around the kitchen of this fourteen-room mansion belonging to Elizabeth Van Lew and her mother, Eliza. Its central feature was a floor-to-ceiling hearth. Miss Lizzie (as friends and family called Elizabeth) had visualized for Jana how the hearth would roar from dawn until long after dusk when the mansion hosted elaborate parties or balls. It would bake bread in its ovens cut into its bricks on each side; roast meats and boil stews and puddings over its grate; and slow-cook vegetables in the embers of its floor all at the same time. Ma would be impressed by its cooking capacity, but she'd probably say her woodstove was adequate enough for the number of people she entertained simultaneously. And she loved her woodstove's top for frying and griddling. These days, the Van Lews also used their woodstove mainly for cooking, relegating the hearth as a source of heat. This kitchen, though, paled in comparison to the size and elegance of the chandeliered parlors and dining room, some of these with brocaded silk walls. Bathed in a thousand-fold more splendor and comfort than the Yankee prisoners she was here to help escape, Jana shuddered with guilt. She also felt the added remorse of not telling Ma and Pa her exact whereabouts in her last letter home this past Christmas. She'd written that she was in Virginia tending the wounded. If they knew she was in the heart of Rebel country, they'd probably send out a posse with a reward on her head.

Seated near Jana at the head of a long, wood table, Miss Lizzie drew a mug of steaming tea away from her lips. "Are you cold, dear? Shall we stoke up the fire?"

"The fire is fine, thank you, Miss Lizzie," Jana said, pushing aside her half-eaten bowl of porridge.

Concern draped Miss Lizzie's striking, blue eyes, behind which hid a brain wise beyond its forty-six years. "Are you ill this morning?"

Jana looked down at her lap and picked at a glob of grits on her pale-green dress. Her only comfort at the moment, besides her shelter with the Van Lews, was in being a woman. She loved the silky touch of her feminine garments and the tips of her auburn tresses back to tickling her shoulders. Over the sound of sweet, vanilla-flavored custard bubbling in its kettle, she said, "I feel badly about being well treated when our soldiers are freezing and starving to death in the prisons here. I'm anxious to do something about it."

"The South's starving its own people too. With Union ships blocking almost all of our ports, we can't trade our cotton, tobacco, or anything else with Europe or elsewhere for food." Miss Lizzie curled her upper lip in scorn. "Slavery is no longer fashionable. Even if the South won this war, which they won't with the North's superior manpower and materials, most nations have abolished slavery and will eventually see the hypocrisy in trading with a nation that yet supports it. Already England refuses to recognize the Confederacy as an independent country for that very reason. The South is too idiotic to see … their cause is lost."

"Please don't mistake me. I'm very grateful to you and Eliza for taking me into your home and sharing what little food you have with me," Jana said, knowing it was a strain for them to feed one more mouth. The two women had custody of Eliza's two granddaughters.

Miss Lizzie's brother had entrusted his daughters to the care of his mother and sister about two years ago because he knew he'd be drafted into the Confederate service sooner or later and because his staunchly Confederate wife constantly neglected their children to indulge in her own amusements. And, sometimes, they had to feed an escaped Union prisoner who they hid in a secret room in their mansion. Jana had fasted right along with the Van Lews several times since her arrival. Not wishing to be wasteful with so many around her starving, Jana slid her bowl back toward her and forced down another mouthful of cereal.

"Mother and I wish your visit could be under happier circumstances," Miss Lizzie said.

"I hope General Butler didn't pressure you too much to add me to your underground network," Jana said, dabbing the corners of her mouth with a napkin. She purposely avoided labeling her intelligence operation a spy ring. Miss Lizzie didn't see how what she was doing could be called spying against her country when she was trying to help save it.

With a toss of her dark blonde ringlets, Miss Lizzie said, "I didn't need coaxing from General Butler. Your merits by way of Colonel Kilpatrick sold me on your promise as an agent amidst my ranks."

"Well, I hope I haven't made a nuisance of myself."

Miss Lizzie's eyes bore into Jana's. "Why don't you remind me what you've accomplished in the month you've been here?"

"Well…I've cared for Rebel wounded in the hospitals. And I've collected dresses and other cloths from ladies all around the city and delivered them to the hospitals to be used as bandages."

"Why?"

"To make myself known as a Southerner who's loyal to the Confederate cause, but who happens to be married to a Yankee imprisoned here."

Miss Lizzie was teaching Jana the art of deception. She professed to spy for the Union you either faked your allegiance to the

Confederacy or paraded your loyalty to the Union. Miss Lizzie practiced the latter, banking on the Confederacy marking her as too obvious to be a spy against it. She had Jana practice the former to show she stood by her man no matter what, hoping to gain sympathy from the ladies of Richmond. They were a powerful group that could help or hinder a person's cause. They left Fanny Ricketts alone and guaranteed everyone else did too when she came to Richmond to care for her Yankee husband. And *she* was a Unionist.

"What else have you done?" Miss Lizzie asked, drumming her well-manicured fingernails on the tabletop.

"Told you everything I've overheard from hospital guards or patients about Rebel troop movements."

Miss Lizzie reached over with her small hand and patted Jana's. "It takes time to build deception. I've been at it since the beginning of the war."

Even though she yearned to see Keeley, Jana knew it took time to plot against any prison guard who would try stopping them from helping Union prisoners escape. Her road to Richmond had crept along. For one, her wound had taken longer than expected to heal. Then she had to wait while General Butler recruited Miss Lizzie and they set up their military intelligence operation. She had to admit, that last part happened fast. They didn't call General Butler the Beast for nothing. He had a reputation for being quick and callous when he wanted something done. And it helped that Miss Lizzie had already had a group formed, working to help Yankee prisoners escape.

Miss Lizzie winked and said, "We're just about where we need to be to get you in to see your husband."

Whoosh! The kitchen door swung open, startling both women. Uncle Henry stepped in with winter's blistering cold busting in behind him as though it sought shelter away from its own frigid self. He set a basket of eggs on the table, no doubt from the Van-Lew farm a quarter of a mile below Richmond, opposite General Butler's headquarters on the James River. His dark cheeks and nose were red with frost. "I got some troubling news for you about the prisoners, Miz Lizzie," he said through chattering teeth.

Jana squeezed her shawl tight around her, a chill of dread making the hairs on her arms stand up.

Rising, Miss Lizzie pushed away her ladder-backed chair and scuffed it across the groaning floor planks to the fireplace. Patting it, she said, "Come sit, Uncle Henry. Tell us your news after you've warmed up some." Moving to the stove, she set a strainer of tea on the rim of a mug and poured water, still softly boiling in its kettle, through it. Finished, she whisked the filtered brew over to her servant.

Gazing tenderly upon Miss Lizzie, Uncle Henry accepted her offering and said, "I'm gonna keep saying it 'til the day I die. I'm mighty grateful to you for setting me free. And I thank you now for this tea." He blew hard on his beverage, putting his cold face into its steam.

"And I'm indebted to you, Uncle Henry, for risking your life every day on my account to help the Union soldiers."

Until Jana saw it for herself, she never would've believed how many lifelong residents of Richmond were antislavery and pro-Union. Miss Lizzie and her mother had taken their sentiments one step further; they'd freed their slaves after the death of Mr. Van Lew. To protect them, they kept their act of kindness off Virginia's books because a law decreed freed slaves had to leave the Commonwealth within one year of being freed or be re-enslaved. Miss Lizzie had told Jana it would kill her and her mother if any of their liberated people were kidnapped back into bondage while crossing other slave states on their way north or out of the country. There'd been too many cases like this even when the freed slaves had their manumission papers. On the books, their slaves were still that; off the record, they were servants, loyal to the Van Lews and eager to serve in Miss Lizzie's secret missions.

Uncle Henry slurped the last of his tea before reporting, "Military's moving Yanks from the crowded prisons here to someplace in Georgia soon. They've already sent butchers and bakers on ahead."

Jana felt a ball of panic wadding up in her stomach. She couldn't let Keeley escape her reach. It would be impossible to make connections so far away and deep within the South.

With calm resolve flickering across her high-cheek-boned face, Miss Lizzie said, "We must get word to the Union officers digging their way out of Libby Prison to quicken their pace. And to Keeley to fake an illness and get himself sent to the hospital where we're more likely to be allowed in to see prisoners."

Jana didn't doubt Miss Lizzie's messages would be delivered within minutes of leaving the mansion. She had agents everywhere, even high up in the ranks of the Confederate War and Navy Departments.

When Uncle Henry started to rise, Miss Lizzie put a gentle but firm hand on his shoulder to keep him in his seat. "Don't leave until I've given you a dispatch for General Butler. From what I've learned about the city's defenses, now might be ripe for him to take Richmond." She went to the custard, stuck a ladle in it, and stirred it around. "Perfect." Her eyes bubbled like the pudding, only with mischief as she remarked to Jana, "It's thick enough to oblige me with a bribe into the hospital. I'll have Cook transfer it to a hot plate." With her petticoat rustling beneath her skirt, she hustled off to the study, where she coded all of her missives in private using a cipher chart and then wrote them invisibly with milk or onion juice, later made visible by applying acid or heat. Over her secret message, she'd write a phony letter to a friend or relative. As far as Jana knew, the only people who knew how to decode her dispatches were General Butler and his chief of military intelligence.

Jana understood Miss Lizzie's need for secrecy. To be caught as a spy meant death, even for a woman. No female had hung yet. Once, Miss Lizzie had been investigated by military detectives regarding her pro-Union activities. She'd taken a Northerner into her home to protect her against threats from Richmond's society and treated her better than Swedish Opera Star Jenny Lind, one of her most famous guests. Jana found it incredulous that the woman had treated Miss Lizzie in kind by blabbing all about her doings. Luckily, nothing came out of the military investigation. Jana hoped she'd learned well from Miss Lizzie, the master at not leaving even a morsel of proof behind.

When Miss Lizzie returned, she handed Uncle Henry a paper, folded into a tiny cube.

Uncle Henry removed his brogan and pried free a block chiseled into its heel. After he tucked the message into the hollow and replaced his ankle-high boot on his foot, he went to the kitchen door, whipped it open, and plunged back into the cold.

"While I'm off sweetening up our provost marshal with custard for permission into the hospital, I have a practice mission for you," Miss Lizzie said.

Later that morning, Jana strolled down the sidewalk of elite Clay Street with its iron-balconied residences. As she approached the gray, brick mansion of Jefferson Davis, the president of the Confederacy, she sensed someone following her. Slowly, she turned around in time to see a stranger duck into a side street opposite. Miss Lizzie had warned her to be mindful. If military detectives followed her every now and then, surely they'd follow anyone connected to her. Fear and exultation wrestled around inside of Jana. While she prayed not to get caught and jeopardize Miss Lizzie's underground network, she was excited about her mission. Successfully completing it meant being entrusted with the next—to help free Keeley and other Union prisoners. She wanted that more than anything. It was why she was here.

With the sun's beams brightening the surroundings and bolstering her confidence, she sucked in a deep breath of frosty air and marched up to the mansion's front portico, a much smaller and less elegant version than the one that graced the front of Miss Lizzie's mansion, though still imposing. She had to get across it and inside. Her mission: to personally deliver the basket of eggs swinging on her right arm to Mary Elizabeth Bowser, one of Miss Lizzie's loyal servants who she'd gotten inserted onto President Davis's household staff to spy. Jana had taken tea with her and Miss Lizzie a few times when Mary had come to the mansion with important news for Miss Lizzie.

Jana was certain President Davis would love to discover how Miss Lizzie and Eliza had sent Mary north to Philadelphia to be educated when they recognized her intelligence. Mary had a mind that could capture the details of conversations and maps the way Matthew Brady portrayed people and scenes through his camera. When serving in the White House dining room, she listened intently to President Davis's discussions with his executive staff and generals about military strategy. When dusting his office, she memorized maps of troop movements sprawled open across his desk. In fact, Jana presumed it was Mary who'd sent word to Miss Lizzie about the sparseness of Rebel defenses around Richmond, making it ripe for a Union attack.

As Jana started up the portico's steps, she hoped Mary would come outside to greet her.

A uniformed guard appeared from around the corner of the house. "State your business, miss," he said. His soft voice and the laugh lines bursting out from the corners of his brown eyes gave him a gentle, jovial appearance.

Jana stepped down, praying he was a soft touch. Whether he was or not, she had to stop him from inspecting her eggs, especially the one tucked beneath the straw. It had been cracked open with its contents replaced by a coded message and its shell glued back together; the seam was made invisible by a white-dye extract from flowers in Miss Lizzie's backyard garden. She drew back her hood to let the guard see her face. She didn't want him thinking she was trying to hide her guilt and thus anything else from him. "I've come to deliver fresh eggs to President and Mrs. Davis, compliments of Miss Elizabeth Van Lew," she said, making herself shiver and hoping he'd feel sorry for her and let her by to warm up inside without any dallying.

The guard guffawed. "You mean Crazy Bet, the wealthy woman who walks around the market in shabby clothes talking to herself?"

"She may be crazy, but she's the most generous person I know. She helps anyone in need without discrimination," Jana said. Miss Lizzie wasn't crazy; she just wanted people to believe she was so they'd stop threatening her and her family because of their pro-Union sentiments. In the short time Jana had lived with Miss Lizzie, she'd seen her go to great lengths to confuse everyone as to her political and social leanings. Besides making herself look crazy, she'd care for the Rebel wounded and ill while subtly caring more for the Union prisoners. That, at least, had put a stop to the *Richmond Dispatch* inciting riots against her for not assisting the ladies of this city with sewing clothes and blankets for the Rebel soldiers. Before Jana's arrival, Miss Lizzie said she'd once housed the Confederate military's overseer of federal prisoners in Richmond while she hid an escaped Union prisoner right under his nose. Other than military detectives watching her once in a while, the government mostly left her alone. Miss Lizzie speculated it was because they too regarded her as crazy and because they still considered her one of Richmond's elite who may yet have money to donate to their cause. Jana knew they'd be scraping off the bottom of the barrel—Miss Lizzie's riches were dwindling with many of her properties sold off and the money donated to the Union cause.

"Are you sure those eggs aren't poisoned? I better inspect them before you take them inside," the guard said.

"Oh, please hurry, sir. I'm awfully cold." Jana removed the basket from her arm and exaggerated the cold and trembling of her gloved hand as she held it out. When the guard grabbed for it, she moved it toward him in a way to make it appear as though his hasty, clumsy hand had tipped the basket. She let about half of the eggs spill out. One by one they hit the sidewalk with a splat and a splatter.

As Jana and the guard stared at the slimy mess, footsteps pounded down the portico steps.

To Jana's relief, Mary Elizabeth Bowser jumped off the steps on the opposite side to avoid the mess and came rushing over. Her dark, chubby cheeks were like those of a cherub. Jana prayed she also had the magic of one.

Mary waved her duster about. Thousands of dust specks escaped from it in a whirling cloud. "I's dustin' the parlor and saw what happened," she said, purposely speaking poorly to mask her intelligence.

"Miss Lizzie won't be pleased," Jana said and gazed down at the eggs with a pretend sniffle.

The guard said to Jana, "I'm sorry, miss." To Mary, he said, "It's my fault. I shouldn't have grabbed for the basket with her hand shaking so."

Mary turned her back to the guard and winked at Jana. "Why ya *is* shivering, miz," she said while cleverly sliding the basket off Jana's arm. "Don'ts ya fret 'bout the mess. I'll cleans it up. Let's gets ya inside where it's warm."

Sounding frustrated with herself, Jana said, "If you don't mind, I'd rather go home. I wouldn't want to make any more messes, especially in the president's house." She retreated several yards before turning back to wave at the guard, hoping to distract him from seeing Mary hurrying into the mansion with the remaining eggs. Heading home, Jana chortled to herself. She couldn't wait to tell Miss Lizzie about her and Mary's performance. When she arrived at the mansion, Miss Lizzie's informant, the man who'd been following Jana, had already apprised her of it.

"From what I hear, you and Mary were masterful. I think you're ready for the next act," Miss Lizzie said. She told Jana how she'd put no message in the secret egg—her mission had been a dress rehearsal for what was to come.

Jana leaned back against the cane-backed rocker in front of the kitchen's hearth. Feeling triumphant with her dress rehearsal, she prayed to stage her real performance just as flawlessly.

General Hospital #13

Richmond, Virginia

Late January 1864

A few days later, Jana flung her heavy wool cape over her shoulders and stepped down onto the front portico of Miss Lizzie's mansion. It was far less grand than the piazza to the rear, adorned with six gigantic columns. In the spring and summer, they stood guard over well-manicured blooms of magnolia trees, hedges of privet, and box bushes, which cascaded down in steps toward the James River. Miss Lizzie was proud of her garden. It had been awarded top honors many times by the Henrico Agricultural and Horticultural Society in their annual competition for the finest in the city. Jana had seen the newspaper articles, which Miss Lizzie kept to prove it. Wouldn't Richmonders be appalled if they knew her flowers worked against them now to produce a dye that made the glued-together seams of cracked-open eggshells invisible and perfect for carrying coded messages to Union lines?

Uncle Henry parked the Van-Lew carriage curbside and jumped down to hold the reins of their last horse not confiscated by the military. The week before, with Rebel cavalry scouting the city for substitute horses, Jana had helped Miss Lizzie take a drastic measure to keep the roan from getting stolen. They led it to an upstairs parlor in the mansion where they piled a thick layer of straw on the floor to mute the echoes of its clomping hooves against the wood planks.

Hearing Miss Lizzie's small footsteps, Jana twirled around.

"I'll be right with you, Uncle Henry," Miss Lizzie called out, her soft voice carrying to him on the wings of a biting wind.

The wind nearly tore off Uncle Henry's wide-brimmed cloth hat. He held it down and hollered, "Take all the time you need, Miz Lizzie." He was waiting to drive Miss Lizzie to her farm about a quarter of a mile south of Richmond for a secret meeting with one of her underground agents. Jana deduced he was a farmer who lived out that way.

As Miss Lizzie pulled Jana's hood over her head, she said, "We can't have the mist running the rouge on your cheeks. And we especially don't want it to flatten your curls. The iron labored long enough to put them into that thick, straight hair of yours."

Jana felt her short, lazy curls, swept up and dangling from a silk ribbon, pressing against her neck. She hoped her hood wouldn't flatten her well-groomed hair. She wanted to look her best when Keeley saw her for the first time as a woman.

Miss Lizzie drew and tied Jana's hood strings into a floppy bow and stepped back to take a look. "Aren't you pretty?" In contrast she appeared unkempt with her natural blonde ringlets unbound and tangled and wearing her buckskin leggings, mismatched rumpled blouse and skirt, and canvas coat.

Although different, each woman's costume would play the same role to undermine the Confederacy today: Jana the devoted wife; Miss Lizzie the poor country woman.

The silky feel of a petticoat hugging her legs and the rustle of her skirt were magical to Jana. She'd never imagined herself loving wearing women's attire. What a relief not to be slinking around in men's apparel anymore. Jana drew a long breath and asked, "Any last-minute advice?"

Miss Lizzie looked around. Her pro-Union sentiments had yielded enemies of her neighbors and friends. They constantly spied on her, hoping to catch her in something underhanded and turn her in. Seeing no one lurking about, she leaned in close to Jana's ear and whispered over her clove-scented breath, "We have to be watchful and circumspect—wise as serpents—and harmless as doves, for truly the lions are seeking to devour us."

Biting her lower lip, Jana almost made it bleed. The mist prickling her cheeks reminded her about the last time the sky threatened more than a mere mist when her impatience got herself and nearly Keeley hurt back in Bladensburg. Over the past eight months, she'd practiced great restraint in getting to Keeley. The day was finally here, and her heart was bursting with eagerness to see him. She had to caution herself to keep a cool head. It was one thing if only she faced the consequences of getting caught spying, another if her actions hurt sweet Miss Lizzie, her family, or her network of agents.

Seeming to sense Jana's worry, Miss Lizzie said, "It's natural to be apprehensive before a first assignment, especially one as important as this. I know you'll do just fine."

"I hope I don't let you down. And I hope to repay you and Eliza some day for all of your kindness, Miss Lizzie."

"You already have, dear. You've graced Mother and me with your presence. Now"—Miss Lizzie whirled Jana around, nudged her down the stairs, and whispered with patriotic fervor—"go. The general and your gentleman await your joyful tidings."

Marching to the white picket fence, Jana pushed open and stepped past its gate and onto the sidewalk along Grace Street.

Uncle Henry nodded at Jana to wish her luck. He knew she headed off to the hospital with a scheme to bust Keeley and other Yankees out of prison.

Jana leaned into the wind, praying only the drab morning made her sense doom in her mission. Not wishing to look rushed and stir up suspicion, she purposely strolled down Church Hill, the highest of Richmond's seven hills in regards to terrain and social status. She strayed a few blocks over from her destination to the corner of Carey and Eighteenth Streets, where stood Castle Thunder Prison. Unlike Miss Lizzie, too superstitious to pass this prison for spies, Jana stood on the sidewalk opposite. She wanted to get a good look at it and a stern reminder not to get caught spying. She shivered, not from the frosty wind whistling across the James River, but under the prison's icy gaze.

Castle Thunder Prison's faded façade gave the impression that the building was old and frail. But its well-mortared bricks and iron-barred windows taunted her to test its will. The city's residents claimed this was the last stop for federal spies before the gallows. Two males caught with war materials against the Confederacy had been imprisoned here and already hanged.

Jana patted her midsection, feeling the bump that was the tintype image of her, Keeley, Leanne, and Charlie beneath her corset. When she touched it, she felt more courageous and not quite so alone. She doused the flames of her silly fears and raised her chin skyward. Tucking the *Holy Bible* under her arm, she stepped off the curb and proceeded the few blocks over to General Hospital #13 that, excluding smallpox cases, kept the ill and wounded inmates of Castle Thunder Prison.

To Jana's approach a sentinel cried, "Halt!" He put his rifle diagonally across his chest and stepped sideways a few feet to block the entrance into the four-story brick building with a flat roof. Overhead, a yellow flag that marked the long, narrow structure as a hospital snapped in the wind.

Jana shoved her signed permission under the guard's nose. As provost marshal general of Richmond, General John H. Winder had jurisdiction over the prisons and their affiliated hospitals. Given the shortage of medical and nursing staff, he was more likely to grant prospective volunteers into the hospitals than he would visitors into the prisons; though, his guidelines were loosely defined. In the case of Alfred Ely—Congressman from New York who as a spectator at the first battle of Bull Run was captured and imprisoned for a time at Libby Prison—he allowed guests based solely upon his fame. Miss Lizzie knew it would require more than her being a prominent citizen of Richmond to secure a pass, especially when it would favor Union prisoners. Pumping the provost marshal full of kind words and custard had helped her get her way.

Moving closer to her, the guard gave Jana an unwelcome dose of his nauseating breath. Some of his teeth were missing; the rest were stained brown from tobacco chewing. He had a sizeable plug in his mouth that made his cheek bulge like a squirrel packing nuts. Snatching the paper from Jana's hand, he studied the signature. "Appears real enough," he muttered, then turned a suspicious eye on her. "So you're a Yank, are you?"

Jana said, "I'm a Southerner…born and raised in Maryland, where Yankees and Rebels live side by side…not in harmony, of course. I was cursed the day I fell in love with a Yankee, but I do intend to love, obey, and honor my husband 'til death do us part." She scowled as though resigned to that loathsome fate.

The guard grinned at her in a patronizing way. "I admire a lady loyal to the cause and her man."

Inside Jana fumed. She wanted to spit in his face for his anti-Union, chauvinistic sentiments.

Spying the book tucked under Jana's arm, the guard said, "I'm to inspect everything carried inside."

Jana smothered her anger beneath a sugary smile. With both hands she held up the *Bible*, clamping it closed to keep the blueprint to Castle Thunder Prison, torn into many numbered squares and tucked between the pages, from falling out. She prayed Miss Lizzie had calculated right about the guard not associating anything disloyal with a holy book flashed in his face. To sweeten the punch, she said, "I hope to show my husband the way through God's words." Hah! She'd show Keeley the way all right—right out of prison.

For a long minute the guard studied Jana. She knew he was waiting for her to twitch an eye muscle or chew on her tongue or do whatever else to give away her guilt. She didn't flinch.

The guard took on a bored expression and spun around toward the prison's entrance. Inserting a key into a large iron padlock, he turned it until a click and then a heavy clank was heard before the bolt dropped open. He pulled the door wide open, waving her inside.

With a reverberating bang, the door shut behind Jana. There was no turning back. She was determined not to let anything go wrong.

A second guard intercepted and led her through the halls and up the stairs of the old factory past rooms where slaves once worked the tobacco rolling and packing machines. The wood or brick of the floors, ceilings, and walls still reeked of the raw plant even though they'd gotten a good whitewashing.

Jana only despised the otherwise pleasant, earthy smell of tobacco because, to her, it symbolized the cruelty of enslaving a people.

Stopping before a wooden door, the guard made it screech on its rickety hinges as he pulled it open. He motioned her inward with the snap of his head.

Inside, the stench from unwashed bodies, excrement, vomit, and bloody and gangrenous wounds seized Jana's nostrils. Her legs grew shaky, though not from the odor or a fear of what she might see and hear. She'd grown used to just about everything horrible from her nursing days in Fredericksburg. If she had the time and permission now, she'd care for these wounded and dying, Yankee or not. But how would Keeley react to her? He'd been briefed his wife, Jana Cassidy, would visit him and not to show surprise when he recognized her by her alias—Johnnie Brodie.

Following Jana in, the guard closed the door behind them and took up a post there. He pointed to the opposite end of the room and said, "Last cot on the left," obviously having been briefed about whom she came to visit.

Jana's nerves settled some when she noted no other guards or hospital attendants in the room to gawk over her shoulders. As she strolled down the main aisle between cots, those not too weak from their wounds or illnesses sat up, looking hopeful she'd come to visit them. They sank back into their straw mattresses when she passed by. The sight of their starved, pain-stricken, homesick expressions saddened Jana. Right now, she could only offer them an encouraging smile to keep fighting for their lives. She prayed her secret material would help all of the Union men escape. Fixing her eyes forward, she caught her breath. Could that be Keeley on the cot up against the back wall, his hair dulled from copper-red to burnt-orange, his face chalky white with gaunt cheeks and sunken eyes? She got her answer when he broke out that old toothy smile, which caused his cheeks to dimple and his emerald eyes to sparkle.

Keeley rose on legs that looked as though they were going to buckle beneath him. When Jana got close enough, he drew her to him, playing the role of a husband away from his wife too long.

Feeling his throbbing heart against her own and his weak but loving embrace, Jana knew he wasn't just acting.

Keeley whispered in her ear, "How are ye, Johnnie?"

Jana pulled back in confusion. Maybe she'd misread him and he really was acting. She searched his face. Did he believe her to be a woman or Johnnie disguised as a woman?

Whispering in her ear again, Keeley said, "I'm relieved to know y'are a woman and a beautiful one at that."

Jana felt her cheeks, already dusted pink with rouge, turning the color of claret.

Still whispering, Keeley said, "I prayed ye were alive and well. And now I pray to live nigh long enough to know ye as a woman." He pulled back, and his emerald eyes danced with adoration for her when he exclaimed loud enough for all to hear, "Y'are a sight for sore eyes, Jana lass."

Jana wanted to dance an Irish jig now that she was sure he loved her. She'd never been happier in her whole life, but she had to quell her ecstasy. Any celebration of their love would have to wait until after Keeley was sprung from prison. With great restraint, she perched on the chair Keeley scraped across the floor to his cot. "Shall we practice our native language, Mr. Cassidy?" she asked, glancing around the room with nervousness.

Keeley flicked a look to signal no one around them understood Gaelic.

Over the next hour, they created deception. When discussing spy matters, they spoke in Gaelic and smiled and laughed. When discussing make-believe family and friends, they spoke in English, feeding off of each other's stories as though they'd grown up together. And, when they took a breath, they doted upon each other as would a husband and wife separated too long. It felt as though they'd never been apart. Jana enjoyed playing Keeley's wife as much as he seemed to enjoy playing her husband.

At one point, Keeley smothered Jana's hand in his and then squeezed it gently when he said, "I hear and see all about meself how the Irishman has elevated himself in the eyes of this country through his fierce fighting and with an eye to his new country. I'm ashamed not to have done that meself. Ye were right, Jana. The only way to make things better is to take a stand with your heart in it."

Jana's jubilation soared; she could fully embrace him as a man with whom to spend the rest of her life now that she was assured he could fight for more than just himself. She squeezed his hand tight. "Your heart's in it now. That's all that matters."

By the end of their visit, Jana warned Keeley he must now show himself recovered from illness. It was urgent that he be moved from the hospital back to Castle Thunder Prison so he could get to work using the blueprint to find an escape route. Any day now he and other Yankees were to be transferred from Richmond's overcrowded prisons to a newly built prison in Georgia, making it impossible for

Jana to rescue Keeley. Also Miss Lizzie was hearing that Union officers were nearly finished digging a tunnel out of Libby Prison. Even if only one officer escaped, a great posse would be raised—officers were at a premium in the exchange of prisoners. Should that procedure be reinstated, the mastermind behind the tunnel's excavation, a colonel, could yield fifteen Confederate privates. Such a city and countrywide manhunt would hinder Keeley's simultaneous flight from Richmond.

The guard circled his index finger in the air, signaling the end of their visit.

In a hurried, hushed tone, Jana recited directions to Miss Lizzie's mansion and stood up to leave.

Keeley rose too. As he moved to embrace Jana, he began teetering from his weakened state, and he fell back toward his cot. His flailing hands knocked the *Bible* from Jana's grasp.

The book sailed into the air. Its pages opened, freeing many of the blueprint squares, right before it smashed onto the floor planks and seized the guard's attention.

With scraps of parchment fluttering all around them, Jana felt the floor trembling under the guard's heavy footfall down the aisle.

Jana and Keeley shared looks of horror and helplessness when the guard pinned bits of the paper beneath the sole of his boot, gathered them up, and began shaping them into a jigsaw puzzle.

Within seconds, the guard's head rolled upward, and his evil grin latched onto Jana.

Waves of terror crashed against Jana's insides. The lion was about to devour its prey. She feared not for herself but for Miss Lizzie, her family, and all of her underground agents. Had she put a stake in the heart of Union intelligence? Or worse yet, sent them all to the gallows?

Castle Thunder Prison

Richmond, Virginia

April 15, 1864

In a long, narrow room in the uppermost story of the prison, Jana carried a basin of warm water over to the next cot and set it on the floor before fetching her stool and drawing it close to her patient. She blew a wisp of her hair away from her face as she soaked a cotton cloth and dabbed her patient's fevered, bald head. Dizzy from hunger and fatigue, she pressed on because she loved to make people well. Ever since her imprisonment, she'd volunteered to nurse the less severely ill and wounded prisoners right here to save the city's hospitals from overcrowding. She didn't mind putting in the long hours to keep herself busy, and she was determined not to dwell on her impending execution. A military tribunal had found her guilty of having materials against the Confederacy and had sentenced her to hang. No date was set yet.

Jana thanked God every day for having convinced the judges who presided over her court martial of Miss Lizzie's innocence. In her testimony, she confessed to the following: She'd come to Richmond posing as a Confederate to make it easier to secure permission into the prisons. She kept it from everyone, including Miss Lizzie, so no one could slip about her being a Unionist. Then she preyed upon Miss Lizzie's known generosity by acting desperate for a place to stay while she cared for her Yankee husband. About a month into her deception, the prison's blueprints arrived anonymously, with no note. The sender must have figured that a woman like her, devoted to her husband, would be motivated to free him and would know what to do with the secret material. And she did—she alone plotted the breakout of her husband. She hoped Miss Lizzie would forgive her for using her to get a pass into the prison hospital so she could pass her plan along to her beloved. They bought it and, unfortunately, Miss Lizzie had to stiffen her guard.

Meanwhile, following Jana's imprisonment, Keeley had returned for a few days to share confinement at her prison, only in a separate building. His proximity had made her hopeful of at least catching a glimpse of him. Before she could, he had escaped on the heels of Libby Prison's tunnel breakout. With Libby's guards imprisoned on suspicion of being bribed in order for over one hundred Union officers to get free, General Winder borrowed guards from Castle Thunder to help guard Libby and hunt down the escapees. The shortage of guards at this prison allowed Keeley to yank out some wallboards in his ground-floor cell. He pretty much strolled to Miss Lizzie's mansion with the manhunt shifted from the city to the country. The last message from Miss Lizzie, smuggled in to Jana a few days ago, reported Keeley was still with her, helping to plot Jana's freedom.

Jana was losing faith. After the great tunnel escape, the prisons had become more heavily guarded. Those sentinels who would have been bribed before couldn't be now as they feared a hanging themselves if they were caught aiding in freeing Yankee prisoners. And Miss Lizzie seemed to have no scheme to spring her yet either. Jana felt caged, having to wait and rely on outsiders for help to escape, but she managed to quell her fright so she could live her last days fully.

In a weak voice, her patient, who was about her pa's age, said, "Thank you, miss. You've been kind to me and the other patients here."

Jana couldn't believe it when Mr. Gowdy had told her he'd been imprisoned for stealing only a loaf of bread to feed his starving family. A tailor by trade and a productive member of society, he didn't have much work these days. There was no material to make new clothes, and there were no old clothes to alter because they were being cut up for bandages. His only real crime was he'd stuck around in support of his native city. The very officials who'd jailed him had brought him to stealing with their lost cause.

The patient in the next cot over hoisted himself up onto his elbows. In a murderous tone, he said to Jana, "I'm not letting any Yankee touch me." He was a Richmonder too, locked up recently for stabbing a man to death in a saloon fight. His victim had given him a nasty gash down his cheek with a serrated knife, and the wound oozed blood now through its cloth bandage.

Remembering Leanne's words to the steward who'd refused to help Clara back at Chatham Manor, Jana said with utter fearlessness, "And when you're bleeding to death from your wound, don't come crying to me." Theatrically, she looked around the room before turning back to him. "By the looks of it, I'm all you have. I wouldn't burn a bridge just yet if I were you."

Mr. Gowdy's voice strengthened and ranked severe when he said, "Don't mind him—misery enjoys company. Anybody who takes issue with even a Yankee who works as hard as you do caring for us and keeping our ward clean ought to be committed to the lunatic asylum."

The murderer's mouth twisted up with anger. "Why I'll show you who's crazy," he said, lunging at Mr. Gowdy with his hands poised to choke him.

Jana was relieved when the two guards, assigned to the room, rushed over and surrounded the troublemaker.

They aimed their rifles at him, and one said, "Twitch a finger, and I'll blow your head off!"

Someone stepped up behind Jana; she knew it was the prison commandant by his voice when he said, "I don't know why we trouble ourselves to fix you when you'll be broken soon enough where you're heading," reminding the criminal of his date with the gallows.

Fear conquered the criminal's expression, and he sank back into his cot and closed his eyes.

Jana speculated he was picturing the noose around his neck as she did many a sleepless night since she'd gotten here.

Captain Lucien Richardson patted her shoulder and said, "Come now, Jana. It's late."

Amazed to see a sky full of glittering stars through the window across the room, Jana asked, "What time is it, sir?" *The days sure went by fast when you were counting them down,* she mused.

"It's nine o'clock," Captain Richardson said.

It was no wonder her stomach was gnawing at her. She hadn't eaten since noon, and, even then, she'd had only an ounce of vile beef, one small turnip, and a sliver of stale cornbread, all of which she'd forced down with some tea. She wanted to vomit just thinking about that meal but gulped instead when she contemplated the starving all around her. Even Captain Richardson had trimmed down some since she'd first met him.

Captain Richardson said, "You need your rest. You're going to kill yourself."

Jana gave him a wry glance as though to say she'd already done that.

"I didn't mean to put it that way," Captain Richardson said, flustered.

Mostly for the murderer's sake, Jana said, "Don't worry, Captain, at least I'm going to heaven." Before she rose, she patted Mr. Gowdy's hand and promised to visit him tomorrow—if fate allowed.

"I'll be right here waiting for you to come, and I'll pray for your freedom," Mr. Gowdy said with an optimistic smile.

"Come now, Jana." Captain Richardson took up her arm and circled it around his. The rough wool of his pant legs scratched together like sandpaper as he whisked her out of the ward.

Leaning heavier on his arm, Jana said, "Not too fast, Captain. I'm feeling a little tired and dizzy."

"I'm not letting you leave your room until noon tomorrow," he said.

"But—"

Captain Richardson interjected. "No buts. Enough is enough. You've been keeping long hours for two months. You can't keep it up forever." He threw up his free hand and said, "I keep right on putting my foot in my mouth."

Jana gave him a small smile and said, "You don't have to mince words with me, Captain. Please, be yourself. Trust me; I've landed myself in prison pretending to be what I'm not."

When they hit the top of the stairs, Jana whiffed the lime and loam, spread on the steps and floors early that morning, still lingering in the air. The disinfectant had grown immediately more pleasant to Jana when it proved capable of keeping down the number of smallpox cases. A clean environment, she'd learned from Clara Barton, was important. She took pride in sweeping and mopping her hospital ward every day to eliminate the noxious gases along with their health hazards.

As the commandant guided her down the warped, creaky steps, Jana noticed an unusual lightness in his walk. "You seem excited about something, Captain." A sudden impulse made her twirl around in mid-step. Facing him, she said, "Please tell me there's a pardon in my room."

"I do have a surprise for you there—nothing anywhere near as monumental as that. I'm sorry if you translated my eagerness too deeply."

"Whatever happens to me, I'll never forget your kindness. In the time I've been here, you've spoiled me to death." Jana giggled. "You see, even I find it hard to avoid that subject."

He nodded his understanding.

"Where were we? Oh, yes, you've spoiled me by giving me my own apartment. You've somehow managed to sneak me real coffee or tea when there's none to be had anywhere around the city." Her lips puckered to the taste they knew better of the bitter brews concocted from edible plant roots, twigs, or leaves Jana forced across them and she drank more often. "And, every morning, right on schedule, you've seen to my hot water for my washbasin. I feel like a pampered guest at the Spotswood Hotel." Each day, after she'd sponged herself off, she soaked her hands until the water turned cold. The grime under her fingernails and embedded in the cracks of her hands was long gone. The cracks were healing with the help of some lotion Miss Lizzie had smuggled in to her. Still, she worked hard to get rid of her calluses. She needed all kinds of diversions to keep her going; she was determined to have soft, delicate hands for the first time in her life.

"I wish I could do more." He settled his dark, somber eyes on her. "President Davis ought to give you a pardon for what you've done here. You've organized the sick ward and pretty much run it all by yourself with an occasional visit from a doctor. And most of your patients are your enemy whom you care for without any complaint and half the time while you yourself are unwell from hunger."

Jana winked and said, "That's the only complaint I have. The food in your grand hotel is pretty poor." At Captain Richardson's frown, she figured she'd better change the subject as it was a sore one for him. He'd griped, only to her, about it being a crime for the military to hold back boxes of food, clothing, and blankets sent from the Northern civilians and its Sanitary Commission for the prisoners. It was an even bigger crime to allow the shipped food to spoil when so many were starving. He wouldn't tell her, but Jana imagined in these boxes of food was the good coffee and tea the captain somehow managed to bring her every now and then. Turning serious, she said, "I don't feel I deserve a pardon for doing what comes natural to me. When a man is sick and needs my help, in my eyes he's just a man, neither Yankee nor Rebel."

"Not many people think and act as kindly as you do. You heard what the murderer said; though he's not a good example ... he doesn't like anybody. And most of my charges are roughnecks, deserters, thieves, and murderers who don't deserve your attention."

"They have some bad traits too," Jana said, to which they both snickered.

Captain Richardson sobered. "Your bravery alone to nurse these dregs of society merits your pardon."

"There are some good people, like my last patient, who shouldn't be here."

"I know, I know. I'm doing all I can to get them out. In the meantime, I'll do my best to keep them away from the bad guys."

When they neared Jana's first-floor apartment, a guard posted at the door saluted his superior. From his leather belt, he drew a metal ring on which jingled the key to the door's small iron lock. The captain had a guard posted outside her door, which he ordered locked even when she was inside. He wasn't about to risk any rowdies getting into her room to molest her or her things. He'd even taken care to separate her from the other female inmates—poor Southerners arrested for stealing food set at prices they couldn't afford. Because they blamed *all* Yankees for their starvation, he feared they'd scratch Jana's eyeballs out.

Jana appreciated the captain's trust in her. He allowed her to tap on the door for the guard to open and let her come and go as she pleased.

The guard inserted the key into the padlock and turned it until it clanked open. Then he stepped aside.

Captain Richardson told Jana to cover her eyes while he swung the squealing door outward. Nudging her through, he said, "You can open them now."

The adjustment of Jana's eyes from the black backdrop of her eyelids to the dusky, gas-lit room coupled with her fatigue and hunger made her dizzy. She put her forearm over her suddenly clammy forehead as her eyelids fluttered shut and she began sagging to the ground. Before she hit the floor, she felt muscled arms catch and carry her over to her cot. And before she fainted, she heard a familiar female voice say, "Step aside, Captain." The next thing she knew, she was sputtering and coughing at something pungent near her nostrils. Her eyelids batted open. A small hand holding a vial of smelling salts disappeared from her sight and was replaced by a memorable face. Jana couldn't suppress her exhilaration. She tried to rise and greet her friend from the wintry days of tending the wounded at Chatham Manor.

Coaxing Jana back down, Dr. Mary Walker said, "Stay still, miss, until your heart's stopped racing."

Jana grew bewildered when Mary didn't recognize her. Then it dawned on her. Mary had only known her as a soldier!

Captain Richardson moved into Jana's view too and said, "Meet your surprise—Dr. Mary Walker. She's your new roommate. I assumed you might enjoy having another Yankee around for company. And now I'm very glad she's a doctor." He looked to Dr. Walker and said, "I've got business to tend to. I'll leave her in your capable hands, I trust. And I'll have some dinner sent up right away."

"Make it a feast. It's no wonder she passed out. I can see her ribs poking through her blouse," Mary said with a flip of her head.

"I'll do better than my best," Captain Richardson said and left the room.

Jana smirked. Mary's caustic tongue hadn't changed a bit. She still wasn't afraid to speak her mind. But her attire had become purely masculine—she'd ditched the skirt that she used to wear over her tight-fitting, black pants, which color she had matched up to a long coat.

When they heard the lock click into place, Mary went to the window that opened onto a balcony and pushed up its lower sash. "You could use some fresh air," she said. "Who would've ever dreamed a prison room would come with one? I'll bet you're happy about that too."

"Yes," Jana said, truly grateful to the captain for it. The window wasn't kept locked, and she could crawl onto the balcony whenever she pleased. This gave her some semblance of freedom in her final days here. Unluckily, it offered no viable escape route with a guard posted below it at all times. He wasn't there just for Jana; the captain required all entrances and exits to be patrolled around the clock.

"I stood out there earlier and watched the sun's fading rays making the colors of the rainbow in the ripples of the James River. That sure was a pretty sight," Mary said.

Jana knew all about watching from the balcony. Every day when she returned to her apartment around noon, she stood out there for a spell, praying the Yankees would come and set her and their own free. They'd nearly done it a month into her confinement. While she was outside on that day, the window behind her rattled, and the smell of smoke wafted to her from the clash between the Union and Confederate cannon on the outskirts of the city. Nonetheless, the Yankees had to retreat because they hadn't heeded Miss Lizzie's warning to come with forty-five thousand troops and attack from the west.

With a gleam in her eye, Mary said, "I'll talk the mayor into tearing down those old tobacco buildings to our front. Then we'll have a nice view of the city."

Knowing Mary, Jana was confident she'd find her way to the mayor's mansion before dawn tomorrow.

Shuffling over to the woodstove in a corner of the room, Mary threw some logs into it, lit them with a sulfur match, and set a kettle of water on the cook top. "We'll have some tea soon," she said.

Jana sat up on her cot. "Mary,"—she began, pausing to Mary's quizzical look at her familiar reference of her—"we've met before. Do you recollect Leander and Johnnie who helped you in surgery back at Chatham Manor?"

"Do I ever! Those were some sensible, hard-working boys."

"Well, I'm Johnnie. I disguised myself as a soldier because I wanted to fight for my country too."

Mary scurried over and took Jana's face in her hands, angling it up into the glow of the gaslight's globe, hanging above Jana's cot.

Recognition flickered in her eyes. "Well, I'll be. You are Johnnie. You know, back then, I had a notion you were too pretty to be a boy. Tell me, what brought you here to hell?"

While Mary resumed making tea, Jana recited her story.

Mary whistled. "My adventures don't hold a candle to yours!" She related how she'd been ousted from a Union field hospital in Tennessee by surgeons jealous of her, even though they were short of hands and could use her help. Afterward, the Confederate army found her roaming the countryside caring for their own people, relegated to vagabonds when their homes were destroyed by artillery fire and then stricken ill from living in the swamps. They didn't know what to make of her, so they shipped her off to prison.

"It goes to show you neither side has any brains," Jana said.

While she waited for the kettle to steam, Mary sat down on a cot that the captain must have sent up sometime after Jana had been in her room earlier. She stared Jana down with a fiery intensity and said, "First, I'm going to fatten you up. Then, if I have to die trying, I'm going to get you out of here."

Jana appreciated Mary's determination. Yet, if Miss Lizzie, the master at scheming with her extensive connections and clout, hadn't come up with anything yet, how could Mary? Suddenly, Jana felt her fears of dying, of never seeing her family and friends again, and of never knowing life as a woman with Keeley come flooding up from the deepest cavern in her heart. She dropped her chin to her chest and held herself as she trembled with every sob.

Mary sat down next to her, cradled her in her arms, and rocked her.

As Jana's weeping slowed, she felt a little less shackled by her fears with Mary here comforting her. She'd never wish imprisonment on any innocent person, but she prayed hard for Mary not to be taken away from her until after she was gone.

In Captain Richardson's first-floor office, Jana squirmed around on the varnished surface of her wooden chair. The early morning sun peeped through the window as though trying to inject some light-heartedness into the dismal mood hovering about the room. Even so, Jana felt her anxiety rising as she watched the captain alternate between dipping his quill pen in the ink well and scratching her personal information onto the coarse, brown pages of his log book.

From behind his small cherry desk, Captain Richardson said, "I need your date of birth, Jana,"—he cleared his throat—"for my records, that is." He kept his somber eyes and pen aimed at his log, appearing unable to face Jana.

"For my headstone, you mean?" Jana asked in a tone sympathetic to his dark task.

Dr. Mary Walker reached over and squeezed Jana's hand, helping to keep her at ease.

"You don't have to coddle me, Captain. You've been overly kind to me these past three months," Jana said.

The captain kept his eyes pointed downward. He'd made it clear to Jana he wanted no part of escorting her—or any woman for that matter, especially the first on either side of the war—to the gallows to hang as a spy.

Jana knew Captain Richardson admired her for helping around the prison instead of sulking in her room as her death crept closer. He'd rewarded her by granting her exercise in the prison's courtyard and Mary permission to bring her back any food she could get her hands on at the market during her strolls there under guard.

When Miss Lizzie had become aware of Mary's living arrangements with Jana and her wanderings outside of the prison, she tried to make contact with Mary in hopes of making her another messenger between her and Jana. It proved too dangerous. From the very day Mary had arrived in Richmond and everywhere she went since, she attracted a cavalcade of onlookers. So they kept to using the woman who occasionally cleaned Jana's room. Through her, Jana smuggled out a letter to Ma and Pa, explaining everything since she'd left home and including instructions for Miss Lizzie to mail it only after her hanging—no sense her family grieving for nothing should her execution be delayed or canceled.

Jana understood Captain Richardson's reasons for prohibiting her from touring Richmond. Unlike Mary who was no threat to the Confederacy, Jana was a spy. The risk of her being swept up and stoned by a mob the guards couldn't quell was too likely.

In a hushed voice, the captain repeated, "Your date of birth, Jana?"

With a quivery lower lip, Jana replied, "The fourth of May, year eighteen hundred forty-five."

Mary caught her breath sharply.

The Captain's head shot up in surprise. "I'm sorry. I didn't know," he said and raked a shaky hand through his thick, dark hair.

Squeezing Jana's hand tighter, Mary conveyed her sympathy.

Jana heaved a huge, sorrowful sigh. "I suppose there's no better day to leave this world than the day you came in," she said, referring to the day's date—her nineteenth birthday.

The captain shifted uncomfortably in his chair while he scratched the momentous date in his log. Placing the pen in its ink well, he rose and scuffed his chair across the wide-planked floor as he pushed it back from his desk. With a heavy sigh, he said, "Time to go. It appears there's to be no pardon from President Davis."

Jana had already resigned herself to that. Any pardon would have come long before now. She could still hope, just as she imagined Timothy Webster, a Pinkerton-Agency operative in Richmond and acquaintance of Miss Lizzie's, had done right up to the moment before he hung in the spring of 1862. As Jana stood to leave, the effort in her fatigued and hungered state sent her heartbeat into a tizzy. She bunched up her blouse over her heart with a dizzying exclamation. Her eyelids dropped closed, and she began collapsing to the floor.

"Not again!" Captain Richardson said. The floor vibrated beneath his pounding boots as he raced to her.

Jana felt him catch her in midair, cradle her in his muscled arms, and lower her to the dusty floor with care. He'd witnessed a few of her fainting spells, with Mary apprising him of others. Though aware of her surroundings, Jana kept her eyes closed, seizing a few more seconds to compose herself. She knew it was Mary pressing her ear against her chest when she caught a whiff of the perfumed pomade she'd only recently started rubbing through her hair. She did it more to perk up her unwashed curls than to heighten her masculine appearance. Luxuries such as soap and a large enough basin of water to rinse out the suds in one's tresses, let alone off the body, were scarce in prison. Mary's closeness comforted Jana.

"She's only fainted, but I prayed her heart took her." Mary's tone dripped acid when she said, "I can't believe the Confederacy's going through with this nonsense. Chivalry's dead in the South."

Ignoring Mary, Captain Richardson asked, "What can I do for her?"

"Set her free."

"Why me, Lord?" Captain Richardson exclaimed. Although he might want to, he couldn't turn a blind eye and let Jana escape. If he didn't produce her for execution, the Confederacy would suspect he'd let her get away and, if the government didn't order his hanging, the citizens of Richmond would stone him to death. They wanted revenge! And they were holding their breath that Jana's heart, rumored to be the cause of her fainting spells, wouldn't give out before the gallows got her.

"What else can I do for her?" Captain Richardson inquired.

With a heavy sorrowful sigh, Mary said, "I don't suppose there's anything else either of us can do for her now."

Jana gagged and coughed on something pungent fanned under her nose. She opened her eyes to Mary's capping and pocketing her trusty vial of smelling salts.

The commandant peered down at Jana and, in a near whisper, said, "You've had another spell, Jana, and Dr. Walker has revived you."

Jana repeated the words he'd once said, "Why let Mary fix me, Captain, when I'll only be broken soon?" She patted his hand to assure him she didn't blame him for her predicament.

A rap on the door sent a thunderous roll around the room.

"Enter," Captain Richardson called out.

A guard stepped in, looking curious; he dared not ask about the gathering on the floor. Instead, he saluted and said, "The escort's here, sir."

Though at a snail's pace, Jana sat up, showing her willingness to get on with matters. She rubbed her dusty hands on the soft fabric of her long-sleeved day dress. Miss Lizzie had gone through great pains to smuggle this dress in to her, specially cleaned and ironed, to wear in place of the tattered, filthy one she'd been wearing since her imprisonment. Respecting this, she brushed the dust away to make it presentable again. A hanging wasn't pretty, but knowing Miss Lizzie, she wanted Jana to look her best for it. Jana was sure she'd chosen this outfit in particular for its soothing pink and gray colors; its feminine appearance would shame the public for hanging a woman; though, Miss Lizzie would be mortified if she knew the blouse's stiff, chin-level collar scratched Jana's neck, reminding her with every move her neck soon would face a far worse fate.

Once Captain Richardson and Mary got Jana to her feet, they linked their arms around hers and kept her steady as they exited the office and progressed through the hallway to the front door.

A sentinel blocked Mary's way when she showed her intent to accompany Jana and Captain Richardson out.

Mary's glare could've turned him to stone faster than a fleeting glance from Medusa.

The guard jumped aside. Terrified of Mary's tirades, the watchmen pretty much gave her whatever she wanted, within their control.

Mary turned her pleading eyes upon the captain.

"I'm sorry, Mary. You've already had your morning outing. Besides, it's for your own good. The swarm out there is thirsting for Yankee blood, man or woman, spy or not. I won't have another hanging on my hands today," Captain Richardson said.

Jana turned to embrace a brooding Mary. She might be labeled odd by her actions and dress; to Jana, she was courageous to sail across uncharted waters. When Mary returned Jana's hug with her own tight squeeze, Jana felt her positive energy flow through her and inject hope. She stepped back. "Don't worry, Mary. I'll be fine," she said, smiling. "I'd never wish prison on you, but I thank God for bringing you here to make my last month bearable. You're an angel of mercy." Jana truly believed divine intervention lurked behind Mary's imprisonment. Why else would she have been foolishly imprisoned?

"I pray another angel guides you to your promised land," Mary said.

Praying for that too, Jana hugged Mary again and turned to step through the prison's open doorway.

Spring's fresh air swooped in, erasing the smell of tobacco and Jana's strongest memory of her temporary home.

Jana's eyes grew teary from the mid-morning sun's blinding rays. With her hand against her forehead, she created a temporary awning until her pupils adjusted to the light, allowing her to proceed safely down the gangplank.

Mounted soldiers in dress coats with spit-shined brass buttons surrounded a black-chromed carriage. They were armed with their rifles, pistols, and sabers, more to thwart any rowdies along the way than to prevent Jana's escape.

Hoisting up her skirt, Jana advanced toward the carriage, struggling not to see it as a hearse with its black curtains tied away from the windows. Behind her, she heard the prison door slam shut to her forever as the captain nudged her up the steps and into the coach.

After he closed her door, Captain Richardson retreated to give the prison guards some last-minute orders.

Through her open window, Jana spied the spire of St. John's Church, diagonally across the street from Miss Lizzie's mansion. There she could almost hear Patrick Henry saying to George Washington, Thomas Jefferson, and the rest of the Second Virginia Convention, "I know not what course others may take; but as for me, give me liberty or give me death!" to spark rebellion against British suppression of American colonists. Jana had no regrets whatsoever about sacrificing her life for Miss Lizzie and Keeley's freedom.

Captain Richardson roused Jana from her reflections when he bounced into the backseat next to her. Knocking his knuckle on the ceiling, he ordered her procession underway.

As the carriage lurched forward, Jana stole a last look at the faded red bricks of Castle Thunder Prison. Whereas before they had gazed upon her in a menacing way, they now seemed to do so sorrowfully. Jana knew from her studies in Greek mythology that Castle Thunder symbolized a place where lawbreakers suffered the wrath of Olympia's gods. She shuddered with fear; she had offended the Confederate States of America and was about to suffer its wrath.

Jana got lost in spring's vibrancy as her conveyance jogged the two miles north and west through the streets of Richmond to Camp Lee. She poked her head through the open window to feel the warmth of the sun on her face, hear the trills of the songbirds, see the white petals of the dogwoods, and smell the sweet perfume of the blue-bells. She never fancied it being fair for anyone or anything to die on a day so alive.

As the carriage veered away from the railroad tracks and continued rattling westward along Broad Street, Jana leaned back in the leather seat to pay her last respects to home. It would be this alive and colorful too. She pictured Pa plowing the fields for planting, Ma baking bread, Rachel and Rebecca in the parlor studying etiquette, Eliza riding Commodore, and Molly jump-roping in the barn. For the first time since she'd left home, she felt a suffocating homesickness. She wished she could say a personal goodbye to her family.

After a right turn and short ride on a rutted, hilly road, the coach slowed to a crawl.

Captain Richardson poked his head out of his window and invaded Jana's thoughts as he fumed aloud, "It's like Manassas Junction all over again."

Jana understood he was referring to the mass of civilians and politicians who'd turned out from Washington with their picnic blankets and baskets to watch the Rebels rout the Yankees in the first significant clash of the war back in July 1861. She looked too. The military camp, once a thriving tobacco plantation and then a fairground for agricultural exhibitions, appeared as a small village. It was set on a high, level plain with over fifty buildings of various sizes. Some were brick, others whitewashed wood, and still others weathered board. Rolling green pastures and forests of oak created the canvas all around the tents. However, the horde of people, probably mostly Richmonders, who had come to witness her hanging, cast a dark shadow over the otherwise picturesque landscape. Pushing and shoving their way toward the carriage, they tried to steal a glimpse of her.

Settling back into her seat to hide in the cool interior, Jana followed Captain Richardson's solemn gaze toward the wooden scaffold set up for her hanging. Its sinister look dredged up those same fears—of dying, of never seeing her family and friends again, and of never knowing life as a woman, especially with Keeley—that she'd felt right before she was sent into battle at Brandy Station. She gagged on a hot wave of nausea and leaned out over the door and vomited.

The crowd heckled, calling her a coward.

Captain Richardson sacrificed his handkerchief to her.

As Jana wiped the sour remnants of her breakfast of cornbread and coffee away from the corners of her mouth, the ride ended in front of a two-story frame house. The mounted sentinels stayed posted around the carriage with their hands resting on their pistols. They were warning the crowd they'd tolerate no one pushing or shoving toward the carriage and their prisoner.

All alone, surrounded by her foes, Jana felt herself crumbling like a dried-up autumn leaf.

A persistent old woman, hobbling on a cane, managed to slip past the guards and sidle up to Jana's window. Her face was tucked inside the hood of her black cloak. "Let's see you escape the grim reaper," the witch cackled.

A familiar, soapy smell drifted Jana's way. She knew the old lady before she tilted her head back and winked. Jana dropped her chin to her chest and began sobbing.

"Off with you, old lady," Captain Richardson commanded.

By the toe of his boot, protruding through a stirrup, a guard nudged her back into the crowd.

"I'm sorry if she upset you," Captain Richardson said.

Jana dabbed her wet eyes on the parts of the handkerchief not soiled by her spittle. Captain Richardson would never know tears of joy ran down her cheeks. Although fleeting, Miss Lizzie's appearance had chased away her loneliness and boosted her courage. "Only the noose can hurt me now," she said.

The front door of the white house squeaked open. An officer Jana knew to be a colonel by the three little gold stars on each side of his blouse collar stepped out and hurried toward Jana's entourage. He was followed by a minister in his black garb and white collar.

Making his way outside, Captain Richardson saluted his superior.

The colonel returned a salute then peered inside and said, "Jana Cassidy, I presume?"

"Yes," Jana said with a sniffle.

Captain Richardson introduced Colonel Shields, the commandant of Camp Lee, to Jana.

She nodded her acknowledgement while staring over his shoulder at the hangman, who was testing her noose for tautness.

Colonel Shields looked behind him. With a somber expression, he turned back to Jana and said, "We'll keep you right where you are until all is ready. No point exposing you to the crowd any sooner than we have to." He gestured the minister forward.

Flurrying to Jana's side, the minister cleared his throat nervously before saying, "Shall we ask the Lord to forgive your sins?"

Jana couldn't tell to which faith he belonged. Did it matter? Last rites were likely the same whatever the religion. Setting her jaw with firmness, she said, "For all my sins, except spying for the Union."

"May God forgive you for doing what you considered was right." He dropped his eyes, cueing her to do the same. He prayed for her soul not to be damned. When he uttered, "Amen," Colonel Shields nodded, signaling her hour of reckoning had come.

Jana found solace in the minister's words. It was important for her to have her soul in good standing with God when she went into the life of the everlasting. She'd prayed alongside the minister to make sure of that.

While Colonel Shields ordered the guards to dismount and their horses tethered to the hitching posts in front of his cabin, Captain Richardson ushered Jana from her sanctuary. Linking arms with hers, he held her steady.

Sensing his trepidation, Jana patted his large, leathery hand. "Thank you, Captain, for all of your kindness." She fixed her eyes forward and said, "Now, shall we get on with it?"

Colonel Shields led the way, and the soldiers stationed themselves all around Jana.

As they marched onward, Jana saw a photographer fiddling with his camera. It called to mind Miss Lizzie's warning about not having her likeness taken or else risk Ma and Pa seeing her hanging on the front page of a newspaper long before they received her note. If she successfully avoided this, the papers would report that a Jana Cassidy had hung, and Ma and Pa would be none the wiser. She faced downward at the grassy path, making a clear shot of her impossible as she passed the camera.

The crowd taunted Jana as she passed. Some said, "Death to the spy!" Others said, "Hang all Yankee aggressors!"

Jana felt something small and hard strike her cheek. As she rubbed it, she saw pebbles being hurled at her from every direction. It got her blood boiling. She wanted to shout: Isn't my hanging enough for you?

"Get these people under control!" Colonel Shields ordered the guards, who aimed their rifles into the masses to subdue them.

More bothered by her noose, which was swinging in the breeze and beckoning her, Jana looked away. Instead, her eyes followed the sun's beam downward with the hope that it would find her earthly angel. Intent on her search for Miss Lizzie, she didn't see the wooden steps of the scaffold before she stubbed her toe and tripped up them.

Captain Richardson righted and guided her up onto and across the platform.

The masses elbowed their way forward.

After the hangman tested the rope and noose for tautness one more time, he tied Jana's wrists together so tight her fingertips went numb.

Jana wished he could deaden her rising fear too.

A ruckus arose. The black-cloaked old lady was clearing everyone aside with a tap from her cane. If Miss Lizzie were caught anywhere near Jana, she'd resurrect the Confederacy's suspicions of her role in the Castle-Thunder-blueprint affair and heighten their surveillance of her, jeopardizing her intelligence operation.

Why would she risk her life by especially drawing attention to herself? Jana wondered as the noose settled around her dress collar, making it scratchier against her neck.

As Miss Lizzie hobbled up into Jana's near vision, the crowd averted their attention to the scaffold, forgetting the crotchety old woman.

Again, Miss Lizzie tilted her head back and winked.

When it dawned on Jana, Miss Lizzie had risked her life in coming here today to show her how to be brave, she was certain there weren't enough words in any existing dictionary to describe her admiration and appreciation for this very, special woman. Although it had cost Jana a huge price to fight for her country, she'd never regret the path she'd chosen. Angling her face heavenward, she prepared to meet her fate with pride and courage. She suddenly knew what she had to do to meet it on her own terms.

Camp Lee, Virginia

May 4, 1864

The snap of cloth drew Jana's eyes to the hangman. He waved the black hood tauntingly, showing his eagerness to cover her eyes and pull the trigger that held the gallows in place. "Traitor," he hissed.

His menacing way emboldened Jana even more. "I dare you to pull the trigger and sell your soul to the devil," she said.

The hangman recoiled in surprise; he had expected to terrify not to be terrified.

Inwardly celebrating her triumph, Jana shifted her eyes back to Miss Lizzie's angelic face.

The clergyman began reading a passage from the *Holy Bible*.

Jana barely heard his words as she concentrated on all of the good in her life: her family and friends. She especially smiled when she dreamed of Keeley encouraging her onward with his dazzling dimples and sparkling emerald eyes. She only heard the minister when he clapped closed the good book and left the platform, followed by Captain Richardson.

The hands of the now humbled hangman trembled as he pulled the hood over Jana's head and started to tighten the noose around her neck.

His jittery nerves calmed Jana while the darkness brought focus. Right before he tightened the noose all the way, she threw herself into a convulsion. She discharged a raucous gurgle while subtly drawing her head back through the noose, so her chin rested on it. With enough give on the rope, she gave the illusion that she was collapsing when she maneuvered down into a kneeling position. The caps of her knees ached under the strain of holding herself up; she couldn't have the rope cutting into her chin or slipping back around her neck and strangulating her. She drew blood as she bit the inside of her cheek to keep herself from whimpering aloud. Her spittle diluted the iron taste in her blood as some of it trickled down her throat, the rest down her chin.

A collective murmur erupted from the spectators.

"What's happening?" a woman frantically called out.

"She's hanging herself!" a man answered with incredulity.

Jana felt the platform vibrating under a heavy stampede of boots up its stairs and across its floor. The familiar, muscled arms of Captain Richardson lifted her. When the noose was slid off, she dropped limp into his arms.

"She's probably had a heart attack." Mumbling, Captain Richardson added, "I hope."

When a hand reached under her hood, Jana held her breath. By the practiced touch, she knew a doctor's fingers groped for a pulse at her carotid artery.

"She's dead," the doctor declared and removed his hand.

Jana sucked in her elation. The doctor had missed her pulse through her dress's rigid collar. Or had he? Maybe he couldn't bear to see a woman hanged either.

Colonel Shields hollered, "It's over. You all go home, now."

As the crowd receded, their grumblings faded to murmurs.

The satiny hood caressed Jana's face as it was slid off.

Jana had to keep her focus razor sharp to deliver a few more scenes before she could escape the Confederacy's clutches. She made her head floppy like a rag doll's and lolled it to the side. Staring at the black backdrop of her eyelids, she kept her eyeballs still.

A set of hands rolled Jana's body onto its side and cut the ropes around her wrists, bringing instant pin-prickles to her fingers.

With her face pressed against the rough, dew-dampened floorboards, Jana stole a quick breath before being rolled back and draped in a heavy wool cloth, probably a uniform coat. She struggled to keep her breathing shallow.

"Move her into the coffin," Captain Richardson said in a rushed, nervous tone.

Jana wondered, *Had he detected some movement to suspect I'm alive?* Perhaps he'd just been blessed with his own miracle to turn a blind eye and let her get away.

Multiple hands reached beneath Jana's head, back, and legs and lifted her.

Jana relaxed, making her body feel heavy when carried down the stairs and, with surprising tenderness, placed on a hard, smooth surface. Her head, arms, and feet rested up against the coffin's walls, making the space cramped, but she wasn't about to complain.

The heavy cloth was removed.

Again, Jana held her breath and kept her eyeballs motionless until the coffin's lid slammed shut. She inhaled some much-needed, sweet air over the racket of nails hammering her coffin's lid into place. Never having feared closed-in spaces before, she suddenly felt claustrophobic in the sheer darkness and with no air streaming in. She hoped she'd escape her pine box before she suffocated to death.

The pounding stopped and the coffin lifted with some grunting. Shuffling feet carried it a short distance.

Jana didn't mind being jarred as the coffin was shoved hard up onto a wagon bed. When the wagon hatch banged shut and joggled her brain, she scolded her eardrums for their ringing, dizzying tantrum. Didn't they know there were worse things—like a hanging— that could happen to them?

A voice, probably belonging to the wagon driver, inquired, "Where to, Captain?"

"Oakwood Cemetery," Captain Richardson answered. His familiar voice comforted Jana in her lonely, pine-smelling box. Then he said, "I'll be getting on, Colonel. Thanks for your help during this trying time."

"Unfortunately, it's my job, Captain," Colonel Shields said.

Captain Richardson instructed the wagon driver further. "I'll follow you as far as Eighteenth Street. Then I'll head back to the prison."

"Yes, sir," the driver said, right before Jana felt him bump into his seat and the wagon lurch forward.

After what seemed like an eternity, the captain called out in a more relaxed tone, "See you back at the prison."

"Yes, sir," the driver said.

With sadness, Jana whispered, "Goodbye, Captain." She wished she could have known him under better circumstances, though she doubted she'd ever see him again.

After a short ride, the wagon pulled to a stop, and the driver called out, "Where do you want her?"

"In the dead house," countered a weary voice, probably belonging to the cemetery's caretaker, who had by now seen enough burials to span many lifetimes. "Her interment will have to wait until tomorrow. I have those to do today."

The coffin was dragged from the wagon and, in short order, landed with a thump on a solid surface.

Two pairs of feet retreated and a door slammed, leaving Jana in absolute silence until some digging started up nearby.

Jana couldn't believe it—her acting had fooled them all! Seconds before the noose was pulled taut, it had struck her that since everyone believed she suffered from a heart malady, maybe they could be duped into thinking she had a heart attack. Back home at a church supper, she'd once heard a woman describe in gory detail her husband's death from such an assault. Acting out those words was easy. She never dreamed she'd be pronounced dead. Just as incredulous, no one had questioned the doctor's verdict. It must be too much for anyone to suppose death could be faked under their watchful eye.

Exhaustion waved its wand over her. She had to ward it off. Her only plan—to kick the lid off her coffin—would have to wait until the caretaker's work day ended. She'd need to get started as soon as she heard his shovel silence.

Richmond, Virginia

May 4, 1864

With a jolt, Jana awakened gasping. The air in her confinement was nearly gone. Droplets of sweat ran down her upper lip and into her mouth; she tasted her panic in it as she admonished herself for making a potentially fatal mistake. *How long have I been asleep?* she wondered. Praying she had enough oxygen and hours before dawn, she remembered to listen for the caretaker's presence before she set to work.

Only the night bugs were singing.

She began kicking at the lid of her coffin, but her cramped quarters prevented her from getting into a position of force. She pounded and pushed on the lid until her hands throbbed. Her chest grew heavy as it deflated. "Think! Think!" she commanded her brain. If only she had a crowbar for leverage. She scoffed at herself for wasting valuable time dwelling on tools she didn't have. Then it hit her to use her body as a crowbar. Quickly, she rolled onto her stomach, rising on her hands and knees as best as she could. Arching her back against the lid, she strained to push.

The nails squealed as they began to loosen their grip.

Jana's exuberance was cut short when she heard the dead house door creaking open. She stilled. With her pulse drumming against her eardrums, she barely heard the dull thud beside her. *How crazed with the Confederacy's cause did someone have to be to make sure I'm dead?* Jana pinched her lips together to keep herself from screaming her silent fears, *I'll hang for sure this time!*

Screech! Her coffin was being pried open.

Jana plugged her ears against the vexing sound and squeezed her eyelids shut in case there were flying splinters.

The lid lifted, and the night's crisp, pure air blew her dampened hair away from her face.

A familiar voice said, "Well, I'll be. Miz Lizzie was right. You ain't dead."

Opening her eyes, Jana sprang up. She threw her arms around Uncle Henry and began to cry with joy.

Uncle Henry stroked her hair and said, "There, there, Miz Jana. You cry all you want. It's good to get it out."

Between sobs, Jana said, "I can't believe I'm free."

"I can't either. But Miz Lizzie said she'd heard of some bizarre escapes over the years, and she was sure you'd have one up your sleeve." Pulling away, Uncle Henry said, "Now, Miz Lizzie warned for us to move fast. Help me get this dummy in there." He lifted its head and waited for Jana to climb out of her wooden box and lift its feet.

Jana stood up, her legs wobbly. She shook them until they felt stronger.

As they tossed the dummy into the coffin, Uncle Henry said, "Miz Lizzie doesn't want anyone suspecting you ain't dead because of a light coffin."

"Miss Lizzie sure covers all of her tracks," Jana said with a sniffle and a giggle.

With Jana's replacement tucked away and the nails to the lid tapped back into place, Uncle Henry gave Jana some men's clothes to slip on over her own.

She'd sworn off ever again wearing men's clothes; to refuse them now would mean death if she were seen. As she hurried to tuck her hair under a hat, stuff her dress's skirt into the baggy trousers, and button the wool coat up to her chin, Uncle Henry crept to the door, opened it, and peeked out. "Follow me and mind your steps," he said.

Not a soul stopped them as they stole out of the cemetery under a dazzling moonlight and found Miss Lizzie's horse and carriage hidden off-road.

The horse hurried the carriage to the isolated garden behind Miss Lizzie's mansion, only a few blocks away; although, it seemed to Jana an eternal distance.

Once there, Jana got goose pimply all over when she spied Keeley waiting for her on the rear grand portico. Not wishing to greet him playing a man, she knew Uncle Henry must have seen her scowl at her clothes because he said, "It's all right, Miz Jana. Meet your man as a woman. Miz Lizzie has guards posted all around the house. Anybody who comes pokin' around will get a good bump on the head." So Jana hurried to strip off her disguise and leap from the carriage, holding her skirt above her ankles as she ran up the steps.

When Keeley met her at the top, his adoring smile, with its dazzling dimples and sparkling emerald eyes, conquered her.

Jana stopped short, stunned by his transformation. Miss Lizzie had fattened him up to where he seemed fitter than when she'd first met him. She wanted to throw her arms around him, but she considered herself a lady now, and it wasn't proper for her to make a romantic overture. Instead, she curtsied.

Keeley bowed. When he rose, he pulled her to him in a tight squeeze. His tender lips brushed her cheek, and then he whispered in her ear, "Y'are the most amazing woman. I love ye, Jana lass."

Flushing all over and feeling giddy under his loving embrace and declaration, Jana put her lips to his ear and whispered, "I prayed to live nigh long enough to get to know ye as a woman. And I love ye too, Keeley lad."

Keeley tilted his head back, roaring with laughter at her mimicry of him.

Standing in the shadow of one of the great pillars, Miss Lizzie stepped forward. Her hands were clasped with delight. "I hate to rush your happy reunion; we must take advantage of the night to get you two out of here."

Jana hugged Miss Lizzie, smelling the familiar soapy fragrance that had comforted her in her hour of need. "You're my angel of mercy. I'll never be able to repay you for helping me with Keeley's escape, giving me courage just when I needed it the most, and rescuing me from my coffin."

"All I wish is for you two to land safely in General Butler's hands," Miss Lizzie said, stroking Jana's hair.

"I didn't survive a hanging for nothing. The time I spent in the coffin was only a dress rehearsal for a role I don't wish to take on until I'm one hundred years old. I'm through with acting!" Jana exclaimed.

"Are you sure? Your performance was far greater than any John Wilkes Booth ever delivered," Miss Lizzie said.

"Oh no! I just thought of Mary—she doesn't know I'm alive," Jana said.

"Not to worry, dear. I'll get word to her as soon as I know you're back in Union hands. Speaking of Mary, I'm hearing that she might be freed soon," Miss Lizzie said.

"I'll pray for that," Jana said.

Miss Lizzie held out Jana's farewell letter to Ma and Pa. "It's so thoroughly and beautifully written, I think it would make a perfect substitute for having to explain everything to your ma and pa when you get home."

Gazing down at the envelope, Jana caressed its wax seal and said, "That's a wonderful idea." She lifted her head, and her eyes met Miss Lizzie's smile. Tears welled up in her eyes. "I'm having trouble saying goodbye to you, Miss Lizzie."

"Then just say you'll come visit me when the war is over."

"What about this dress?"

"You look beautiful in it. You must keep it."

Jana was elated to share with Miss Lizzie the miracle in the dress's stiff collar.

"Well, then, perhaps you'll remember me whenever you wear it."

"I need nothing to remember you by. I will never forget you, Miss Lizzie."

Tears cascaded down Miss Lizzie's cheeks. After Keeley thanked her with a hug, she nudged them both toward the steps and with a sniffle said, "I'll miss you both." She pointed to the wagon, standing in place of her carriage and driven by a stranger. "Now, you must go."

Jana glanced back to take in Miss Lizzie's angelic face one last time. She blew her a kiss and turned away, hoping she'd become even half the woman Miss Lizzie was. That would be glorious enough for her.

Keeley offered her his arm.

As Jana circled hers around his, she caught sight of her hand. She was proud of how hard she'd worked these past months to make her hands soft and delicate. Daintily, she held up her skirt with her free hand as she walked down the steps. *Yes,* she contemplated aglow with pride, *Ma and Pa will be proud of the woman I've become.*

Epilogue

Jana and Keeley's angel of mercy arranged for them to be sneaked out of Richmond on a wagon bed with a false bottom topped with manure. No picket in his right mind would come near the wagon to check for deserters or escaped prisoners.

Beneath the putrid cover, the fugitives lay on their stomachs, sucking in clean air sifting through the slits between the floorboards. The wagon's rattling southward along the eastern side of the James River threatened to give them away; Jana hoped never to make a journey like this again.

Their driver carted them as far as the first checkpoint in Miss Lizzie's underground network—her vegetable farm—before passing them off to another of her couriers. Both were farmers who understood the tremendous danger in carrying people rather than coded messages. Nonetheless, when it came their turn, they considered it an honor to hide the runaways in their wagons and share in taking them the remaining thirty-five miles to General Butler's headquarters at City Point.

Though it took several days to outflank the Rebels, Jana and Keeley cherished their time together. When held up, they were hidden in secret rooms, corn cribs, and haylofts. They felt the same fears a runaway slave would about getting caught and losing his liberty. Jana knew for her to get caught meant death; the Confederates would make sure she didn't get away a second time. All along their escape route, the sweethearts huddled together, holding hands in their cramped, dark places. They laughed and talked about the hearth and home they'd build in Elmira. Jana was glad when Keeley declared he'd like to have children.

Their last ride was a harrowing crossing over the swiftly flowing James River in a rowboat. Shortly after reaching Union lines, Keeley was returned to the Porter Guards. Before he turned to go, he looked weary and scared but assured he was determined to see his duty through to the end. And this time, he'd be fighting for his country too.

With a twinkle in his eye, Keeley said, "I'll send ye most of me soldier's pay to put somewhere safe. When we marry, God willing, we'll use it to build our hearth and home in Elmira."

With a twinkle in her eye, Jana said, "I know Ma and Pa are going to embrace you as the son they never had. I'll bet they even parcel off some of their land to get us started." When Jana reached for his hand, she felt a twinge of pain in her bad arm. She suddenly grew alarmed.

"What's wrong, me Jana lass?" Keeley asked, tenderly brushing his hand along her cheek.

"I have something I need to show you. I didn't think about it until now. It seemed so long ago and not significant, at least, to me." She pushed back her sleeve and revealed her awful scar. "I was shot in the arm when I was racing back to you in the ditch at Brandy Station. I thought I should give you one more chance to turn away from me." As her eyes settled upon her blemish, she said, "I'll understand if it's too hard for you to ever see this without thinking of me as Johnnie." She couldn't bear to look up; she'd die if she saw rejection in his eyes. Instead, she felt him swooping her up in a loving embrace.

"I adore ye all the more for it, Jana. Y'are the woman of me dreams."

"You've just made me the happiest woman alive!" Jana cried.

On a steamboat bound for Washington and its hospitals, Jana kept busy nursing the wounded. Having found her life's calling in caring for people, she decided that, after a brief stay home, she'd return to nursing in the field hospitals. One day she hoped to become a midwife and bring beautiful babies into a peaceful world. For the rest of the war, however, she'd make sure she got a nursing assignment somewhere near Keeley and alongside Charlie.

Jana recalled Charlie's correspondence to her, which had been smuggled across Confederate lines while she was living with Miss Lizzie. He'd claimed to be happy with his assignment as a hospital steward and with collecting a pay to support his ma, little brother, and the two newcomers to his family—Leanne and her ma. He was relieved to have Leanne in Buffalo, watching over everybody. And as it turned out, Leanne hadn't needed to stand up to her pa. Her ma had willingly slipped away from Elmira with her one night, long before her pa could make any trouble. Leanne had set up her own blacksmith shop and rejoiced in providing for her new family too.

In Granville, Pennsylvania, Jana boarded the last train on her journey home. Before settling onto a hard bench in her empty compartment, she made sure Maiti was comfortable in her stall car. Jana couldn't wait to introduce her to Commodore; she knew they'd become lifelong pals.

A feeling of contentment swept over Jana as she rested her head against the window and reached into her coat pocket for the photograph that had been her companion. While the train rocked along, she gazed with great fondness upon the faces of Keeley, Leanne, and Charlie. Mostly, her gaze settled on Keeley. She couldn't wait to show Ma and Pa the likeness of the man who'd won her heart. She sensed Keeley would survive the war, and they'd fill their hearth and home with a gaggle of children. She'd also point out to Ma and Pa her own likeness in the tintype, outfitted as a cavalryman, to help tell them her tale. At first, they'd be sore at her for running away and shocked by her enlistment. In the end, though, she knew they'd be pleased to see she'd found her way to womanhood.

When the train steamed into Elmira's station, Jana shifted on her seat and reached for her carpet bag, eager to be reunited with her family at last. Hearing her petticoat rustling beneath her skirt, she smiled at the irony: dressed as a man in the cavalry she had begun to discover the sweet glory of her womanhood. Now, dressed as a woman, she couldn't wait to embrace marriage and babies. She promised herself never to abandon her adventuresome spirit. After the war ended, besides assisting with the birth of babies, she'd take up the fight to help her country mend and provide equal rights for all. She felt excited by the challenges ahead of her and knew Ma and Pa would be proud of her plans. More importantly, with Keeley by her side, Jana believed she could train as a midwife, raise their children, and travel the lecture circuit to tell about her experience in a soldier's uniform. She imagined a satisfying life filled with love— and plenty of adventure!

Acknowledgments

I thank the women who bravely stepped out of their traditional roles as homemakers and into soldiering, nursing, and spying during the American Civil War and for giving me exciting material around which to craft my story!

Every writer has special people who influence their work. For me, they are:

Kevin O'Neill, associate professor at SUNY Plattsburgh, bequeathed me tools that unleashed my right brain.

The Institute of Children's Literature (Connecticut) gave me my building blocks.

The Highlights Foundation set me up in beautiful Honesdale, Pennsylvania, and Chautauqua, New York, to learn from the masters.

Susan Campbell Bartoletti, award-winning and honored author of *Black Potatoes: The Great Irish Famine, 1845–1850, Hitler Youth: Growing Up in Hitler's Shadow*, and the popular historical novel *The Boy Who Dared*, taught me so much about developing my scenes, plot, and characters and inspired me on my way.

My writer friend, Susan Hoffman, led me into her greenhouse and showed me how to arrange words into colorful bouquets. Her direct influence yet blooms in the final pages of *Sweet Glory*.

Christy Wightman assigned my novel draft as her book club's reading and discussion. From these parents, attentive to their young adults' readings, I gleaned invaluable comments. And she led me to my writing coach.

Karen Knowles, author, teacher, and writing coach, taught me everything I know about editing when she guided me through a thorough revision of my novel draft. Without her, I would not be published!

Emily Hensler and Mia Simon stole time away from their homework to read and critique my story.

Theresa Rizzo, writer and cofounder of the Crested Butte Writers (Colorado), reminded me of the elements important to any great story opening in her training to judge novels as the coordinator of the Sandy Writing Contest; these skills have sharpened all of my words within.

Capital District Society for Children's Book Writers and Illustrators, especially Eric Luper, Kyra Teis, Lois Huey, Nancy Castaldo, Linda Marshall, and Lyn Miller-Lachmann, pirates with a treasure chest of advice about writing, marketing, and publication, kindheartedly shared some of their gold with me.

Every writer has research to do. Special people and resources that advanced mine:

The keepers of historical Elmira, New York, armed me with facts, fiction, and walking-tour maps. And then they allowed me, a perfect stranger with no prior appointment, to comb through and photocopy their archives. This city rivals any in the United States for painting a picture of progress with its numerous, awe-inspiring landmarks dating back to the Revolutionary and Civil War eras. It is a goldmine for educators and history buffs!

No greater regimental history than that recorded by Civil War Veteran Noble D. Preston can possibly exist. From it, I extracted almost everything I needed to know about the Tenth New York Volunteer Cavalry Regiment.

Ron Matteson, through his book *Civil War Campaigns of the 10ᵗʰ New York Cavalry*, bolstered my research where Noble D. Preston was vague or silent, and he authenticated my words about this regiment.

Higginson Book Company of Salem, Massachusetts, has kindly permitted me to reproduce maps from their 1998 reprint of Noble D. Preston's book.

The park ranger at the Gettysburg (Pennsylvania) Battlefield led me to people and places familiar to the Tenth NY during their seventy-two-day layover in this town before they were shipped off to war. These insights into this regiment's beginnings helped me to define their character.

A Brandy Station (Virginia) Foundation member left her board meeting to welcome my husband and me in at closing time and give us a private tour of the Graffiti House (where convalescing soldiers scrawled their names, pictures, and slogans in charcoal all over the second-story walls). And then she armed us with facts, fiction, and a driving-tour map for the battlefield. Another goldmine for educators and Civil War enthusiasts!

Teacher Mary Radom examined my story for age appropriateness and helped me study my book market.

Writing is often a lonely venture. It is key for every author to surround themselves with people who believe in them. I have many family and friends to thank and little space to do it in. Those I fail to name should know that they are no less important to me. Some rose above.

My mom, Patricia, instigated my love of history when she dragged me on tours, and then she drove the getaway car while I hopped in and out of it to research my protagonist's hometown. My mother and father-in-law, Anita and Ed, waited patiently to read my completed story, and they have championed it ever since. All three have kept me aware of the outside writing community through their wealth of contacts and newspaper clippings.

My twin sister, Lita, who shares my passion for historical fiction, loved my novel right from the start—her wink and nod is important to me. My other "sister," Heidi, and my friend, Judy, already have some grand markets lined up for me. My brother-in-law, Al, and his family kindly allowed me a glimpse into yet another Civil War soldier's life through their kin's memoir. My other siblings (in-laws and outlaws): Doug and Garth committed their time and kind words for my novel's review and Greg and Christine cheered me on during every phase of composition alongside nieces and nephews Christopher, Cara, Courtney, Kylie, Brent, Brandon, Weston, Devyn, and Blake. Special thanks to Courtney for her gazillion encouraging e-mails and great efforts to recruit book reviewers.

Through their knowing eyes forever etched in my heart, I know that my dad and grandparents can see that what they stood behind—my lifelong dream to write and publish a novel—has come true.

Just like Civil War regiments had mascots I had my cuddly keeshond Hadley throughout my war with words. He inspired me through his boundless energy as a puppy and his will to survive as a troubled octogenarian. Bless him for licking an empty water bowl and holding his own water when I was too engrossed to notice.

My husband and best friend, Jed, really heard my countless edits as evidenced by his insightful questions and suggestions for improvement. He summoned the rain during my more frightening creative droughts, and when he noticed my writing engine running in high gear, he let me be, even taking on my share of chores. He is the greatest person in the whole wide world!

Amazon customers who kindly reviewed my novel's excerpt for the 2010 Amazon Breakthrough Novel Award Contest and influenced its advancement and exposure on a worldwide stage: Barb/Craig F., Cathy/Ken R., Cara H., Christopher G., Courtney G., Dannie B., Dan/Susan H., Doug G., Garth H., George P., Heidi G., Jed P., Jennifer/Whitten L., Joan L., Judy S., Karen/George H., Karen K., Linda F., Lisa K., Lolly F., Lynne H., Lynne/Rick G.,

Marsha P., Mary R., Mary W., Pam G., Rachel N., Richard P., Rick S., Ron M., Ryan C., Stephanie C., Theresa R., and Terry F.

I thank my mom, Patricia, my mother-in-law, Anita, my friends, Lynne and Marsha, and my critique-group buddies (Cathi, Kate, and Sarah) for volunteering, with very little time allotted, to proofread my novel before it hit the press.

I thank my team at Tate Publishing for caring about me and *Sweet Glory:* Joey Garrett, acquisitions editor, saved us from the slush pile and then went to bat for us. Lauren Downen, director of copy-editing, and her staff tidied up my story while arming me with new tricks of the trade. Hannah Tranberg, senior technical editor, waved her wand and helped me to turn my Cinderella into a princess. April Marciszewski, graphic designer, translated my head and heart onto the best cover I have ever seen. Nathan Harmony, graphic designer, preserved the historical ambiance of the cover in designing the interior pages and labored to make my Civil-War era maps presentable. If the marketing representative, publicist, and media department are just as exemplary in their work, we cannot lose.

I am honored that Tate Publishing has taken a chance on me and my story!

Fact and Fiction

In writing fiction, an author sometimes takes liberties in sketching historical places, events, and people but only where the facts are vague or silent. The following are examples as they pertain to *Sweet Glory*:

It is fact that John Jones, a former slave who escaped from Virginia, was embraced by the citizens of Elmira, New York, and became a highly productive member of this community. In his greatest work—aiding nearly one thousand slaves to freedom—he could have eluded a slave catcher.

It is fact that Clara Barton, Dr. Mary Walker, and Walt Whitman all tended to the wounded at Chatham Manor following the battle at Fredericksburg in mid-December 1862. Given the narrow window of time that the wounded were cared for here, it is likely that these three persons crossed paths.

It is fact that the opposing armies farmed their nurses from within their ranks. Although the Tenth New York Volunteer Cavalry Regiment did not fight at Fredericksburg on December 13, 1862, they were in the vicinity—a small portion standing in reserve on the Union's left with the remainder scouting. One or more of these troopers could have been assigned hospital duty at Chatham Manor.

It is fact that Dr. Mary Walker was a prisoner at Castle Thunder Prison in Richmond, Virginia, April-July 1864. In a letter to her mother, as published in the *New York Times* on June 16, 1864, she claims she has "plenty to eat and a clean bed to sleep in." Further, it is fact that Dr. Walker was permitted by extant Captain Richardson, Commandant of Castle Thunder Prison, to tour this city's streets under guard. Dr. Walker may have been given preferential treatment during her confinement, but it is fact that Union prisoners were starving. Jana was put on equal footing with the majority to lend credibility to her fainting spells.

It is fact that after March 1863 the ill and wounded prisoners of Castle Thunder Prison were removed from the prison to their own building called General Hospital #13. As most hospitals in Richmond were constantly overcrowded, it is possible that the less severely ill and wounded prisoners were held and treated at the prison instead.

It is fact that 109 officers escaped from Libby Prison in Richmond, Virginia, on February 9, 1864, via a tunnel that they had dug. And it is fact that Yankees incarcerated elsewhere around the city escaped in many different ways, including as easily as yanking out flimsy wallboards in their ground-floor cells. Although there are no known flights from Castle Thunder Prison simultaneous with the Libby-Prison breakout, they could have happened.

It is fact that Elizabeth Van Lew, a lifelong resident of Richmond, Virginia, was a spy for the Union and that she softened up General John H. Winder, Provost Marshal General of Richmond, for his permission to visit Union prisoners and bring them food and reading materials. She could have called upon those of Castle Thunder Prison and General Hospital #13.

It is fact that all military personnel, including Surgeon Roger W. Pease of the Tenth New York Volunteer Cavalry Regiment, mentioned in my novel existed at the time!

Bibliography:

Adams, George Worthington. *Doctors in Blue: The Medical History of the Union Army in the Civil War.* 1952; rpt. Baton Rouge, Louisiana: Louisiana State University Press, 1996.

Alden, Henry M., and Alfred H. Guernsey. *Harper's Pictorial History of the Civil War: Contemporary Accounts and Illustrations of the Greatest Magazine of the Time.* New York: The Fairfax Press, 1866.

Angle, Paul M. *A Pictorial History of the Civil War Years.* Garden City, New York: Doubleday and Company, Inc., 1967.

Bartoletti, Susan Campbell. *Black Potatoes: The Story of the Great Irish Famine, 1845–1850.* Boston, Massachusetts: Houghton Mifflin Company, 2001.

Bial, Raymond. *The Underground Railroad.* Boston, Massachusetts: Houghton Mifflin Company, 1995.

Bolett, M.D., Alfred Jay. *Civil War Medicine: Challenges and Triumphs.* Tucson, Arizona: Galen Press, Ltd., 2002.

Blanton, Deanne, and Lauren M. Cook. *They Fought Like Demons: Women Soldiers in the Civil War.* New York: Vintage Books, 2003.

Chemung County Historical Journal: A Civil War Anthology. 1964; rpt. Elmira, New York: The Chemung County Historical Society, Inc., 1985, 1993.

Chemung Historical Journal: Elmira Prison Camp. 1964; rpt. Elmira, New York: The Chemung County Historical Society, Inc., 1990, 1997.

Davis, William C. *The Civil War*, 3 vols. 1990; rpt. London, United Kingdom: Salamander Books Ltd., 1999.

Elmira City Directory, 1860. Elmira, New York: Chemung County Historical Society, Inc.

Elrod, Mark, and Robert Garofalo. *A Pictorial History of Civil War Era Musical Instruments & Military Bands.* Missoula, Montana: Pictorial Histories Publishing Co., Inc., 1985.

Fletcher, William A. *Rebel Private: Front and Rear, Memoirs of a Confederate Soldier.* 1908; rpt. New York: Meridian, 1997.

Garrison, Nancy Scripture. *With Courage and Delicacy, Civil War on the Peninsula: Women and the U.S. Sanitary* Commission. Mason City, Iowa: Savas Publishing Company, 1999.

Garrison, Webb. *Amazing Women of the Civil War.* Nashville, Tennessee: Rutledge Hill Press, 1999.

Haskins, Jim. *Get On Board: The Story of the Underground Railroad.* New York: Scholastic, Inc., 1993.

Hesseltine, William B., ed. *Civil War Prisons.* 1962; rpt. Kent, Ohio: The Kent State University Press, 1997.

Holland, Mary Gardner. *Our Army Nurses: Stories from Women in the Civil War.* Roseville, Minnesota: Edinborough Press, 1998.

Holy Bible, King James Version, 1611. Reference Edition. New York: American Bible Society.

Janowski, Diane L., and Allen C. Smith. *Images of America: The Chemung Valley.* Charleston, South Carolina: Arcadia Publishing, 1998.

Jaquette, Henrietta Stratton, ed. *Letters of a Civil War Nurse: Cornelia Hancock, 1863–1865.* 1971; rpt. Lincoln, Nebraska: University of Nebraska Press, 1998.

Kagan, Neil, ed. *Eyewitness to the Civil War: The Complete History from Secession to Reconstruction.* Washington, D.C.: National Geographic Society, 2006.

Katcher, Philip. *Union Cavalrymen, 1861–1865.* London, United Kingdom: Osprey Publishing Ltd., 1995.

Lonn, Ella. *Desertion During the Civil War.* 1966; rpt. Lincoln, Nebraska: University of Nebraska Press, 1998.

Madden, David. *Beyond the Battlefield: The Ordinary Life and Extraordinary Times of the Civil War Soldier.* New York: Simon & Schuster, 2000.

Matteson, Ron. *Civil War Campaigns of the 10th New York Cavalry: With One Soldier's Correspondences.* Lulu.com, 2007.

McCutcheon, Marc. *The Writer's Guide to Everyday Life in the* 1800s. Cincinnati, Ohio: Writer's Digest Books, 1993.

McPherson, James M. *What They Fought For, 1861–1865.* 1994; rpt. New York: Anchor Books, Doubleday, 1995.

Morris, Richard B., and the editors of *Life. The Making of a Nation, 1775–1789.* Volume 2. 1963; rpt. New York: Time-Life Books, 1969.

Noe, Robert S., Jr., Town Manager. *Exploring Leesburg: Guide to History and Architecture.* Town of Leesburg, Virginia, 2003.

Palmer, Richard, and Harvey Roehl. *Railroads, In Early Postcards, Volume One, Upstate New York.* Vestal, New York: The Vestal Press Ltd., 1990.

Phillips, David. *Maps of the Civil War: The Roads They Took.* 1998; rpt. New York: MetroBooks, 2001.

Preston, Noble D. *History of the Tenth Regiment of Cavalry, New York State Volunteers, August* 1861 *to August* 1865. 1892; rpt. Salem, Massachusetts: Higginson and Company, 1998.

Rodgers, Sarah Sites. *The Ties of the Past: The Gettysburg Diaries of Salome Myers Stewart,* 1854–1922. Gettysburg, Pennsylvania: Thomas Publications, 1996.

Roth, Margaret Brobst, ed. *Well Mary: Civil War Letters of a Wisconsin Volunteer.* Madison, Wisconsin: The University of Wisconsin Press, 1960.

Rummel III, George A. *72 Days at Gettysburg: Organization of the* 10th *Regiment, New York Volunteer Cavalry.* Shippensburg, Pennsylvania: The White Mane Publishing Company, Inc., 1997.

Scheel, Eugene M. *Loudon Discovered: Communities, Corners, & Crossroads, Volume 2, Leesburg and the Old Carolina Road.* Leesburg, Virginia: The Friends of the Thomas Balch Library, Inc., 2002.

Sills, Leslie. *From Rags to Riches: A History of Girls' Clothing in America.* New York: Holiday House, 2005.

Smith, Julian. *Virginia Handbook, First Edition.* Emeryville, California: Avalon Travel Publishing, 1999.

Stanchak, John. *The Visual Dictionary of the Civil War.* New York: DK Publishing, Inc., 2000.

Taylor, John M. *While Cannons Roared: The Civil War Behind the Lines.* Dulles, Virginia: Brassey's, Inc., 2000.

The Timechart of the Civil War. St. Paul, Minnesota: MBI Publishing Company, 2001.

Towner, Ausburn. *A History of the Valley and County of Chemung: From the Closing Years of the Eighteenth Century.* 1892; rpt. Elmira, New York: The Chemung County Historical Society, 1986.

Varhola, Michael J. *Everyday Life During the Civil War: A Guide for Writers, Students, and Historians.* Cincinnati, Ohio: Writer's Digest Books, 1999.

Varon, Elizabeth R. *Southern Lady, Yankee Spy: A True Story of Elizabeth Van Lew, A Union Agent in the Heart of the Confederacy.* New York: Oxford University Press, Inc., 2003.

Ward, Candace, ed. *Walt Whitman: Civil War Poetry and Prose.* Mineola, New York: Dover Publications, Inc., 1995.

Whitelaw, Nancy. *Clara Barton: Civil War Nurse.* Berkeley Heights, New Jersey: Enslow Publishers, Inc., 1997.

Wilbur, M.D., Keith C. *Civil War Medicine:* 1861 *to* 1865. Old Saybrook, Connecticut: The Globe Pequot Press, 1998.

Wiley, Bell Irvin. *The Life of Billy Yank: The Common Soldier of the Union.* 1971; rpt. Baton Rouge, Louisiana: Louisiana State University Press, 1998.

Williams, T. Harry, and the editors of *Life. The Union Sundered:* 1849–1865. Volume 5. 1963; rpt. New York: Time-Life Books, 1969.

Williams, T. Harry, and the editors of *Life. The Union Restored:* 1861–1876. Volume 6. 1963; rpt. New York: Time-Life Books, 1969.

Woodhead, Henry, ed. *Echoes of Glory.* 3 vols. Alexandria, Virginia: Time-Life Books, 1998.

Internet Sites

"Beaverton.k12.or.us: Underground Railroad Code Words and Phrases." David Leahy of Greenway Elementary School. 14 August 2000. http://www.beaverton.k12.or.us/

"Civil War Richmond." Civil War Richmond Inc. 2008. http://www.mdgorman.com/

"Historical Marker Database: Duels in Bladensburg Dueling Grounds Marker." F. Robby. 6 June 2008. http://www.hmdb.org/

"History.com: This Day in History 1820: Naval Hero Killed in Duel." History.com. 22 March 2008. http://history.com/

"Library of Congress.com: America's First Look into the Camera: Daguerreotype Portraits and Views, 1839–1862. Library of Congress. 23 April 2002. http://www.loc.gov/

"National Park Service.com: Chatham Manor." Mac Wyckoff. 4 April 2006. http://www.nps.gov/

"Prairie Ghosts.com: Bladensburg Dueling Grounds." Troy Taylor. 1998. http://www.prairieghosts.com/

"Rarey.com: The Complete Horse Trainer." John Solomon Rarey. 2 February 2006. http://www.rarey.com/

"Wikipedia.com: Postage Stamps and Postal History of the United States." 10 January 2011. http://www.wikipedia.com/

"Wikipedia.com: Tintype." 2 July 2011. http://www.wikipedia.com/